When the City is Safe Again

When the City is Safe Again

Sean Mejias

TINY FROG
PRESS

Published in the United States by
Tiny Frog Press
Rochester, NY
TinyFrogPress.com

ISBN (Paperback): 979-8-9951986-0-4
ISBN (eBook):   979-8-9951986-1-1
Library of Congress Control Number: 2026907233

10 9 8 7 6 5 4 3 2 1

Edited by Aaron Lelito.
Cover and interior design by Tiny Frog Press.
Author photo by Sparks of Light Photography, LLC.

For the One Most High

And to my wife, my mom, my sister, and mother-in-law:
the heroes.

"To every thing there is a season, and a time to every purpose under the heaven:"

— Ecclesiastes 3:1 (KJV)

Chapter 1: The Support Group

It started like most nights: alone.

Days and nights felt as if they folded in on themselves. The quiet, weighted air of the place would have been jarring to most others, but it settled over him like a mutual understanding. The radiator repeated its clunky rhythm, an unsettling loop of an offbeat drum. Solitude had nearly become a tradition, though one that he still struggled with the majority of the time. The house settled around him. A gentle breeze brushed against the windows, as if the building itself was taking slow, methodical breaths for the man inside. The coffee pot in the kitchen broke the silence with a tone that let him know the brew was finished.

It signaled the beginning of something new. Although he prompted it, deep inside, he was unsure of its validity. The smell of strong coffee pierced through the air, and there was a faint aura of a long-loved perfume that competed with the coffee to warm the room.

Outside of the front window and across the street, the neighborhood cat stood guard on the neighbor's stoop where water was left out. The cat didn't stir as it watched the first man enter the house, or the next, or the next. It acted as if it expected them to show up, although they never had before. It sat like a quiet audience too polite to interrupt the parade, and blinked slowly as the night spiraled inward.

The four men gathered in a lopsided circle on creaking metallic folding chairs in the living room of a Kew Gardens home. Two among them held a styrofoam cup of steaming, caffeinated sludge. Another slumped back into the chair as if to tempt just how much more the aged chair might be able to take before it collapsed. The last leaned forward into the circle.

His forearms rested on the bouncing knees that shook the chair like it was a mechanical bull that fought its rider. One of the men who held the beverage in question began the meeting. He wore a faded zip-up hoodie that remained open. The zipper broke long ago, but he was too stubborn to replace it. He wore dark-wash jeans and shoes that fit the rain-infused fall chill and his tired eyes. He inhaled deeply before speaking as if he needed to methodically choose his words.

"Boys, thanks for coming," he yawned.

"All of you know me, but I know you all don't know each other just yet. All of our spouses are super. What this group is meant to do is provide us with the opportunity to support one another while our better halves are off... well, doing better. We don't have to have any secrets. So, I'll start."

Attentive quietness overcame the room. The only thing that broke through it was the creaking of the chair that lay underneath the owner's bouncing legs.

"My name is Davey. My wife is SolaRae. The one with the tight gold and black striped bodysuit, black boots, a cape to match, and a picture of the sun across her chest. She can harness both the heat and force of the sun through her hands and channel burning projectiles. She also flies, which is fun. We actually grew up together, and I was one of the first people she told when she realized she had the H-gene. But we've only been married for a year. It keeps me up at night knowing that she puts herself in harm's way… so, yeah, that's me. Cass, how about you next?" He pointed to the man next to him, who also held a cup of coffee.

"Sure. Thanks, Davey." Cass had a short-cropped beard and hair to match. When he lifted the disposable cup to his lips, the other men could see the shining glint of a watch that they couldn't guess the brand name of. He wore a slim tan suit that paired well with his darker complexion and spoke decisively. "I'm Cass. Davey and I went to college together. My wife is Echona; she went to college with us, too, before she chose to become a hero. She wears the nondescript, baggy black pants and a gray hooded tank with the picture of a small microphone on it. She has the power of mimicry, volume control, and a photographic memory. I used to be the big-shot attorney breadwinner, but she's been getting a lot of endorsements. I'm almost embarrassed to say my ego is taking a hit, and that's why I'm here. I have less free time for my work because I also act as her agent. I'm happy for her though… mostly."

"Thanks for sharing, Cass, and thanks for coming," Davey said reassuringly. "I know the H-gene is only something that has been around for a short time, but it evolved in women, and we should support them. Of course, that's easier said than done. How about you, Jose?" Davey asked as he pointed to the man bouncing his knees.

"Alright," he sighed. "Name's Jose, good to be here, meet the rest of you. I'm a pro triathlete, or at least used to be." His tan skin hid behind a baggy gray pullover sweater, and his legs bounced in black sweatpants that were cuffed at the ankle. His long, unkempt hair was back in a bun. "Davey and I used to go to the same gym and have kept in contact. My wife is OwlHeart. She flies, and her outfit looks like a bunch of feathers. She has frills on the bottom of her arms to look like wings, but she doesn't need wings to fly. She's also ridiculously quiet, like it scares me sometimes just how quiet. But it's good for the kid. We just had a baby a few months ago. She's back to saving the city now, pumping when she gets a break, and I get to be home. I love her. I love the kid. But man, it's a lot of work. Diapers suck, man, and I haven't been to the gym in weeks." He looked down. His legs stopped bouncing, and he slouched a bit. He almost appeared defeated.

"That has to be tough, Jose. Thank you for sharing. I don't envy you, but as the saying goes, 'this too shall pass.' How about you take us home, Eric?"

"Uh, okay." The slumped man began. "Name's Eric, and I'm not actually married. My fiancé is LunAva, SolaRae's younger sister. So, that's how I met Davey, too. Ava introduced me to Rae and Davey last Thanksgiving, and he invited me here. I'm trying to be a streamer, but I haven't started yet." Eric wore a mismatched flannel jacket and gray sweatpants. His shaggy facial hair matched his unkempt hair. "Ava can enhance the abilities of the moon's lunar energy. She manipulates light, the gravitational pull of things, and other stuff. She wears a silver and black bodysuit with a crescent moon on her chest. I don't really know how to be a husband or whatever. Just here to try and live up to her expectations."

"I hear you, Eric. Thanks for sharing, and welcome to the family."

Jose scoffed and shook his head.

"Something you want to add, Jose?" Davey remarked, and his lips embraced the Styrofoam again.

"Nah, man, it's cool."

"Alright, anybody else?"

There was silence filled by the low hum of traffic as rush hour began to end and the city moved around them.

"It's just…" Jose started again. "If I had free time, I would be in the gym training, not playing something for fake friends."

"Technically, not playing for anybody," Cass added, and Jose motioned his hand in agreement. Eric stared at them, a look of loss crossed his face.

"We don't need to judge how Eric spends his time, guys. He'll figure it out. Maybe since you guys have it all together, you can help him."

"Hang on, who has it all together? I'm drowning in a sea of piss, crap, and spit-up without enough sleep to tread the current. It's like I forgot how to swim laps, and I'm just hanging on to a buoyant diaper. I'm just bobbing up and down on… poop, trying not to get it in my eye again. I'm just lucky my mom could watch the kid for an hour today."

"Again?" Cass questioned with a laugh.

"Don't ask."

"Fair enough," Cass shrugged. "And I hardly have enough time for myself anymore."

"So, it sounds like maybe we can insert our opinions a little less on what Eric does? I'm sure he could use a friend, too. There are not very many heroes, but more women are coming to face the H-gene that lies dormant in them. For now, we're the only ones, at least that I know of, in similar boats in this city. We might as well try to be here for one another."

There were nods of agreement.

"Question," Cass started.

"What's up?"

"How did you even bring us together?"

"Dumb luck, honestly. LunAva brought home Eric. That was easy. When I saw one of Echona's ads on my phone, I had a hunch. She looked similar to the girl I knew you dated in college. We hadn't talked since graduation a few years ago, but I thought I recognized her, despite her attempt to hide herself, and I threw out a prayer. You all know SolaRae doesn't try to hide herself. So, when Jose saw her, he actually reached out to me and filled me in on his wife."

"And you thought a support group would be a good idea?"

"Absolutely. I'm a therapist, and I know how much connecting with another person can strengthen your own life. Talking is valuable."

"What about their secret identities?"

"Well, it's up to you guys. Knowing who the husband is doesn't exactly make finding the wife, or fiancé, difficult. If we see somebody out and about with their spouse, we'll automatically know. You all know that SolaRae doesn't care. Her name is Rae, clever, I know."

"I suppose that's true," Cass added.

"My fiancé is Ava Selene. Rae's younger sister, but I said that already," Eric remarked without a second thought.

"My wife OwlHeart's real name is Sara."

The three men looked at Cass. He felt as if he shouldn't share. He had safeguarded her name and their marriage for years.

He caved.

"Jazmine. Echona's name is Jazmine."

"Thanks for sharing, Cass. I could tell that was not easy."

Davey paused for a beat.

"Anybody have anything they'd like to discuss? It could be anything, doesn't have to relate to our wives. We can just talk about anything."

"I feel…" Jose began. "I feel like I constantly smell crap."

"That's some…" Eric started.

"Don't. Just don't." Jose cut him off and put his face in his palms. He dramatically slapped them on his knees and hung his head back.

Davey was glad to see the group come together so effortlessly. Some therapy groups he worked with in the past took some getting used to. But this one felt natural.

"Solid or mushy?" Cass questioned.

"Bro…"

"Brown or green?" Davey added.

Jose sighed as if he had exerted himself.

"Brown. Mushy. Somebody else go."

The three other men shared a hearty laugh.

"What are you playing nowadays, Eric?" Davey changed course after sipping on his coffee.

Eric sat up and leaned forward in his chair. "There's this really cool new MOBA that I've been trying out. I think I'm actually pretty good at it, too. Might try to grind it and see if I'm good enough to stream."

"Sounds fun."

"You don't have to be good enough to stream, bro. Just do it," Jose responded. "When I first started competing, I knew I wasn't going to win. I just did it. You'll get there too."

Eric contemplated Jose's encouragement.

"I don't know. I'm not ready. I don't even have a good webcam."

"Work with what you have," Cass added.

"I agree with them, Eric. Sometimes, just starting and putting yourself out there is the best step. Could be worth considering, right?"

"I guess so."

"When the stream starts, we'll all tune in, I'm sure. How about you, Cass? Anything on your mind?"

There was a moment of quiet before the man responded. "How about you, Davey?" The host wasn't prepared for the flip.

"Uh…" he sipped his coffee. "Thanks for asking," he paused. "Well, I'm really mad the Mets missed the playoffs again."

"That happens most of the time, bro. Come on over to the Bronx," Jose joked.

"Then I'd have to sell my soul, and I'm not quite there yet. But I'll let you know. Anyway, I might be joining you in the mess soon."

Jose and Eric looked confused.

"You guys are trying?" Cass asked.

Davey pointed a finger at Cass and then touched his nose.

"No way, bro. Nice," Jose added.

"You're right, there's no mess. It's all yours," Eric remarked.

Jose gave him a glance that ensured Eric knew it wasn't funny, despite him finding it hilarious internally. Horns of traffic beyond their meeting filled the momentary silence.

"Rae and I agreed to start trying around three months ago, but really, we haven't been outside of a few times since that conversation. She's been kicking butt and loving it, but she's been too tired. I can't ask her to take a break from what she loves. The endorsements make us more than my therapist's salary, too. I'm sure it was similar for Sara, right?"

"Actually, no. It was mostly her idea. I was just there for a good time…"

"And a short one?" Eric joked and earned another of Jose's looks.

He ignored him. "I always thought I'd be a good dad and all. Timeline was just never something I thought about."

"You should have that conversation with her," Cass added. "Open and honest. That's what Jazmine and I believe."

"I appreciate the sentiment. Maybe I will someday. I'm okay with being her sidekick for now and letting her do what she does best."

"Just don't put your own goals to the side and wake up one day without realizing them."

"I'll keep that in mind."

Another beat of silence filled the room and its lopsided chairs.

"How about you, Cass?"

"Nothing. Work is a lot with being Jaz's agent too, but it's not a big deal."

"It's okay to acknowledge when you're burning out, man."

"You'll be the first to know, Davey."

"Hey, Davey," Jose asked.

"What's up, Jose?"

"I'm burnt the heck out."

"Like a sack of dog crap on fire?" Eric joked.

"Look at that, Davey. You got the next Jerry Seinfeld as your future bro-in-law. Not funny." Jose tried to stay serious but gave in to a small chuckle. "Alright, it's a little funny."

"When he finds a joke he likes, he really sticks with it. Can't exactly blame him," Cass added.

"We're here for you, Jose. Seriously, guys, it can be a lonely world in a big city. For now, we can at least begin to understand each other." Davey's phone buzzed, and he stopped to check it.

A text from Rae came across the screen, which read: "Will be home late tonight. Robbery-Homicide in Sugar Hill. NYPD needs help. Fled on the train. Can't find him yet. Love you."

Davey sighed quietly in disappointment before he composed himself. "Well, guys, looks like tonight's not the night yet either. Wife is heading to kick some butt. I was going to make us dinner, but does anybody want a pizza?"

The sun began to set over the Queens residence. An illuminated newspaper clipping of SolaRae apprehending a criminal began to dim. Jose's phone went off.

"Looks like Sara is probably joining in on whatever SolaRae has going on. Would love some pizza, but I have to go get the kid before it gets too late. Maybe next time. Thanks for the invite, bro. This should be good." Jose stood from his unsure chair and said his farewells before leaving the house.

"I should get back too," Cass said, "I haven't heard from Jaz yet, but maybe that means she's home tonight. Thanks, Davey. See you next time." He followed behind Jose.

"Thanks for coming, guys. Try to stay awake on the train, Jose."

"Yeah, we'll see. I should really take up drinking coffee." He yawned.

"Where you headed, Cass? Want to walk to the train?"

"I'm good. I worked from home today and drove from Flatbush.

Get home safe."

Jose and Cass left the home and headed down the sidewalk in opposite directions.

"I like pizza," Eric added.

"Yeah… yeah, I know."

Davey ordered pizza for the two men, and it arrived before long.

"So, no text from Ava? Not joining her sister this time?"

"I forgot my phone at the apartment. Probably?"

"I'll check with Rae." He texted her back to see if the sisters were working together, but no response came. He hovered his fingers over the screen and considered sending a clever response, but thought better of it. Chances of a response were lower than the chances of a squabble when they were able to reconnect. The men finished the pizza, and the night had taken the city.

"You might want to get home, Eric. Ava might be waiting for you."

"That's probably true." Eric stood and burped. "Hey, can you call me a ride? I don't have bus money."

Davey took a deep breath through his nose and released it. "Sure, Eric, that's fine." He ordered the ride for his future brother-in-law. "It's around the corner. Turning onto 127th now."

When Eric left, Davey watched as the car's taillights left his vision to turn down Metropolitan. The smell of a struggling exhaust filled the street. As he turned to clean from the night, he thought he saw a glimpse of gold over the night skyline illuminated by the streetlights and advertisements. It looked to be moving quicker than a shooting star. Yet, in the same thought, it was gone, and he returned to his chores. He washed the last plate, turned off the light, and settled into the quiet house. It was routine, but he never quite got used to the feeling of waiting. He thought of the chairs again. Standing, creaking, but resolute. They weren't built to last forever, but they held nonetheless.

He started to rinse the old coffee pot, stained with a deep brown that never left despite several thorough washes over the years. As the warm water splashed, Davey allowed it to cascade over his hands like a soft waterfall. The water reminded him of his college years, when, as a freshman, he and Cass had been dared by upperclassmen to go for a swim in the nearby park's fountain. The fall semester had just begun, and the season's chill had not yet taken its hold. The water that looped through the piping of the fountain was an endless warmth. The water splashed down on their heads and joined in the shallow pool at their feet before it was sucked back into the center. The men were encouraged to strip down to their undergarments so as not to return to their dorms with soaked clothing.

Davey decided to take the older men's advice and proceeded to get into the fountain in his briefs. Meanwhile, Cass declared he would rather risk soaking the old carpeted halls of the dorm. The swim did not last too long before a security guard from the park came to stop them. They hurriedly climbed out of the fountain. Davey to retrieve his clothes from the ledge where he set them. But, in the rush of it all, he hadn't noticed that some of the upperclassmen took his clothes. The two young men ran through the park back to campus. One was soaked, the other was nearly nude. Davey wasn't entirely sure which was worse, but the two men laughed the entire time as they ran from their evening dip. He recalled it as one of the first instances of their budding friendship. They went from assigned roommates to having shared experiences in a matter of minutes.

He snapped back to his chores as water filled the coffee pot and splashed down to the bottom of the sink. He nearly dropped the coffee pot into the hard basin, but caught it before it fell. In the same motion, he accidentally knocked over a plate he had yet to put away from earlier in the day. It shattered on the floor with a loud crack. He let out a deep sigh and carefully set down the coffee pot. Then, he retrieved the broom to carefully sweep the shards. Davey considered trying to glue the plate back together, but decided that this particular broken thing could not be fixed.

Chapter 2: Central Sausage

The host finished cleaning and folding the chairs that not even a full can of WD-40 could save. He had already tried the trusted substance. Twice. But the chairs were still mostly functional, which meant he wouldn't send them on their way. They weren't perfect, but they were his, and he took the best care of them that he could. He stayed up for a while and kept an eye on his phone for news from his wife. None came, and he attempted to distract himself by finishing the notes from his clients earlier in the day. Davey could only bear so much forced diversion and failed attempts to occupy his mind.

The tiredness that the instant coffee staved off was beginning to return, but he felt that even if he lay down, he wouldn't sleep. He took some melatonin. He wondered if Rae ever thought of him when she was being the savior of the city. Then he took an edible. Together, they usually helped him sleep when she was gone. He never shared his drug use with any friends, not even with Rae. He didn't want to admit how much he needed the assistance to quiet the stream of anxiety. It was easier to blame the gummies than admit he was afraid of the phone ringing. Easier to be a little foggy than fully awake in the moment someone told him she was gone from some accident. So, he took a shower and went to bed. It was all he could do to try to ease the anxiety. Quiet the restlessness. Try to let the night take him.

He stared at the different shapes made by shadows as cars passed his window. The city didn't rest even when he finally attempted to. The cracks of the blinds allowed momentary light to enter the room, and each time a new shape came with it. As he continued to lie awake, the smell of her perfume entered his nose. He had been familiar with it since they were children. She never changed her scent. He listened attentively for the sound of a door unlocking and boots being removed, but it never came. His mind was playing tricks on him, pulling the scent from memory. It happened often. Some nights, it felt like the home remembered her better than he did. The pillow and walls held on to her longer than his tired mind could. Eventually, he fell asleep to the faint sound of the train and the traffic that became his white noise after living in Queens for his entire life.

He woke to honks the next morning. Not an unusual bit of life, but still not a pleasant one. The sheets on his wife's side of the bed had been tossed, and the light in the bathroom was on. So, he knew she had made it home the night before. He hadn't missed a phone call from the hospital or NYPD to let him know his wife had been taken from him in his drug-induced sleep. She was super, not invincible. While she could endure more than any average man, safety was still a necessary practice.

He climbed out of bed, groggy. Sunlight peered through the blinds, stronger than the night's headlights. He shuffled to the bathroom and opened the door to find her. Seeing her braless in a baggy t-shirt and a pair of his old gym shorts made him stir like it always did. She was curling her long brunette hair and letting the strands drop to frame her caramel skin.

"Morning," she said in a cheery voice and offered her husband a smile that always made him swoon. It seemed like she had plenty of sleep, but he had no clue when she made it back home.

"I made you some coffee, but it got cold." She motioned with her lips toward the cup of coffee on the bathroom counter as her hands were occupied. It sat next to an empty mug, and he wondered if she had intended to share a cup, but couldn't wait.

"Thank you." He kissed her cheek and went to grab the mug.

"Oh, hang on." She dropped the lock of hair she held and picked up the mug. A faint brightness came from her hand. Suddenly, the mug began to steam again as if it were a fresh cup. He had seen her do that trick many times before, but it never stopped being a wild feat of mysticism to him. Miraculous became routine in their marriage. He still caught himself waiting for the mystery to fade, for the light to flicker out one day. For him to be left with nothing but a cold mug and an ordinary life.

"Thanks, babe. Want some breakfast?" He blew on the coffee a bit and took a sip that nearly scalded his tongue.

"Not today." She put down the curling iron and checked for any spots she missed. "I have to run down to the precinct to make sure everything is squared away from the chase last night. I'll plan to grab a bite with Ava. She was there too."

Davey wondered if his sister-in-law ended up going to the scene. He never heard from Eric, but that wasn't anything out of the ordinary. "Right. How'd it go? Catch the guy?"

"Of course we did." She gave him a smirk. "OwlHeart was able to get a good vantage point, and Ava and I caught the guy. Echona was busy with something else, I believe."

"Sounds like a good night then. No injuries?"

"Not to me." She smiled at him again. "Can you do me a favor? Grab my other suit from the closet? I need to wash the one from last night."

He set his coffee cup back down and went to recover her suit.

"Be back tonight?"

"Planning on it." She took off her clothes and began to slither into the bodysuit adorned with her logo. "You had something last night, too, right?"

"Oh, yeah. Just some guys over and some pizza. Nothing crazy." He didn't tell her about the support group. He didn't plan on withholding that information. It was a result of instinct rather than a developed lie.

"I'm glad you weren't alone." She smiled at him. "Zip me?"

Davey obliged, squeezing her waist before kissing her cheek.

"Love you," she said as she looked into his eyes.

She studied his face as if it wasn't already ingrained in her mind. She liked to linger before departing, even when time was tight.

"And I love you."

She sat on the bed to put on her boots, then walked to the window. She raised the blinds, opened the window, and gently flew through it. He watched her disappear toward Manhattan before he closed the window and retrieved his coffee. The bathroom smelled like a mix of her patented perfume and hairspray. The baggy shirt and old shorts clumped on the floor, a reminder that loving her as much as he did meant learning to live with her lifestyle, and he felt up to the challenge. The room cooled the moment she left, like the air had been holding tight around her and finally let go. He continued to drink his coffee and quickly tidied up the clothes his wife had left behind. He prepared for the day himself as a private practice therapist. Comfortable, welcoming, but still professional was his go-to attire when he was in the office.

He made himself a slice of toast that melted the peanut butter before he could eat it. After rinsing his plate of bread crumbs, he grabbed his old hoodie that clashed with his aura of inviting professionalism and faced the brisk chill of a fall Queens day. Then he left for the train. Walking. He locked the door and stepped into his rhythm. The door closed with the same soft click it always did that told him the day was beginning, or ending. He descended the stoop of one of the city's first true superheroes. Sirens from somewhere else in Queens thinned in the air and faded to their destination. The smell of her perfume clung to him and joined the light coffee scent on his breath.

It wasn't a long trip to the station. He was well acquainted with it. From his house, he would catch the Q80 bus to get to the Union Turnpike–Kew Gardens station easily. Perhaps, this routine was the simplest thing in his life. From there, he would take the E to Queens Plaza and walk to his office. The usual faces of morning commuters boarded the train with more people standing than normal. An unhoused man under a jacket lay across one of the benches on the train, and people would just as soon leave him alone.

He was lucky to have a short commute.

Lucky to be able to afford a small office in a small building due to his wife's income.

He loved Queens, and as far as he knew, it loved him too. Or at least the people there loved being able to see a therapist who was married to an actual superhero. She was never careful with her identity. If somebody wanted badly enough, they could find out where they lived. But this was SolaRae, the darling of New York. Beloved, or feared, by all. Davey considered himself lucky to be able to call her his own. Some days, it felt like he borrowed her. Like the city had checked her out of a library he shelved in their small Queens bedroom.

He mostly didn't mind the general fascination with his wife. It bothered him more than it bothered her whenever the media decided to criticize her well-doing on a slow news day. It continued to bother him when they thought they would be able to sexualize her whenever they chose. It was so bothersome that Rae had to talk him down from reaching out to Cass and filing a lawsuit on behalf of the superheroes. He did, however, find a certain comfort in being able to see his wife every day. Even when she was home and gone in the night. He worked across from a building that had a large mural of his wife and sister-in-law painted on the side. Davey thought it didn't quite capture her likeness as well as it could have, but it was passable. The echo of the train under his feet followed him to his office. He subconsciously tried to match his steps to its rattle.

He parked himself in his small square of an office. Enough for a desk, some chairs, and a small bookshelf. The sounds of the city silenced as he climbed the stairs, and an uneasy silence found him. There was no quiet in his beloved borough. He propped his laptop open and saw that the notes he had attempted to work on the night before remained open. He checked his calendar and saw he didn't have many sessions today. Two regulars and an intake. His office, while small, did have a nice view from its single dirty window. He could spot the mural, some of Queens Plaza, and his favorite hot dog cart that sold the SolaRae Dog: a plain hot dog with spicy mustard. The vendor, a middle-aged Eastern European man named Boris, thought he was clever.

Davey never purchased his wife's namesake. In principle, he also never had the LunAva Dog. That one just had cream cheese, like a bad take on a Seattle Dog. Or the OwlHeart Dog: a fried egg with ketchup. Boris cut the tip of the ketchup bottle to look like some demented heart, and would squirt them on one at a time. There wasn't an Echona Dog yet. Davey thought the name might have just stumped their local hot dog artist. Despite the creative options, Davey's daily dog was only ketchup and mustard; regular, not spicy.

When he tried to focus his attention on preparing for his intake, his phone chimed, and Rae texted him: Are you at the office? The phone's buzz pulled him out of the awkward quietness of the office.

It wasn't like her to text him while at the office, and his heart skipped a beat when he saw her name.

Davey: Yeah, what's up?

Rae: What are you wearing?

Davey: A khaki sweater… why?

Rae: Just messing. Come to the roof.

Davey hid any excitement he began to feel and took the short journey from his office to the roof. He left the small fluorescently lit office space and headed for his wife. His heart beat faster. It felt like he was doing something he wasn't meant to. After arriving, he waited a moment before seeing his wife appear in the sky and land gently on the roof next to him. At one point, her suit aroused him, but now he preferred seeing her in her natural state, though he wasn't sure which was which. She moved to kiss him, and he matched.

"What's up, babe? Just in the neighborhood?"

"Yes, and no."

The wind shifted around the roof, barely noticeable.

"Hey, bro," a voice came from behind Davey. He jumped and turned as Rae giggled.

"I hate when you do that, Ava."

"Yeah, I know, but it's too fun not to." Her hair was shorter than Rae's, but the same deep brunette. Ava preferred a pixie cut. There was also a stark height difference between the two. Davey was a tall man, and Rae could nearly look him in the eye without making him look down. Ava was far shorter. Their suits matched, but Ava chose to wear a black mask in addition. They both were athletic, which came with the activity levels of heroes.

Davey went to hug her. "Just because you can control gravity doesn't mean you need to."

"Yeah, yeah… great power and all that."

"Eric made it home last night, by the way? He was over, but I didn't hear from him. Said he forgot his phone."

"Yup." She looked at her wrist as if checking the time on a watch that had never been there. "Right about now he's promptly settled into his game, slouched in his chair. Dishes, unwashed."

"You really need to talk to him," Rae added.

"I will. I just don't want to crush him."

"Am I missing something here?" Davey questioned.

Rae looked to Ava and waited for her to answer.

"I don't know how much longer I'll be with Eric. I love him, but he shows no motivation. He just wants to play his games."

"Have you tried talking to him about it before ending things?"

"Are you billing me for this session, doctor?"

"Not a doctor, and no, of course not. I'm just saying, you could try to talk to him and see what he's hoping for. Maybe you'll be able to help him get there and do it together."

"Maybe. I don't know."

"Thanks, babe, but we're actually here to see if you could talk to someone."

"Oh, yeah? Go ahead, tell me."

"Well, the criminal from last night: his attorney is trying to get him off on an insanity defense. I'm hoping you might be an expert and just talk to him."

"I'd love to help, but that's a conflict of interest, Rae."

"Told you," Ava interjected.

Rae channeled a small orb of bright energy and tossed it at Ava's feet playfully. It scorched the roof, and Rae smirked.

"Would you still talk to him? Off the record? Not for the lawsuit?"

"I mean, yeah, sure. It's usually harder than that for random therapists to talk to random criminals."

"Babe… I'm SolaRae." She played up her confidence and winked at her husband. "I make things happen." She kissed him again, and then the heroes of the city were off to do what they would.

The light breeze of the women leaving to circle the city took his breath away. He thought of himself as remarkably unremarkable in the face of incredibleness. He was fine with that in the name of supporting his wife, at least for now. He could strive to be a remarkable househusband, therapist, or hot dog connoisseur.

He returned to his office with the light breeze hanging onto bits of his hair. He pulled up his notes for the client he was scheduled to see before lunch. A young Midwestern transplant with goals of grandeur who had been chewed and spit out by the city on more than one occasion. They were making progress on realistic goal setting, prioritization, and negative self-talk, as well as her anxiety. Davey thought she was only coming to him to tell her small-town parents they knew SolaRae's husband. But he was proud of the work they were doing. The transplant didn't show. He doomscrolled until his stomach told him it was time for lunch.

He meandered down the steps to his home-away-from-home. His stomach spoke again and reminded him that he should speed up a bit. He was thankful to return to the comforting noise of the streets. Boris's hot dog stand, more commonly known on the internet as Central Sausage. Davey crossed the street as Boris sat on a lawn chair next to the stand in a plain white shirt and black pants. He was a large man, imposing on anyone who didn't give him a chance and speak with him.

"David, my friend! Welcome to Central Sausage, all hero eat here!" He stood and opened his arms to greet Davey as he crossed the street. Davey was welcomed to the sound of the sizzling hot dogs and the smell of grease that made them just that much better.

"Just Davey, Boris. How's business?" He asked Boris this every day. It was part of the charade that they didn't already know they would not be in each other's lives outside of 12:15 p.m. on a weekday.

"Good, David, good. You try new dog today?"

"I'm good, Boris. Just the regular."

"No, today is a new day, da?"

"Yes, Boris, but I don't want to try a hero dog." He eyed the SolaRae Dog picture and firmly declared again that he would never choose it.

"I come up with a new one. The Echona Dog, sweet chili. You feel the aftertaste at dinner."

"Clever. But, no. Just the regular."

"How about the Bratislava Dog? It's sausage, not hot dog. Sauerkraut and mustard, good, yes? You try? I use secret Slovak squeeze technique."

Davey was interested and, for whatever reason, opted to try something new.

"Sure, Boris. Why not? A regular, and I'll add a Bratislava Dog."

"Yes! My grandmother say one full belly, one full heart."

He paid the vendor and left Central Sausage until the next day. He took the two hot dogs back up the steps and returned to his office. He sat with his lunch and first ate the new option. That's when he remembered he didn't even like sauerkraut.

He was particularly hungry and decided to stomach it before embracing his other old friend. The afternoon stretched on before him, and his next appointment time arrived. It was with an entrepreneur who seemed to have more failed business decisions than successful ones. But Davey applauded his persistence, especially since work was clearly an avoidance technique for the crippling depression that he refused to acknowledge. The entrepreneur, unfortunately, was a no-call, no-show. Davey wasn't entirely disappointed with how lackadaisical his day became. Before he wasted too much more time, he forced himself to review the intake. It was a young Black man from the Bronx. He was slim, with a cut jawline, dark eyes, and a shaved head. He was referred to Davey by an inpatient program that specialized in working with at-risk young adults who might not have access to the proper mental health services necessary for success.

His phone chimed. Another text.

Rae: I got you access. Come down to the 30th Precinct. I can come fly you over if it would take too long.

Davey: It's okay. I'll be there soon, but I need to be back for an intake later this afternoon. What's his name?

Rae: Sounds good. I'll fly you if time is too short. Name is Simon Cribb. Thank you <3

Davey looked at his phone. Simon's name seemed familiar, but he wasn't running around the city mixed up with criminals. He started to close his laptop, then he saw it again. Simon Cribb was meant to be his intake appointment. For a moment, the city felt smaller, like all its chaos was quietly circling the same few people and had decided he belonged in the middle.

Chapter 3: Say Something

Davey sat on the rickety train to Sugar Hill and continued to be in the presence of greatness. The recorded track that encouraged safety on the train came over the loudspeaker, and it was SolaRae. She turned the charm up for the announcement, but he knew his wife's voice was warning him to "say something if he sees something." He answered her prompt in his mind with a yes, Babe, will do. He offered a silent chuckle to the blank faces around him in the crowd of the train that, naturally, went unanswered.

He heard the automated track play another two or three times before he approached his stop. The last time it played, he changed his answer to Rae, I don't think I will, in a joking manner. The train stopped at the 145th Street station, and the train brakes overtook the automated messages. He disembarked and thought about how the inner dialogue he had with the loudspeakers on train rides was the most he spoke to his wife some days. Sometimes he liked it when the train was delayed for whatever reason. It meant he was able to sit with her a bit longer.

He navigated his way to daylight and climbed the grimy steps to the street. He rarely found himself in Manhattan after he graduated from college. The sound of the vibrant borough felt sharp to him. The noises cut across his ears like a nail on a chalkboard. It felt as if he moved slowly against the waves of vendors, tourists, financiers, and the unhoused. The air felt dense. It was as if the social ladder that many found themselves climbing in Manhattan contributed to being thousands of feet above sea level. Above Queens. At one point, he loved it nearly as much as he did his home borough, but that thought was quickly dispelled. He continued and took in the distinct atmosphere that came with the lengthy borough. The sounds were similar but foreign; they weren't his own. Not the ones from Kew Gardens.

As his feet took him down St. Nicholas Ave., children playfully ran past, acting as if they were flying. He smiled as they passed him, and OwlHeart quietly flew overhead. She descended and swiftly vanished behind the short skyline of W. 151st St. Davey continued to walk until he turned the corner for the precinct. A crowd had already gathered. Not of justice seekers but of media outlets and fans. They weren't asking about the criminal; they were asking for the heroes. Cameras flashed to be outdone only by SolaRae's natural brightness. He saw her as soon as he turned the corner. She was buried in the crowd. But to Davey, she looked just like the girl he knew as a child. She stood tall between LunAva and OwlHeart, who had just arrived. News seekers shouted questions as the lights of emergency vehicles added to the controlled chaos. But he only cared for her. He had already learned to, mostly, live with the excitement that followed.

He walked closer to the precinct entrance. His peripheral vision filled with movement, and his eyes narrowed. His wife saw him now. She winked at him, and his steps felt a little lighter. He got a closer look at OwlHeart for the first time, or the woman he learned was Sara. She had wide hips and light, neutral-colored frills that popped. She appeared to be a true owl, and fans couldn't tell where her suit ended and her tan skin began. Davey thought it looked magnificent. He continued to walk past them and noticed only a small, single out-of-place item on OwlHeart. The white of a breast pad just revealed itself over the seam line of the frills. In her excellence, Davey forgot that she had just given birth a few months ago. He maneuvered into the building and welcomed an acceptable level of noise as he paused. He wasn't quite sure if it was her heroics, her suit, or her ability to do her job while intermittently pumping for the child she just welcomed into the world that made her most magnificent.

As he acquainted himself with the precinct, he took in the atmosphere. Keyboards competed with phones and voices to see which might be the loudest. Officers briskly moved around him as he navigated the traffic like an old video game and made his way to the desk sergeant.

"Hey." He didn't get the attention of the man in uniform.

"Excuse me!" he tried to speak up.

The desk sergeant, who was leaning over paperwork, peered at him through his glasses.

"No need to yell, sir. Can I help you?" Davey didn't quite comprehend how he seemed to talk flatly but loud enough to conquer the noise around him.

"I'm here to see Simon Cribb."

"You're not his attorney."

"No. I know that."

"So, you can't see him."

"I'm the therapist."

"I'm the desk sergeant."

Davey, exasperated, put his hands on his hips gently and looked at the ground.

"SolaRae sent me." He didn't like pulling the hero card, but sometimes it was necessary.

"Yeah? God sent me." He wiped his nose.

"You don't believe me?"

"Should I?"

"It would be nice, yeah."

As the back and forth continued, the heroes left the admiring crowd on the street and strutted into the building. It felt like things simply stopped around them. Rae approached her husband and the desk sergeant. LunAva and OwlHeart hung back and started down the hall. Davey caught a shift in the air of the room.

"He's good, Gary." She addressed him.

Gary didn't stop staring at Davey. "Sure thing, SolaRae. Thanks for the help last night again."

SolaRae tapped Davey's shoulder and motioned for him to follow her. They proceeded in the direction of the other heroes as Rae called back, "Any time, Gary!"

The precinct parted for the hero as the path to the back room that held Simon Cribb was easily navigable. He caught himself being in awe of his wife again. A state that he was realizing might as well be a constant. The smell of her perfume filled the narrow hallway. He wanted to kiss her as the longing he routinely felt in her absence was amplified in her presence. But she wouldn't appreciate it while working, so he didn't.

"Ava, OwlHeart, and I will be on the other side of the glass in case you need us. Just talk to him. Get a feel for what's going on. Sounds alright?" She turned to face him as they reached the room.

"Sure," he said, staring into her eyes.

"Love you," she whispered with a smirk.

He winked at her and entered the room. Simon Cribb sat with his arms folded on his stomach. His head slouched so his chin touched the top of his chest. As Davey entered, the suspect was unmoving, and a notepad sat on his side of the table. He sat in his spot and noticed Simon's hands were cuffed. He observed the captive in silence for a beat before he began.

"Hey, Simon. Looks like you might have found yourself in some trouble. My name's Davey, I'm a therapist. Just here to talk. No judgment whatsoever."

There was no response. Rae said the DA cleared an informal wellness consult, but he wasn't sure if Simon was ready to talk.

"They told me you were involved in a robbery that went wrong?"

Silence.

"You know what, Simon? I think I was supposed to meet with you today, regardless. You were a referral of mine. I think it might be beneficial if you chose to talk, Simon, since we were going to anyway and all."

He lifted his head.

"What are you thinking about, Simon?"

"I'm scared."

Davey paused for a brief moment to see if the young man would continue his train of thought. But there was nothing added.

"That makes a lot of sense. It's totally natural to be scared. I can only imagine the handcuffs and cold dark room don't help. Is this your first time in cuffs?"

"No."

"And what was the first time like for you?"

"The arresting cop let me go. Connected me with mental health people or whatever. I didn't think I needed it."

"That's fair. Can you tell me about your first experience?"

"It was nothing."

"Sure. That would explain being let go. I could find out from the officers, but I'd rather hear your side."

"Fine."

"Thank you, Simon."

"I had a stressful day and was mad at the world. I don't remember doing it, but somebody called the cops on me. They said I was screaming on the street in a threatening voice. They said I had a knife. The cop didn't find one. That's all."

"I hear you. What do you think happened?"

"I don't know. I remember thinking my vision got blurry."

Simon looked at the corner of the room and squinted as if something caught his attention. Davey was taking notes.

"Your pen is kind of loud. Did you know that?"

"Sorry, Simon. Thanks for letting me know."

Simon's breath was slow. Methodical.

"You have to live on the street, is that right?"

"Yeah."

"Sorry to hear that. If you'd like, I know of a few shelters that can help during the cold months."

Silence.

"So, what happened last night? Again, I just want to hear your side."

"I was hungry and they told me that stealing some food would be easy enough."

"I see. Who is 'they'? The street and train cameras only saw you alone."

Simon paused and stared at the corner again. "Nobody."

"Sure. So you broke in to steal some food."

"And a blanket."

"And a blanket. What happened next?"

"I was in the kitchen, and some lady walked in."

Davey continued to take notes and attempted to do so quietly.

"She scared me when she screamed. I tried to tell her that I just needed some food. I didn't realize anybody was home. She just kept yelling. It was too loud. I grabbed a knife and stopped the yelling so I could focus. Some other girl walked in, and I ran back through the door with food."

"I'm sorry that happened, Simon. It sounds like that was a really tough situation for you. Is there anything else you'd like to tell me?"

"No."

"Well, thank you for talking with me."

Davey stood from his chair and left the man in the dark room. The door closed with a soft click behind him, and he found himself thankful that he had the flexibility to freely move. Exiting the adjoining room, Rae joined him in the hallway.

"What do you think?"

"Well, he definitely killed someone, but he also definitely needs some sort of assistance at the same time."

"You think he should be let go?"

"Not at all, babe... SolaRae. There needs to be justice for the life he took, but I'm fearful that he will get lost in the judicial system. I'm just saying that I think there should be a balance. He needs help."

"That's fair. Thanks for coming. I'll see you later."

"Yeah." He didn't entirely believe that he would be able to see her tonight.

They walked together through the noise of the precinct and back to the crowd outside. Rae squeezed his arm before they separated.

"You're doing good work, Rae."

She smiled at him. "You too."

She walked through the door to the flashing lights of her adoration. He waited a moment and slinked out behind her back into the open streets. He returned to the comfortable hum of the busy city.

Later that evening, the sisters SolaRae and LunAva patrolled the night skies of New York. They were hardly ever dim. If anything, the night made it easier to see certain occurrences that required their attention. As they neared the end of their watch, an unfortunate accident took place on a nearby overpass. Smoke billowed into the night sky as one car was flipped and threatened to fall onto the road beneath it. The sisters flew into action. They cut through the sky with precision and grace. When they arrived at the scene of the accident, SolaRae took the lead.

"Check on them," she pointed to the car at risk of falling. It teetered slowly like a seesaw forced to move by a slight breeze. The clicks of the car across the flimsy railing nearly sounded as if the vehicle itself was screeching for help. "I'll take care of the other one."

LunAva did as her sister instructed. In the past, she might have interjected with her own plan. But she had started to become amenable, and Rae was right. It made sense for the hero with control of gravity to check on the car about to fall. Ava didn't like it, but she knew her sister was right. She floated down to check on the occupants of the swaying car.

"Hey, guys… how's it goin'?" LunAva asked.

The passengers were too stunned to speak.

"Hanging in there?" she joked.

"I don't really know that now's a great time, LunAva," the driver responded.

"I mean, I guess not."

She flew around the car to make sure it was safe to lift when she heard Rae check in.

"How does it look, LunAva?" her older sister yelled.

"Peachy. You?"

"Easy fix."

Ava flew back down to face the driver.

"I'll get you out of here in a jiff, bud. Just… don't go anywhere."

"Wasn't planning on it!" The driver's voice was shaky.

LunAva flew to the side of the car and focused on it. She began to alter the gravity of the car, so it would float off the overpass and toward an open patch of road. As she did so, a piece of rebar that she hadn't noticed was pinned down by the car sprang back like a pinned doorstop.

It struck her across the side of her head.

Her vision blurred as the car began to drop.

She attempted to compose herself and successfully ensured the safety of the car.

Her vision became gray, and ringing filled her ears.

SolaRae went to check on her sister and noticed something was off. LunAva began to fall out of the air. It wasn't a far drop to the road below, but it was still one that would be painful. She flew to her sister and barely caught her in time. A slow stream of blood started to leave Ava's ear as Rae lifted her back upward. Rae's chest began to rise and fall sharply. Her shoulders tensed and her eyes widened.

"Ava!" she called out.

There was no response.

The honks and headlights of rushed travelers waiting for the debris of the accident to be cleared filled the night sky.

"Ava!" She tried to be louder. She touched her sister's warm blood that stuck to her fingertips.

Ava lurched forward.

She fell out of Rae's arms and then stabilized herself. Her jaw started to turn a shade of black and blue that would rival a cool dusk.

"What the heck, dude?!"

She grabbed her jaw.

"Dang, that hurt."

"Hospital?" Rae asked.

"I'm fine," she rubbed her jaw after she spoke.

"Ava, I really—"

"I'm fine, Rae. Just remind me not to listen to you again."

"You've been saying that for years, sis."

"And yet you continue to not remind me."

"And I'll continue that trend. Are you going back to your apartment tonight?"

Ava avoided eye contact with her sister, "No. Mom's tonight. I still haven't talked to Eric yet."

Rae gave her a look that only a big sister was capable of giving her little sister.

"I know, I will." Ava attempted to reassure her.

"Don't wait until it's too late, Ava."

"Yeah, yeah. See you tomorrow," Ava started to fly off for their parents' house.

"I'm texting mom about your accident, so she can check you out!" Rae called after her before heading for her own home.

By the time she arrived back in Kew Gardens, the day had become tomorrow. She flew in through the bedroom window and tripped on her entrance. Davey shot upwards from their bed.

"Babe?" he said groggily. "Everything okay?"

He reached for a lamp on the nightstand.

"Sorry, yeah," she sniffed. "I mean… no."

He yawned, "Want to talk?"

"It's okay. You can go back to bed."

"It's fine, Rae. What's going on?"

She didn't say anything.

She moved to the bed, superhero suit still on, and collapsed onto Davey. She buried her face into his shoulder and started to cry quietly.

He let the quiet keep and put his arms around her, stifling another yawn in the process. He rubbed his hands down her sweaty hair and held on until she didn't need to be held anymore.

"Want to tell me what happened?" Davey asked, "Or is that a conversation for another day?"

"It's really not a big deal. It was just…"

"Rae, if it made you cry, it's a big deal."

"There was a car accident. Ava and I were taking care of it. She didn't see a piece of rebar pinned under the car; she moved it, and the thing smacked her across her head. She started to fall out of the air. I caught her, but then I couldn't wake her up. I just… I thought I lost her."

"I'm sorry, babe," he yawned, "that must have been scary. She's good now, though?" Rae nodded.

"Good. That's what matters. Need help with your suit?"

"I'm good. I'm going to take a shower, and I'll be in bed soon."

He turned off the lamp and gave her a thumbs-up as he collapsed back down onto the bed. Rae's breathing slowed until it matched his own. She pulled away and disappeared into the bathroom. The shower started a moment later, steady and distant. Davey listened to the sound of water on tile as he lay and attempted to fall back asleep. It reminded him of rain on glass, the same rhythm that used to calm him when he was young. He thought about the car crash, about how many lives she had to hold together so she didn't fall apart herself.

The water stopped. Steam drifted under the door and into the room. It carried her scent with it. He felt it settle around the bedroom, warm and nearly electric. For a moment, he imagined the sound of the train again, her voice coming through the speaker. Say something if you see something.

He looked toward the bathroom door and whispered, "I see you."

When she came out and slid into bed beside him, she was quiet. He could just feel the magnetic pull of her body. He heard her try to quietly clear her throat and just barely reached out his hand for her. Davey thought that maybe this was what love really looked like when no one was watching.

Chapter 4: Quick Realism

One week later, the circle of resolute chairs formed again. The room smelled of burnt coffee and rain. The men welcomed the soft pitter-patter of raindrops falling against the front window of the Kew Gardens home. Pumpkins littered the stoops of 127th as the community readied itself for Thanksgiving in the coming weeks.

"Welcome back, guys. Glad you all decided to come back for a second get-together. How's everybody been doing?"

"Dude, I got myself a better webcam and I think I'm ready to start streaming!" Eric shared excitedly.

"That's great, Eric. Way to dive in."

"Yeah, I think it'll go well."

"Just don't be disappointed when it doesn't," Cass added.

Eric's smile faded.

"Really, bro?" Jose questioned Cass.

"I'm a realist."

"That's kinda messed up, bro," Jose called him out.

"If messed up is being real, then…. whatever." He paused. "Listen, Eric, I'm glad you're doing this. I'm just saying that I know streaming is oversaturated. From what I've heard, it can be difficult to grow a fan base, let alone have a revenue stream."

"Doesn't mean you shouldn't start, Eric. Just don't get discouraged." Davey shared.

"I can try. Also, things seem to be pretty good between Ava and me. So, that's cool."

Davey shifted uncomfortably in his chair and recalled the last conversation he had with his sister-in-law. He pondered whether she ended up talking to him or not. "Glad to hear it, Eric. Anything else on your mind?"

"Nope. I think things are looking up for me."

Jose gave Eric a fist bump in support.

"Heck yeah, bro."

The smile returned to Eric's face.

"Not trying to be the bad guy here."

"Just good at it?" Jose responded to Cass.

"Maybe I should just go." He stood up to leave, as the quiet room filled with the sound of the rain, and he threw his Styrofoam cup in the garbage. He caught a glimpse of his warped reflection in the front window, which was cluttered with raindrops. Frozen in the doorway, he had to decide if it would be better to brace the rain or sit back down. Davey watched the tension roll through his shoulders and recognized the look. The quiet collapse of a man too tired to fight his own performance. Cass wasn't angry. He was frayed. A streetlight outside of Davey's home hummed as if it were chiming into the conversation with the men in the front room. It hummed for a beat too long before Davey took over for it.

"Come on, Cass. It's alright. Realism is helpful. Nobody can be optimistic all the time. With that being said, I think most of us face the harshness of real life on a regular enough basis to leave some at the door. You help us stay grounded."

"Just messing around, Cass," Jose added.

"It's all good, dude," Eric remarked.

Cass considered the men's responses.

"You guys made me throw out my coffee."

He took a second before sitting back down.

"It's fine. It's bad coffee anyway." Cass started to warm up. "Speaking of which, Jose, how's it going?"

"Funny."

"My coffee is fine." Davey sipped it and tried not to smirk behind his lie.

"Na, man. It's not."

"Really not selling me on the whole coffee thing, fellas." Jose yawned. "I think I'm gonna have to bite the bullet and figure something out. The four-month sleep regression is killing me."

"Just have an energy drink, dude. I have one or two a day and I'm good." Eric suggested.

"Bro, do you know how bad those things are for you? I can't be

putting that stuff into my body. I'm an athlete... or at least used to be."
He took a long exhale.

"Get back into the gym recently?" Davey questioned.

"Na, bro. Not really, at least. It's been kinda fun though. I love that little dude."

"Looks like parenting suits you, Jose."

"Yeah, I think so. I'll be able to get back to it at some point, I'm sure. In the meantime, I started jogging with him. Sara pumps on top of buildings and then tries to figure out a good spot to meet and hand it off to me without a huge crowd around. It's a fun game we play. Sometimes I've even been lucky enough to beat her to the spot and try to sneak up on her. The baby usually gives us away when he sees the cool bird that's his mom."

"That's pretty sweet. You guys are adjusting to the new normal, then?" He wondered what counted as normal for him now. Nights without sleep; the continued attempt at learning to love the ache of absence.

"Oh, for sure. She's been limiting her endorsement commitments for a bit, too. So we get her more at home. It kinda puts us in a tough financial spot because I haven't been able to do events for my triathlete endorsements, but we'll get there. She's incredible. I'm just holding it down."

"Yeah, I feel that, Jose." Davey was proud of the man who seemed to be in good spirits. But the idea of adjusting to a new normal was still something that escaped him when it came to his sleep cycle. "How's your new normal, Cass?"

"Same old. Nothing new over here."

"Jaz is doing good? Didn't see her at that press thing at the precinct in Manhattan for Simon Cribb last week."

"Jazmine is fine. She was doing something else."

"Glad she's doing well."

"What about you, bro? ¿Qué te pasa? What's going on in the life of Davey and numero uno, SolaRae?" Jose asked.

"Not much really. We talked, and we're still in agreement to try for a baby."

"Nice, bro. And did you get to?"

"Yeah, dude, did you?" Eric whistled.

Davey chuckled. "As a matter of fact, yes. After the Cribb thing, it was a quiet week, and she was home for two or three days."

"Good to know she could spare thirty seconds from her busy life," Eric responded.

"That's at least fifteen seconds longer than what I've heard about you," he winked, "brother-in-law."

"Hey, man, not cool."

"That was a quick response, Eric," Cass suggested. "Used to doing things… quickly?"

Jose burst out into laughter before he switched back to Davey. "Happy for you, bro. Kids are great. Seeing the little dude grab your finger with his whole hand just makes it all worth it."

"Thanks, Jose. I hope we don't have to try for too long before it happens."

"Bro…" Jose started before he paused.

"What?"

"You absolutely want it to take at least a little bit of time." Jose laughed again and got some chuckles from the other men once Eric caught on to what he meant. "Just sayin' you should take your time." His laughter trailed off.

Davey took a sip of his coffee and stopped himself from laughing again as the heat reached his lips.

"You guys are something else," Cass remarked.

"In the best way possible. You really have nothing on your mind, Cass?"

"Not really. At least nothing that I'm spending time thinking about. I keep myself busy. Court appearances, endorsement deals, briefings, news appearances, depositions, brand negotiations. It just keeps going."

"And you're not burnt out? That's a lot, man."

"Bro is the super husband." Jose chuckled.

"I do what I have to," Cass replied.

"It sounds like you have to give yourself a break," Davey added.

"I will take one when I can."

"Well, you know we're here."

Eric and Jose nodded in agreement with Davey, who looked at his phone to check the time.

"Hey, anybody want to watch the Nets game? It starts soon."

"The Nets, bro? The former New Jersey Nets? The fake New York team? Bro, the Mets and the Nets?" Jose questioned Davey's logic.

"I'm a glutton for punishment." Davey shrugged.

"Don't tell me you're a Jets fan, too?"

"J-E-T-S!"

There was no response.

"What, seriously, no other Jets fans?"

"Of course not!" Jose added.

"I don't follow sports, unless it's e-sports."

"Giants, all the way," Cass added.

"Giants, Knicks, Yankees, Rangers. It's an easy choice, bro."

"Fine, fine. Does anybody want to stay for the game or not?"

"To watch them lose? Sure, can't wait. My mom's domino night was canceled so she can watch him longer. I can stay til halftime, probably."

"I have to get back to work. This was my free hour of the day. But next time, maybe." Cass stood from his chair again. "You want me to put this chair somewhere, Davey?"

"I'll take care of it. Thanks, Cass. Don't work yourself too hard."

Cass opened the door and left for the sidewalk back to his car. The smell of rain on an autumn day filled the air. It challenged the lingering burnt coffee scent for control before being whisked away in the breeze of the door clicking shut. The chair was empty but stood resolute in its position. Partially indented, mostly uneven when not being used, and the metallic gray was now a spotted brown.

"How about you, Eric? Feel like taking up basketball?"

"Not really, but I don't think I have anything else to do. Let me see if Ava is home." He pulled out his phone in a struggling movement that seemed like it took more energy than it should have. "Aw, man, my phone died. Can I use your charger, Davey?"

"Sure, Eric. It's in the kitchen. Bring it over near the TV. There's a plug by the couch."

Davey led Jose to the adjoining room that held a comfortable sectional and a large TV. He pulled up the game and showed Eric where the nearest charger was. Soon enough, the game started, and during the first break in action, an advertisement for a new type of hearing aid came on with Echona as a spokesperson. She was in her suit and given a script full of puns surrounding hearing and echoes.

"Wonder how much Cass got her for that?" Davey asked.

"Not enough, bro. That was bad."

"Places are still figuring out how to best use heroes for revenue, I guess. OwlHeart ever do any bad ads?"

"There was one rep from a fried chicken ad that tried to get her."

"Yikes."

"Yeah, she passed on that one."

"Good."

Eric's phone powered on and started to buzz repeatedly.

"Ah, crap, I gotta go," Eric spoke up. "Ava's waiting for me at home. Thanks for the charge, dude."

"Get home safe, man."

"See you, bro."

Eric wandered out of the house and allowed the chill of autumn to once again breach the entrance. Davey wondered if Ava might end up having the talk with him or not. It wasn't his place to ask. So he would add it to the list of things he would be patiently waiting to hear about.

"So, Sara and you really have a good system going?"

"Yes and no. Her schedule isn't exactly fixed. She's out patrolling right now and hoping that nothing comes up so she can meet me at home with the kid. In a way, the kid's sleep issues have helped us spend more time together."

"That's nice at least."

"Yeah, she was actually thinking about revealing her identity, but decided not to. Just in case some crazy person wanted to come after one of the first babies from a super."

"Understandable." Davey's chest began to feel tight. He felt tension in his forehead and on his shoulders.

Everybody knew Rae's face.

She never attempted to hide it. It made any potential date night a challenge. Most people who cared to know knew who she was married to. A good deal of people preferred to act like she wasn't married at all. Desire sells. So he had been told by a number of public relations people who claimed to have the best intentions for Rae, and by extension for Davey. But if she got pregnant, if they had a child, everybody would know. The media would follow their pregnancy. Try to be there when the kid is born. Maybe even try to follow them home. Be there every day outside of their Kew Gardens home during her maternity leave. He hated himself for the thought, but part of him feared her fame less for what it brought her than what it took from him. Every headline made her brighter, and him a little farther away.

The two men continued to watch the game in silence when the autumnal air filled the space for another moment. Jose couldn't be bothered to shift his attention, but Davey looked to the door as it clicked shut.

It was Rae. In all of her splendor, she walked through the threshold of their familial home in her suit as if it were just another day. To her, it was. She was carrying a bag of takeout and walked to the room. Her legs elongated in the stripes of the suit and tall boots.

"Hey, babe, brought dumplings." She bent to kiss Davey's cheek. "Oh, hey, I'm Rae."

"Ha, yeah, I know." He smiled at her. "Jose."

"Would it surprise you if I said that I knew that already?" She smirked.

"You didn't suddenly develop the ability to read minds, did you, babe?"

"No, but that would be sweet. I just saw your picture. I was sitting with OwlHeart while she was pumping. She showed me your picture and your kid. Couldn't stop raving about how good a dad you are. Kind of made me want one of my own. I think Davey would be a great dad." She rested her free hand on her husband's shoulder. "How do you guys know each other?"

"I'm sure he will be," Jose smirked at Davey. "We used to go to the same gym." He patted Davey and rose from the couch.

"Leaving already? I got extra dumplings just in case."

"Yeah, it's almost halftime, and I really do have to get back. Nice to officially meet you, Rae. I'll catch you next time, bro."

"Thanks for stopping by, Jose." The cool breeze entered the home once more.

Davey watched the door for a moment after it shut. The house fell quiet, the game murmuring in the background like a reminder that the world kept moving. He thought about Jose, the way the man smiled through exhaustion. Before the baby, Jose had been the kind of athlete who could run a marathon and still offer to spot you after. Now his endurance was measured in hours without sleep and bottles prepped by dim light. When Jose talked about "holding it down," Davey knew he meant it in more ways than one. The man was lifting a house with one hand and a life he'd traded in the other.

The quiet pressed in. Davey sat back on the couch, listening to the city breathe through the window seams. The air smelled faintly of rain and reheated coffee.

Davey was alone with his wife. An event that he felt was far too infrequent, but they would develop a routine. Their own new normal at some point. Rae slipped off her boots near the couch, the sound small against the hum of the now-muted TV. She leaned back, eyes closed for the first time that day. For a moment, neither spoke. She rested her head on him and closed her eyes as the two embraced. Her hair was damp against him.

"You look tired," he said.

"I am," she answered without opening her eyes. "But it's a good kind of tired."

He ran his thumb across her hand. It was rougher than he remembered, calloused from fieldwork. The small, human part of her he could still touch. She opened her eyes and smiled at him, and for once, he didn't think about the city, or the lights, or who might be watching. Just her, here, next to him.

"So, dumplings?" Davey stood and put his arm around the waist of his wife.

"Dumplings. Maybe the best culinary invention ever."

He kissed her.

"You know what?"

She kissed him back.

"What?"

"I think dumplings would taste great after…"

She kissed him again and cut him off.

"Did you develop the ability to read minds all of a sudden?"

"Not quite."

He kissed her again. She left him to put the bag of dumplings on their coffee table. Then returned and embraced her husband. She leaned in and whispered in his ear, "Unzip me."

Chapter 5: When Queens Slept

In the morning, Davey woke to find that Rae still lay next to him. Her limbs sprawled out, hair messy, and a bit of drool that tried to leave her open mouth. The sheets just barely covered her naked body. A container of dumplings sat on the nightstand. Open, mostly empty. Some soy sauce fell onto the white rug on the bedroom floor. They brought their snack upstairs while making full use of the free evening.

A loud array of honking entered the room from the street below. To his surprise, his wife continued to sleep. He looked at her and smirked. He wanted to congratulate himself, but he was sure she was just wildly tired. There was something grounding about watching her sleep through the city's noise. The woman who once lit up half of Midtown without breaking a sweat could now snore softly beside him. It reminded him that he wasn't just her support system. He was her landing pad. She was his, and he was hers. She, however, was also the city's.

And the city felt awake as she slept.

Sunlight crept through the closed blinds as if it were a call to action for SolaRae. It hit her face. Her still features shone in brightness. He thought that if he were an artist, she would be his muse. He put on a pair of old gym shorts before leaving the comfort of his bed.

He quietly shuffled out of the room, thankful that she didn't have part of Echona's ability and her sensitive hearing or volume control. He climbed down the stairs, careful not to step on any of the wooden planks that liked to complain when too much weight was put on them. He reached the bottom and stared at the chairs, still holding guard over the otherwise empty room where they were positioned the night before.

The rain stopped at some point and left behind a light dew on the front window. Davey shifted to the kitchen to start some coffee. He drank it black; she drank it closer to a coffee-flavored milkshake. Afterwards, the consideration was to start their breakfast but the question arose if she had to fly off to anywhere this morning. So, he began his climb up the whiny staircase. Now, with an extra level of caution to not spill the full mugs. When he arrived back in the bedroom, she managed to sit up in bed. Her eyes were still groggy, and she stretched out her arms for an exaggerated yawn. He handed her the mug.

"Thanks, babe." She yawned again.

"Sleep well?"

"Amazingly." She set the coffee mug on the nightstand and decided to eat the last surviving dumpling that clung to the container. She washed it down with hot coffee. Somehow, heat didn't seem to bother her much. Davey thought it might be the best benefit of being able to harness the power of the giant fireball in the sky. He smiled at her with an appreciative glance. This level of normality rarely happened, and it was proof to him that his life before she decided to become a hero was still out there somewhere.

"I'm glad. We should do it again sometime."

She blushed, and he loved that he was able to cause that response still after the years they had been together.

"We really should." She drank more of her coffee.

"Anything on the docket for you today?"

"There's some impromptu rally with Election Day next week. NYPD asked for an assist in case it gets out of hand. I'll be there with Echona, while Ava and OwlHeart patrol the skies and see if anybody needs them for anything."

"Wow, be safe. Some of these people have gotten a little emotional."

She shook her head, "Right. As if a politician ever cared."

"Hey, there are some good ones out there."

"Maybe."

He drank his coffee that had reached an acceptable temperature for prolonged sips.

"How about you? Anything going on? I know your Fridays usually have lower client activity."

"I'll be at the office through lunch. Then, I'm open. I was actually thinking about trying to talk to Simon Cribb again. I think I heard they're moving his arraignment up from next week. I was supposed to be his therapist. Maybe I can dig a little."

"I don't know if there's much use, babe. The DA sounds to be pretty sure of the outcome of the trial." She stood from the bed to go to the bathroom.

He observed her walk. A siren sang outside their window and proceeded down the street.

"But, good luck. Swing by the rally when you're done? It should still be going on into rush hour."

"Sure. Where is it?"

"Marcus Garvey Park. They haven't moved Cribb from holding at the 30th, so I think you can just hop on the bus and work your way down Manhattan."

"Sounds right. I'll try to stop by."

"Thanks, babe."

She left the bathroom, still nude, and walked to her husband. She placed her hand on his bare chest, and he felt her knee rub against his old gym shorts. "Seriously, thank you. I couldn't do what I do without you." She kissed him.

"I'm here for you, Rae. Always have been. You know that." She moved to start getting into her suit.

"You know, I'm fully capable of getting in and out of my suit on my own, but it's nice when I get your help. Do you mind?" She finished slithering inside and turned her back to him.

"Not at all." He set his coffee down on the nightstand and zipped her up. He stole a kiss on her cheek and playfully smacked her butt. Then, he started to get ready himself.

His closet had become more extensive than hers since she decided to assume the identity of SolaRae. But there were never enough options to make his daily choices all that difficult. He put on his comfortable professional look and donned the faded hoodie with the broken zipper. They both finished their beverages. He started making the bed before Rae suggested that he might want to wash the sheets first. So, he stripped them and quickly made it with the spare set.

"Flying out today, babe?"

"How about I walk out with you?"

"Is that the safest idea?"

"If people wanted to track me down. It wouldn't be that hard, Davey. If I can get another minute with you, I will."

"Understood." He replied with a smile. "Ready to go?"

"Just about." She went back to the bathroom, and Davey could hear the sound of her spraying her perfume. She walked past him for the stairs, and the smell intoxicated him. They walked down the stairs talking as a normal married couple would. The dew on the window had begun to dry from the morning warmth. Davey rinsed the coffee mugs and set them in the sink as Rae opened the door.

He held it open for her to pass through first and softly closed it behind them as the door let them know their day would now begin with its quiet click. The street was no busier than any other morning. The train rattled in the distance, cars honked, and Queens was alive. She kissed him on the sidewalk.

"See you later. Love you."

"Love you too. Be safe," He responded, and she gently took off into the air. The air formed around her, and he studied her soft flight path. She left to attempt to protect the city from killers like Simon Cribb. He would step into his routine and try to see if he was able to understand him.

Together, they helped the city.

In one distinct way or another.

He focused his attention back on his routine. Although it didn't require much focus any longer. It was the Q80 bus to Union Turnpike–Kew Gardens Station and the E to Queens Plaza. Easy as flying. The subway advertisement was his sister-in-law this time, telling the riders to keep an eye out for dark spaces and be aware of their surroundings. He thought this one was a clever idea. Good job, transit.

He was happy sitting with the usual faces of a weekday morning and the rhythm of the train. Accustomed to the screech of the brakes, the grime on the station's steps near his office, and the climb to an uneasy quietness that, somehow, always shocked him when he arrived at his square of confinement. He opened his laptop to fill the room with the soft hum of the fan whirling inside. He welcomed an email from his 10 a.m. client that needed to reschedule. He started to think meeting with the husbands was good luck for a lackadaisical Friday. So, he did what any self-respecting thirty-something would do with no work and started flicking through videos until lunch. The time went by fast enough for Davey, and by the time 12:15 p.m. came to him, he was off to the races. He left his quiet concealment for the steady hum and Boris. He was sitting in his lawn chair, white shirt and black pants.

"David, my friend! Welcome!"

"Just Davey, Boris. How's business?"

"Good, David, good. You try new dog?"

"Just the regular, Boris."

"You like spice, yes?"

"Not really."

"I have Atomic Crunch Dog. Deep-fried with spicy mayo and diced ha-la-peenos."

"That's going to be an atomic no."

"Okay, David. You like magic, yes? Try Bacon Surprise Dog. It dog, wrapped in bacon, sprinkled with chocolate cookie dust, and icing drizzle." Boris grinned like a man who believed food was science. Every new creation was an experiment in joy or disaster, but never indifference.

"Surprise!" Davey playfully raised his voice. "Two regulars." Standing there made him hungrier. Boris pouted at the man but prepared the two hot dogs and took his payment.

"See you Monday, David."

"Have a good weekend, Boris."

Davey took his lunch back up the stairs to his office as he tried to match his pace to the train beneath him that was just leaving the station. He returned to his office and began to scarf down his two hot dogs. Simon Cribb crossed his mind as he ate. He wasn't entirely sure what he expected from his next talk with the young man. He wasn't even sure that desk sergeant Gary would allow him to see the accused. He just felt compelled to try.

He took the grease-filled aluminum wrappers of the hot dogs with him as he left his office. Lunch was a staple, but that didn't mean he wanted his office to smell like it. It would take far too long for the odor to leave the six-by-six room.

Even if he was able to crack the dirty window that had become stuck in place around the same time he married Rae. He shut his laptop, grabbed his notebook, and descended to civilization. Said his farewells to the large mural of SolaRae and LunAva next door and left them for the train.

The rattle of it was a welcome distraction as his anxieties surrounding Simon Cribb came to light. He didn't hear those announcements or have the capacity to find them funny. He stared out of the opposite window of the train. Through the tunnels of the underground, past stations that were not his own, and his feet subconsciously took him to the transfers he needed.

He arrived at the 30th Precinct and climbed the grimy steps once more. He wondered if the layers of dirt, dust, and occasionally dried gum that covered the steps might be at all similar to how the inside of Simon Cribb's mind felt.

There was no crowd outside the station this time. It remained a quiet street lined with police cars. No sirens, camera flashes, or spinning lights. No heroes as he walked toward the station door and breached the entrance. It was starting to get cold outside, but somehow, the inside felt colder. There was less rush in the air.

No phones or keyboards competing for attention. No officers were navigating around him. Just Davey. And desk sergeant Gary. At Marcus Garvey Park, Rae was in the sunlight, doing what she needed to do for the city. All the while, Davey was about to enter the shadows. Between them, the city turned cyclically between light and dark with love balanced somewhere in the middle.

Chapter 6: He Likes Me

"Excuse me, sir."

Silence.

"Gary?"

The desk sergeant peered over his glasses.

"Do I know you?" he asked.

"Well, no, but…"

"So, why are you calling me Gary?"

"I was here with SolaRae not too long ago and she…"

"So, you're a hero of the city, too?"

"No, I'm a therapist."

"I'm the King of New York."

"I wasn't aware we switched to a monarchy."

Gary stared at him.

"Are you trying to be funny?"

"No, I just…"

Gary raised his arm and stuck out his thumb facing sideways. He paused for dramatics and then tilted his thumb downward.

"I don't actually think kings did that."

"Oh, so you're a historian."

"No. Still just a therapist."

"What do you want, therapist?" Gary enunciated his vocation.

"I'm just here to see Simon Cribb again. I need to speak with him some more."

"Did you become an attorney, too? Historian, comedian, attorney. That's quite the array, funny man."

Davey's shoulders dropped. "Still, only a therapist. I need to speak with him. I think I can help him. It'll be quick."

Gary paused.

"Only because I like you. I'll have him put in the same room as last time. Go on back."

Davey took a moment before working toward the back room. Likes me? he thought. Odd. The hallway lights flickered in rhythm with his pulse. Every visit to a station felt like walking through someone else's nervous system. Flickers, hums, and unseen judgments filled the air.

He proceeded down the corridor, alone this time, and found the room that he had gone to with Rae. It was empty. He took his seat on the sturdy chair that reminded him of what his own used to be like and opened his notebook. After a few minutes, a stern officer walked in with Simon Cribb in handcuffs. The officer didn't address Davey. She sat Cribb down and parted with a, "Don't try anything stupid." Now, it was just Davey and Simon. He wasn't sure if anybody was watching from the adjoining room. In a way, it felt freeing in a frightened but exhilarated sense.

"Hey, Simon. Remember me?"

There was silence as Simon stared into the dark, empty corner of the room.

The same one as last time.

"I'm the therapist who just wanted to hear your side of the story."

"We remember." The young man's eyes didn't shift from the corner.

The plural stuck in the air. Davey felt the room grow colder. He looked toward the corner but saw only faded paint and the faint outline of some forgotten informational poster board once taped there. Whatever Simon saw, it belonged to a place that ignored everyone else. Davey rubbed the back of his neck. He wasn't sure if he wanted to know what lived in that kind of silence.

"I'm glad. How has it been? How are you feeling?"

"Fine."

"That's good, right?"

No answer.

"Have you been able to keep full? Warm?"

"Yes."

"Has your attorney told you what will happen next?"

"Guilty. We're guilty."

"Yeah, I know, Simon. But that doesn't mean you're a bad person. I can tell there's good in you."

"Guilty."

"Does your attorney want you to try to get a plea deal?"

Silence.

"Do you know what the deal is for?"

"Guilty."

"I hear you, Simon. Thank you for sharing. It sounds like you might be looking at going to prison for a bit."

Simon continued to look toward the corner. His eyes never wavered.

"I know your arraignment is coming up. How would you feel if I showed up?"

"Okay."

"One more thing. I have an attorney friend. He's not a criminal attorney, but I was thinking about seeing if he might be able to review your case. It seems pretty much a case closed for everybody involved. But I thought it might be worth a shot to see what he thinks. So, what do you think about that?"

"We have an attorney." Simon's head slowly shifted toward Davey. He stared at the man across from him.

"Right, but isn't he a public defender? They are usually overworked. Could it be worth seeing another perspective?"

"Guilty."

"Simon, is your attorney pressuring you to take a guilty plea to wrap things up and get to sentencing?"

The young man looked back toward the empty corner. A sunken

quietness filled the dark room.

"Guilty."

"Thank you for talking with me, Simon. I'll see you at your arraignment. Keep that belly of yours full." Davey tried to offer Simon a smile, but it felt forced. His words felt small. Like tossing a pebble into a well that had no bottom. He wanted to believe empathy could echo far enough to matter. He wasn't sure it ever did.

He stood to exit the room, and Simon's attention did not shift from the corner. He didn't react at all. Davey opened the metal door and looked back at the young man before leaving him again. Something felt off to him. It felt like Simon needed more help than what was being offered. But Davey wasn't sure how he could help now or if he was capable of helping. He navigated his way down the corridor and heard the door to the adjoining room open. The stern woman in uniform went to retrieve Simon. Davey continued to the entrance.

He turned to Gary before opening the door. "Until next time, King." Davey took a comically exaggerated bow and nearly tripped in the process.

"See you, funny man." The overseer, desk sergeant Gary, responded without looking up from his paperwork. Davey took his leave from the station and left one cold place for another as the autumnal breeze announced itself.

He went the opposite direction from which he came and headed down Amsterdam Ave. toward the M101 bus stop. The city's breath returned in horns, chatter, and bus brakes. He felt it vibrate through the pavement like a pulse. The bus ran every nine minutes, and by the time he arrived at the stop, he just made the next bus. The devoted public transit arrived in a hurry, like it owned the street. To be fair, it might as well have. As he prepared to board, he once again came face to face with his wife. Her dazzling face graced the side of the bus and promoted her next appearance on one of the local late-night talk shows. For a second, he almost waved back at her printed smile. The version of her that never looked tired, never bled, never aged. The city got that one. It took him nearly half an hour to get to the park where his wife was playing security at some political event she didn't care for. The closer he got, the thicker the air became. The smell of sweat, street food, and something metallic hung about.

The city had moods. Within a few minutes, he walked down 5th Ave. to the park, and he could already feel the chaotic energy.

He passed the community pool and the playground toward the noise of shouting. A large grassy area had been wholly filled with people in red shouting at people in blue and vice versa. What he thought was supposed to be an impromptu rally had turned into a competition to see which side was louder. NYPD held a barrier in the middle ground to ensure shouting didn't turn into a melee. Signs filled the air that wasn't already taken by a bullhorn or two. On the far side of the grassy area, SolaRae floated above the crowd. She was attentively watching. Davey thought she was probably just ready for NYPD to call the rally and send everyone home or to a jail cell for the night.

He walked toward the rally, unsure if he actually wanted to set foot into the fray, but he told his wife he would be there. As he arrived, he saw that Echona was standing in the middle ground opposite SolaRae. He knew that she couldn't fly, but it was still a shock to him to see a superhero on the ground with the common folk. Davey moved to stand next to her.

"Jaz..." he backtracked after accidentally starting with her name. "Ja... Jazzercise just finished. What's going on?"

She slowly turned her head toward him, and her eyes took a second to stop staring at the situation in front of her. Her long black hair peeked out from the hood of her tank, which she always kept up. It flowed around her slim black mask perfectly, and her pale skin accented both.

"Davey?" She said as her eyebrows punctuated the question above her mask.

"You know who I am?"

"Of course I do."

Her tone carried no surprise, only a particular hint of exhaustion. Heroes, he thought, must grow tired of being treated like stories instead of people. Davey shouldn't have been surprised, but he was nonetheless. He forgot they went to college together. Then, he remembered when Cass first introduced her to him. The two of them were in the same freshman required class, and he invited her to his dorm to study. Davey felt as if they instantaneously clicked. He was happy they found each other. It reminded him of his relationship with Rae. She had chosen to go to a separate college. It was the first hint of longing for her in the quiet absence she left. Then, he was reminded that the women worked together now, as heroes of the city. But Echona didn't know that he was aware of her real name.

"Right. You work with my wife."

"Talks about you a lot. She's lucky to have you."

He wondered if things were alright between her and Cass.

"You do jazzercise?"

Davey looked to the ground. "Oh, yeah… absolutely… can't get enough of it."

"Didn't think you were the type."

"Well, we all have our secrets, I guess." He stared at her for a beat. "Any idea when this will be over?"

"No clue, but things are getting more tense."

"Yeah, I can feel it too."

"You might want to consider getting out of here, honestly. I can tell her you stopped by. She's pretty focused."

"Sure. Thank you, Echona."

He took her advice and started to leave. He chose to walk around the park rather than through it, but his feet took him down Madison Avenue. Before long, he found himself leaning up against the fence that was next to the grassy area. From there, he saw his wife. As focused as he had ever seen her in their lifetime together. Echona was covered by the crowd on his side, as were the NYPD officers who held the middle ground.

The crowds got louder. The words were more indiscernible.

In an instant, Davey felt like he was watching the event in slow motion. A participant, on one side or the other, threw their megaphone over the police-inhabited divide. SolaRae noticed it in the air. A flick of her wrist, and she channeled a ball of energy from her high position. It looked like the small world that had been developed in the park of angry residents had its own sun. She quickly tossed the ball toward the megaphone. With great precision, the ball met the megaphone in the air as it reached the high point of its trajectory. It burst with a spark and rained down micro-sized bits of electrical engineering. Davey thought it sounded like a starting pistol at an old race and looked like an all-too-bright firework.

That was the catalyst.

It wasn't Rae's fault, he thought. If she didn't act, it would have hit somebody and led to the same outcome. All the same, the small explosion caused a stillness before the storm. Then, the officers bridging the divide were overrun. Neighbor charged at neighbor, mad at something they couldn't control. Instead of coming together for change, they fought one another for what they believed was the lesser of two evils. They clashed like two armies that fought for a general they didn't know.

Rae dove into the fray. Undaunted.

Davey's eyes went wide, and his heart beat faster than it had in years.

She was stronger than most. It was generally acknowledged that the H-gene gave the women who evolved with it a heightened strength.

But she wasn't super strong. She wasn't invincible to any misfired fist. The yelling turned to totally ignorant grunts that held the space and drowned out the nearby noises of the city.

Suddenly, the sound stopped.

He turned his head to the other side of the opening and saw that Echona had jumped backward. If he understood her abilities correctly, she had just removed the sound from the field. She funneled her hands around her mouth, and in the loudest voice he had heard in his life, she conquered the atmosphere. The sound burst forward from her. The crowd was covered in heavy pressure, as if they had been swallowed deep underwater by a wave in the middle of Manhattan.

"Everybody stop! Leave now or be arrested!"

She demanded control, and she got it.

The brawl began to stop, and people started to look at her. Some tried to speak, but no sound could get out of the zone she controlled. A few stragglers threw some late hits at others. But for now, Echona was their leader, and they were her subordinates.

The crowd started to disperse, and Davey walked into the park again. There were a few truly injured parties, but not as bad as he expected. To his surprise, police and protesters of both sides began to help each other up and dust each other off.

He looked for SolaRae.

He checked the air, but she wasn't there.

He looked to Echona, but she was alone.

He tried to shout for her, but couldn't hear himself speak. He kept trying to yell. The sound eventually returned halfway through a scream of SolaRae, so it sounded like he was just calling for his wife. Growing frantic, he continued to search. Then, he saw her. She was kneeling on the grass. Her height diminished as she appeared as if she had shrunk into herself. He ran to her and noticed her hand was covering her upper gut.

"Rae. Are you hurt?" He knelt beside her.

"Um… hey…" She responded, "Thanks for coming… I guess you really do like me. I'll be okay. Help me up." She extended her hand to him from her gut. He took it in his, but something was off. Her hand was covered in blood. He looked her over as he put her weight on him and wrapped her other arm around his neck.

"Rae… you got stabbed."

The words sounded foolish out loud. Like describing a never-ending nightmare. Blood covered his hands, warm and thick, enveloping his hand. The smell hit next: iron and sweat. His mind searched for logic and found none.

She collapsed into him. He picked her up and held her in his arms. He saw her chest rising and falling slowly. Davey searched for an officer in hopes they might be able to call for an ambulance. There weren't any left. Echona was still talking to civilians. In a voice he thought might even rival her powerful yell, he called out to her and tore through the silence that followed the chaos. Somewhere above the rooftops, a plane passed. Ordinary life carried on. The city was unaware that the world had tilted for the couple in the grass.

Chapter 7: That's New

Echona silenced blocks that surrounded the scene, and in an even louder boom called for the closest ambulance to Marcus Garvey Park. Within minutes, Davey carefully carried Rae into the ambulance. The paramedics began to assess her. The sirens filled the air, and for the first time, he felt uneasy while listening to them. Thankfully, it was a quick ride from the park to the Harlem Hospital Center ER. They pushed her out and into the hospital. Her face was plastered on the walls.

For a moment, it felt like the poster version was silently judging the real one. Nurses and technicians alike caught themselves briefly staring at her before getting back to work. In her suit, bleeding, being wheeled to a room, they realized she was human.

To Davey, the ride was both too fast and not nearly fast enough. Every turn felt like it might shake her loose from his world. He tried to count her breaths and kept losing track.

Inside the hospital, the posters of her were smooth and unbothered, all clean lines and perfect lighting. The Rae on the stretcher had sweat at her hairline and blood drying along the edge of her suit. He had the sudden, irrational urge to tear the posters down. If the city wanted her so badly, it could at least have the decency to look at the whole picture.

A medical team swarmed her and began cutting away the tight-fitting suit until the sun split on her chest. Since becoming a hero, she chose not to wear a bra in her suit. It was tight and padded enough for her not to feel like an extra bit of socially preferred clothing was necessary. The smell of blood mixed with iodine filled the sterile place.

It wasn't a large stab wound, nor was it multiple cuts. To Davey, it seemed like a wide and deep one. Blood clouded the edge of the wound, and he was moved out of the room. Her team needed to ensure there wasn't any larger internal damage.

It felt like a lifetime for Davey.

The routine beeps echoed in the unit with the low, vibrating hum of some instrument persisting. The heating unit of the room buzzed, and the old clock on the wall ticked with inaccuracy. Every second took five.

But waiting was something he had become accustomed to.

He thought about texting Cass to see how he and Echona were doing, but decided against reaching out. Cass was probably too busy. He knew enough therapeutic techniques to try to help him cope with the situation in some respects. He didn't use them, but he knew them. The breathing exercises, the grounding, the cognitive reframes. They all lined up in his mind like pamphlets that held a thin layer of dust. He could hear himself giving the talk in his well-trained therapist voice and wanted to punch the guy he heard. None of it touched the part of him that was already planning what he would do if the doctor came out and did not smile.

He grabbed a cup of bad hospital coffee and returned to a chair near where Rae was being worked on. After an hour or so, the early sunset of autumn began, and a doctor came to see him.

"You're Mr. SolaRae?" the doctor asked.

Davey forced a chuckle, "Yeah, that would be me." He stood and shook the doctor's hand.

"She told me to say that, by the way. Which I suppose would give you the impression that she'll likely be fine."

"No internal damage?"

"We're still running some tests, but she's awake. I can take you to her if you'd like."

"Absolutely."

The short walk was a quiet one. The sound of steps was only interrupted by the routine beep of some of the machines that flooded the unit. They arrived at her room, and the doctor swung open the curtain. She was lying on the bed, slightly angled upwards, blankets draped over her chest. Her hands fiddled with the buttons on the hospital bed until she got too frustrated and turned her attention to Davey.

He stared at her in admiration. She was his girl-next-door, and he loved every bit of her. To see her eyes again, which had grown to have just a glint of gold in them, felt like a blessing. The fluorescent lights softened her features.

"Hey, babe," she said. Her voice was the tiniest bit strained.

"Hey, hero." He sat on the edge of the bed next to her after giving her a kiss on the top of her head.

"So, maybe don't go flying into angry crowds again?"

"You know what, I might take your advice on that one. But, I think it's actually in the job description."

"You should talk to HR about hazard pay then."

"Yeah… they've been unresponsive."

He chuckled. She joined him but stopped quickly.

Laughing hurt.

"Davey…"

"Yeah?"

"Thank you for saving me."

"I wish I could've done more."

"You did plenty. You're the superhero's hero." She puckered her lips to suggest that she wanted him to bend toward her and kiss her.

He softly obliged and embraced his wife.

Davey's phone chimed. Rae looked for hers, but they realized in the chaos, she either misplaced it or one of the nurses moved it for her. It was a text from Ava: How is she?

Davey: Will be alright. Thankfully.

Ava: Good. I'll tell mom and dad. She's all over the news. They're freaking out.

Davey: Good idea. Didn't think about reaching out.

Ava: No prob. Tell Rae the city is taken care of. Tell her to get some rest.

Davey: Gladly.

"Your sister says you need to rest," Davey shared plainly.

"My sister can mind her own business." She tried to laugh again, but couldn't.

They sat together into the evening until a nurse came to the room and joined them.

"Mr. and Mrs. SolaRae, how is it going?" The nurse was a peppy young lady who seemed like either the burnout hadn't gotten to her yet, or she truly loved the job. Davey was happy for her.

"Well, I've been impaled. So there's that."

"How's the pain?"

"Not… super."

Davey rolled his eyes and shook his head at his wife, who thought she was hilarious.

"That's good, right?"

"Yes." He answered for his wife to save the young nurse from another attempt at a joke.

"Glad to hear it. We did a FAST exam when you came in, but now that we're all situated, we'll be bringing in the portable ultrasound soon for a better look at things. It shouldn't be too much longer, but just holler if you need me in the meantime."

"Sure. Thank you," Davey said to the nurse as she left.

"I'm hilarious," Rae commented.

"Right… you know what? I actually know somebody who would

really love to hear your jokes." Davey thought back to his encounter with Gary, the desk sergeant.

"Oh, yeah? The good folks at the comedy club?"

"Sure. Yeah, let's go with that."

After a short wait, the nurse rolled back in with the portable ultrasound.

"Alright, super family, let's check out your insides." She carefully spread a cold gel around her stomach to check for internal bleeding. The dark shapes on the screen blurred together like an incomprehensible jigsaw puzzle for Davey. The nurse's focused look eased as she scanned her upper abdomen.

"Upper abdomen looks great. I'm just going to check the lower abdomen and pelvic region to make sure nothing was missed, nicked, or forcibly moved down there. Here's some more of that gel." The nurse began to scan her lower abdomen. Her eyes squinted at the screen, and she hesitated.

"I'll be right back, I'm just going to grab the attending to take a look."

"Is something wrong? It sounds like something's wrong." Davey responded.

"One minute." The nurse vanished behind the curtain and back onto the unit. She returned, in a minute, with a doctor. The nurse squirted another dose of gel onto Rae's lower abdomen and handed the doctor the scanner.

She pointed at the screen. "Is that what I think it is?"

The doctor didn't respond outside of quiet "hmm's" and "huh's." They did a thorough scan of every angle. Then, he returned the scanner to the nurse.

"Anything bad, doctor?" Davey questioned.

"Nothing bad. Although it might not be expected."

"Huh?" Rae asked.

"It's a gestational sac. Early, but in the coming weeks, this little life will be confirmed." The doctor replied.

Rae's mouth hung open, and she went wide-eyed as they started to mist.

"A what?" Davey asked.

"Davey…" Rae placed her hand on his arm.

"It's the first sign of early pregnancy, Mr. SolaRae. Very early, just a few weeks, but it looks like you'll be a dad if things go according to plan in about eight or nine months. We'll have the OB team confirm, but it looks clear to me. I believe congratulations are likely in order. We'll leave you two alone for a bit."

Davey slumped backward in both shock and relief. His wife would be fine. The word dad landed in his chest with the same weight as the word widower had been carrying all afternoon. The two collided so hard that it made him dizzy. What they both wanted but could never find time to work on was set to happen. Then, the emotions flooded them both as they embraced one another.

"We're going to be parents," Rae declared.

"You'll be an amazing mom, Rae. Really."

"And you'll be an amazing dad."

They kissed. The harsh fluorescents seemed to dim around them and allowed the couple to have their own spotlight. They warmed each other more than any heater would. It felt like they weren't in a hospital. The light sheets were their own. In each other's arms, they were home.

"I wonder if the kid will have powers too?" she asked.

"That would be interesting. You can always ask Sara if she has noticed anything new with her kid."

Rae paused for a second and realized what he said.

"First, yes, good idea. Second… and maybe more importantly, how do you know OwlHeart's real name? I mean, I know you had Jose over, but did Jose just tell you like it was nothing?"

Whoops, Davey thought. The lie was not even a lie, just a pocket of air he had never filled with words. "Not like it was nothing, no. I've been meaning to tell you, actually…" He waited a moment.

"Spill it, Mr. SolaRae."

"We've only met twice, but the spouses of the heroes have been getting together. Kind of like a support group. I thought it might be a good idea to try and get everybody together with heroes and the awakening of the H-gene in a handful of women, being so new. It's new for everybody, you know. You ladies just got the cooler end of it."

"Huh, interesting."

"It wasn't meant to be a secret or anything."

"I'm not mad, babe. That's a good idea. But, how did you know who to reach out to? Besides Eric, I guess. Is he included even though he's not technically a spouse yet?" Her voice was light, but he could see the faint shadow under her eyes, the same one he watched deepen every month the city asked more of her. It was the whole reason he had wanted the group in the first place.

"Yup, Eric is included. I went to college with Cass and Jazmine. Remember when we were long-distance for a little bit? I hung out with them. We lost contact after graduation. I saw one of her ads on TV and thought I recognized her. So, I took a shot."

"That's wild. I don't think she's ever mentioned going to college with you. How about Jose?"

"He actually reached out to me. We used to work out at the same gym, and he saw a picture of you on my phone. Apparently, I seemed trustworthy, because the dude just spilled it out for me."

"That's nice."

"Yeah, I thought so too."

"So, spill the details. What do you guys talk about?"

"Yeah, no. Not happening, Rae."

"Aw, you're no fun."

"Hey, I started the group for guys to be able to talk about things. There are so many people who think guys can't talk or have emotions. It's so antiquated."

"That's fair… I guess." She jokingly pouted at him.

"Yeah, I'm also still building trust with them. They don't all like to talk."

"Cass?"

"Wait… how did you?"

"Know?" She cut him off. "I work with his wife. We talk. She talks about how he doesn't talk. Sounds like a support group would be good for him."

"Absolutely. Thank you for understanding."

"Any time, Mr. SolaRae." She winked and invited a kiss.

The night remained quiet as Davey was allowed to stay with her. She asked him to share the bed with her. But he was too worried about accidentally hitting her wound in his sleep. He found the chair and slept better than he did at his own house some nights. The incessant beeps of the machines that wouldn't be forgotten filled the night. Quiet nurses shuffled about, and a chorus of coughs or moans occasionally filled the air. In the morning, Davey woke to grab coffee for them before the hospital breakfast arrived for his wife. He set the beverage down next to her tray. She took a sip of the steaming cup that reminded him of the Styrofoam from group nights. She immediately put it down.

"Wait… I don't think I can have coffee when I'm pregnant. Or was that a myth?" She took another sip instinctively and then another. "I should ask someone."

"I'm pretty sure it's not advised to try and fight crime while pregnant, but I don't think you'll be stopping that after you heal. Am I right?"

"You are correct. At least for the first few months. Man, I'm going to have to see if some of my suits can be taken out."

"You're going to look great, Rae."

"Yeah, tell me something I don't know."

A doctor from the OB team walked in during their conversation.

"How's it goin', Rae?"

She touched her belly and gave the doctor a joking look. "Be honest, how far along do I look?"

It earned a chuckle from the doctor. "Why don't we find out?"

Davey helped move the untouched tray of breakfast from over the bed and Rae's sheets out of the way.

"Here's the gel." The doctor gave the typical warning. "And here's the scanner."

Davey again was completely lost when it came to looking at the screen, while Rae seemed entirely lost in the miraculousness of seeing her insides.

"That's a gestational sac. You two are going to be parents. If you have any questions, we'll always be here for you, SolaRae. I'll let you two finish eating. But, before you go, schedule an OB appointment in two or three weeks. The sac is small. So, we should be able to confirm everything by then. Congrats again."

"Thank you, doctor." They said in unison. They sighed in relief that the doctor from last night wasn't wrong. This was real.

Next, the nurse from last night walked into the room. Still unbelievably peppy. "Alrighty, Rae. We should be able to get you out of here sooner rather than later. Your vitals are fine. You're eating, drinking, and passing urine. I heard you walked the floor last night before bed without fainting. So, that's great. Blood tests came back fine. Pain is good?"

"Pain is good," Rae responded.

"Perfect. Well, in your discharge paperwork, there will be more info, but just be sure to keep the wound clean. Rest and avoid any strenuous activity. Take pain meds as needed, and we'll send a prescription for antibiotics to your pharmacy. You have passed the checklist. If you're feeling up to it, I can help get you out of here. Glad you're doing alright."

"Thank you, nurse. I am very much feeling up to it."

It was a short wait for the discharge paperwork, and Davey started to wheel her out of the unit. One step closer to Kew Gardens. He draped his faded hoodie over her. Both to keep her warm and to hide her hospital gown, which he knew she hated. They got closer to the exit when a security guard stopped them.

"Hey, folks. You might not want to go out that way."

Rae pulled the loose jacket a little tighter over herself. The automatic door opened when another patient left. The antiseptic smell of the hospital gave way to the autumn dampness. As the door closed, she began to see flashes in her direction. The media had encircled the exit to catch pictures or interviews with the hero who was hurt. They did not know they were aiming their cameras at someone who still had tape on her arm and hospital socks on her feet.

"Animals," Davey muttered. He knew that was not entirely fair. They were just doing their jobs. So was she. So was he.

"There's a side exit I can lead you to if you want to give that a shot. I don't know if it's any better, but they might not have found the door yet."

"Worth a shot," Rae said.

He led them through the labyrinth of bright hospital hallways until they arrived at a secondary exit. It appeared empty.

"Babe?" Rae asked.

"Yeah?"

"How are we going to get home?"

Davey hung his head, "Son of a—"

Reporters and cameras came flooding down the alley to the side exit after some of them saw her being wheeled away from the front. He froze as the crowd ran to him. Nowhere to run. The noise entirely cut him off. Davey and Rae retreated inside. A charge nurse tried to shoo phones away.

"Does this hospital have easy roof access?" Rae addressed the security guard.

"Sure, but it's not really wheelchair-accessible."

"That's fine. He can carry me."

"Rae, you can't fly. I won't allow it."

"Allow it? Cute. But I wasn't planning on it anyway. Let me see your phone."

Davey wondered what she had planned, but handed her his phone. She unlocked it and made some calls.

"Take me to the roof, Jeeves."

"You're such a loser."

"And you love it."

He obliged her, and the security guard led them to the roof. She was by no means heavy, but Davey thought he needed to get back to the gym with Jose.

"Thank you, my good man." She motioned a tip of her invisible hat to the security guard who had decided to head back inside.

"So, what's the plan, Rae?"

"Be patient. You'll see."

The fall breeze nipped at them on the roof as the sounds of the city seemed even more like a distant hum at their feet. After a few minutes, LunAva appeared on the roof. Shortly followed by the quick Owl-Heart. "Davey, meet my plan. My plan, meet Davey."

"You can't be serious."

"I'm so serious. They already agreed to it."

"No biggie, bro," LunAva added.

"Relax, hermano, we got it." He hadn't had a chance to speak to OwlHeart, but she carried the same strong aura of confidence that Rae did.

"Alright, sure." She convinced him. "Take her away. Be safe. I'll try and shimmy through the crowd with a hospital mask or something. See you at home." He kissed her before letting LunAva and OwlHeart gently fly off. They carried Rae between the two of them. High, fast, safe, and quiet enough not to be spotted by the lingering cameras.

He watched the air curve around them as they left out of view. For a flicker of a second, it looked like they were taking the whole problem with them. The blood, the cameras, the posters. Just three streaks in the sky and the man on the roof who loved one of them more than he could say. The city noise dulled more so when they took off, a rare moment above the chaos of the last day or so. Davey returned to climb the stairs back into the hospital and find his own way through the crowd.

Chapter 8: Coach's Decision

The commute home felt longer than it should have for Davey. He was used to long transit times. It came with the territory of needing to travel around the boroughs. This one felt excruciatingly long. The announcements on the loudspeaker proved not to be enjoyable. The screeches of the brakes were off-putting. The harsh noises started to remind him of the nonsensical screaming at the park. The subway lights flickered across the windows like camera flashes from a crowd. He blinked them away and told himself it was just motion blur, not memory. He only wanted to be home with his wife. He was always more comfortable on public transit, but he considered starting to switch to rideshares.

He eventually made it to the stoop and his door. It softly clicked open and let him enter his home. Two coffee cups remained in the sink from Friday morning. The rusty chairs continued to hang onto their positions in the living room. They stood like sentinels from another life, waiting for the men who had sat in them to return. The smell of cold coffee and damp air clung to them, a reminder that healing wasn't only happening upstairs. He realized he had never put them away from the Thursday night group and hadn't been home since yesterday morning. He climbed up the loud stairs, not nearly as careful as he had been the other day. He needed to get up to check on Rae. Davey crested the last step and entered the room. The lights were dim, but the blinds were open. She was lying on her back and scrolling through her phone.

"Hey, babe. How was the flight?"

She looked at him and seemed utterly disinterested in life. Uncomfortable with bed rest. "Eh, there were no in-flight snacks. Plus, the flight attendant broke my toy in the seventh grade and never apologized."

"You should write a letter."

"I just might." She returned to scrolling through her phone.

"Need anything?"

"Just for coach to put me in."

"Sorry, the lineup's been set for the next week."

She didn't respond at first. "Just water then."

"As you wish."

He jokingly took a bow and left to grab the water. He returned with a glass and a metal straw, then set it on the nightstand next to her. The dumpling container still sat there empty. He took to tidying the room while she was in bed. Tossing the dirty sheets that lay on the floor in a similar but distinct pile for him to wash when he made it to the laundry room. He filled her water again and fluffed her pillow.

"Hey, babe?"

"Yes?" he said while continuing to move about the room.

"I promise you. I'm okay. I don't need mothering. I will rely on you for anything I need. I will call you when I need to go to the bathroom in case I need help."

He looked at his feet in guilt, suggesting he had been caught.

"Seriously. Thank you, but I will be okay."

"I just can't lose you, Rae."

"Come here."

He obliged.

She pinched his nose with her fingers.

"Got your nose," she joked with him.

"Wow. You really are a loser."

"And you really love it."

"I really do." He bent over to kiss her. "I'm going to do some cleaning downstairs if you need anything."

She gave him a thumbs-up, and he creaked down the whiny stairs. Davey carefully folded and put the chairs away. He was already looking forward to the next group and couldn't wait to share the news. He shifted to cleaning the few dishes in the quiet house. Davey watched leaves fall onto the ground and be whisked away in the breeze. They drifted through the air without a care in the world. The colorful leaves found themselves taken by the wind from one yard to another. They announced themselves to neighbors before they continued onward. Davey had a fondness for falling leaves. He wished he could float through life as easily as they do. He mindlessly put the plates in their places and was startled when he heard a loud grunt from upstairs.

He left the sink running and ran upstairs. His loud feet crashed on the steps as he skipped a few here and there. In the moment, Davey subconsciously felt like a superhero in his own regard. He cut through the air of his home toward the noise. He ran into the doorjamb as he made his entrance to the bedroom and hurt his shoulder, which made him remember that he was, in fact, not a superhero.

He caught his breath. "What? What's wrong?"

"This is ridiculous!"

"You're okay?"

"Physically, yes. Emotionally, no."

"What happened?"

"I just got sent a viral video. It's a super blurry video of me diving into the park. They call me reckless. Say I'm recovering at home after the 'incident.' It wasn't an incident! It was some people who got passionate about something, and then I got stabbed."

"I think that's what an incident might be, babe."

Rae looked at him, and he thought if she could shoot the sun out of her eyes, he would be burned. She was silent. Her jaw tightened, and he saw the flicker of light under her skin. It was an involuntary shimmer that always came when she was angry or frightened. She turned her face to the window until it passed. Then, she slowly turned her head back to her phone. He wasn't sure if he should apologize, try to comfort her, or say nothing. He felt the temperature in the room drop and the air become dense. He realized he had said the wrong thing and slowly walked backward, so as not to make any sudden movements. He retreated downstairs and shut off the water before going to watch TV.

He flicked through the channels as one of the few young people who hadn't cut the cord. He still forced himself to watch the news on occasion. The first story he saw was the grainy footage of Rae diving into the crowd. The first headline he saw was 'Helpless Hero?', which was followed by a video somebody managed to sneak of her being wheeled into the hospital on a gurney. The question mark cut deeper than the word itself. He imagined some intern deciding that punctuation, choosing uncertainty over empathy, and felt something in him grind. Davey started to fume.

They had no idea what she had gone through. What she went through every day in the name of keeping the city safe. Now they were attacking her for getting hurt, and it wasn't even her fault. Not really. They went after her public image like she wasn't the darling of the boroughs. She was his, and she was the city's. Yet, the city opted to start questioning her at the first chance. He could only imagine what might be going through her mind. Guilt for being hurt or for not stopping the tension at the park earlier. Her public image was taking a direct hit, and he couldn't do anything about it. Now, she would have to manage it all as a hero and as a mother. He turned off the TV and sat on the sectional for a few minutes in silence. He went back upstairs quietly and saw that she was still scrolling through her phone. He moved to sit next to her on the bed. He placed his hand on her stomach, below her wound.

"You're incredible, Rae."

She lowered her phone to her side and put her hand on his. She closed her eyes and took a deep breath. When she opened them, he could see her eyes were misty. He didn't say anything but continued to connect with her. She started to cry.

"Rae, you're incredible."

He sat with her as she cried. Heroes had emotions, too.

The doorbell rang.

"Are you expecting a visitor?"

"Nope. But, I did get you a surprise that I think you might enjoy while you're laid up. Stay right there." He took his hand off her stomach and backed away.

"Right. Because I have a choice."

He headed for the door quickly, creaking down the steps, and returned with his hands behind his back.

"Take a guess."

"Chocolate chip cookie dough ice cream?"

"No, but if you want some, I'll get you that too."

"What is it?"

"I thought you might be interested in some light reading." He brought his hands forward and showed a pregnancy book that he ordered on the way home.

She chuckled. "I guess we're starting early, huh?"

"Never too early. Love you." He handed her the book and kissed the top of her head. The weight of the paperback felt ridiculous after everything. It was a manual for something no one could ever actually be ready for, no matter the extent of their readings.

She started to flip through the book.

Half-interested, half-bewildered.

"Chapter Four," she began, "avoid strenuous activity. So, like, crime-fighting?"

Davey didn't answer.

"Chapter Six, everything in moderation. So, crime-fighting. Perfect. Moderate, non-strenuous crime-fighting."

"That sounds like an oxymoron, but sure, yeah, why not?"

"They'll need me out there soon enough."

"You're right. Soon, not today, not tomorrow. You need to heal. You've done enough heroing for the time being."

"Do you think the kid will come out glowing?"

"It's entirely possible, I guess."

"Maybe we should just give them a hero name straight out of the womb."

"Yeah… I don't know about that."

"Superbaby?"

"That's kind of a mouthful."

"The Crier."

"How about the baby doesn't have the word 'the' as part of their legal name?"

"Well, that could be limiting then. 'Crier' doesn't really carry the same weight."

"I'm sure we'll come up with something."

"How about 'Super Crier?'"

"Rae…"

"Davey?"

"Enjoy your book." He watched her read for a moment. The hero and the therapist, pretending the world outside their window wasn't already waiting for both of them. That night's quiet reminded him of another one, years ago, before the city knew her name. Before they had their home. Before they were Mr. and Mrs. SolaRae.

They were in his first apartment. When date nights looked like instant ramen and boxed wine. Rae had spread a dozen magazines across the floor. Wedding planners, flower catalogs, and even one about tropical venues that they both knew they'd never afford. She had highlighters in every color and her laptop open to a spreadsheet.

"You don't even like weddings," he said.

"I don't like other people's weddings," she corrected. "Ours will be different. Efficient. Elegant. Possibly televised."

He laughed and leaned against the couch. "We can't even afford a venue. And I'm almost positive that it won't be televised."

"We'll do it on the rooftop. You fix the lights. I'll build a playlist that makes the neighbors forgive us. No chairs, maybe a few benches, a cocktail table or two."

He remembered her flicking through pages, marking tiny tabs for colors and dresses she would later call too much. The glow from her screen lit her face. Only back then, she didn't glow on her own.

He asked her why she was planning so far ahead.

"Because," she said, "if we don't write it down now, then your mom or mine will fill in the blanks for us."

He smiled at the memory. Back then, the biggest thing either of them had to worry about was whether the cheap fairy lights would stay up long enough for vows. They thought life would wait for them to be ready. That the future would unfold politely in the order they imagined.

He thought of them now, a hero holding a pregnancy book like it was a sacred text. The same woman who once made color-coded tabs for napkins and centerpieces now had to plan her next public statement. He wanted to believe they could still live inside that rooftop dream. Maybe they still could someday. Outside, a siren trailed off into the distance, swallowed by the hum of traffic. Life hadn't waited for them to be ready, but it had still found them here, together.

Chapter 9: Paperwork and Prayer

Over the next few days, Davey continued to help Rae recover. He canceled his appointments for the week ahead. They had been mostly frugal, and Rae made enough through her endorsements. She started to recover, and it was Thursday before he attempted to leave the house. News traveled that the arraignment of Simon Cribb would be happening, and Davey had told the young man that he would be there.

"You're sure you don't mind if I go?"

"Of course not. I really don't think you'll be missing anything, but if you want to go, you should."

"Okay. If you need anything, call your sister. She'll be able to get here faster than I can."

"I'll be fine, Davey. I'm already almost healed. I feel like I could do fifty crunches right now."

"Please don't."

"Davey… leave."

They parted with a kiss. He hesitated at the doorway a little longer than was necessary. He lingered until the quiet settled. The house didn't sound like their home yet, not while she was grounded upstairs. It felt like holding his breath in a dream.

He was trying to convince himself of the fact that he already knew. She would be okay.

He creaked down the stairs and welcomed the breeze of autumnal Queens that he hadn't felt in a few days. The door closed with its usual soft click, and he double-checked that it locked behind him. That it hadn't, for the first time in years, lied to him and left his injured wife upstairs, vulnerable. As if she couldn't blast anyone who wandered into the house for some nefarious reason, despite lying in bed.

He rhythmically headed for transit and found joy in the journey again. The rattle of the train and the screech of its brakes had begun to return to their former glory. The blank faces started to feel warm, but his mind began to shift. What if one of these people is the one who stabbed her? he thought. The suspect was out there somewhere, and he highly doubted they would ever be caught. What if the person was another Simon Cribb? Just scared and full of misfortune. They would still need to answer for their crimes. Simon does too. He couldn't help but start to feel like the system was one giant ball of bureaucratic nonsense that encouraged people like Simon to fall through the cracks, so they didn't have to care for him.

The train screeched to his stop. He disembarked, but the feeling of uneasiness stayed with him. He marched to the arraignment and left one chill for another. Simon was already sitting down next to the lethargically appearing public defender. Davey took a seat as close to him as possible. The courtroom smelled faintly of paper and disinfectant. The benches creaked when anyone shifted. It felt less like a place of judgment and more like a waiting room for consequences.

"All rise for the Honorable Judge Narra." The bailiff ordered as a wiry old man walked in and sat at his bench. The court was in session.

"Good morning, all. From what I understand, this should be a quick session. Will the defendant please rise?"

The public defender nudged Simon to stand. He did, but wasn't looking at the judge. He was staring at the empty jury box. Davey considered that having a jury there would potentially help the young man. He thought that Simon might have wanted a jury, but didn't have the words to ask for one. Couldn't stand up to the public defender who had likely pushed him to take the plea and avoid trial.

"Your charges are as follows: Burglary in the First Degree, Felony Murder in the Second Degree, Leaving the Scene of an Incident Without Reporting, and Resisting Arrest. How do you plead?"

"Guilty." The word landed softly, like it had been practiced. Davey wanted to stand up and ask if anyone believed it. The young man didn't even look like he understood the language of punishment.

"What was the agreed-upon plea?"

"Your Honor, the agreement is for time served, the resisting arrest charge dropped, and for him to be transferred to a minimum-security facility," the public defender answered.

"Mr. Cribb. You should know that I do not find leniency in the act of senseless killing. I would have you serve your sentencing in a maximum-security facility, but your attorney has seemed to strike the right deal. Mr. Cribb, do you understand that by accepting this deal you are hereby waiving your right to a fair trial and that sentencing will be handled by the court?"

Davey silently scoffed; it didn't seem like there was anything fair. It felt like Simon was being forced to proceed in this way.

"Yes."

"Then, I accept your plea deal. Bail is remanded, and the defendant will remain in custody until sentencing."

Davey wanted to interject. To say something for the man who should be meeting with him instead of being forced to avoid trial. One bad mistake, and now he'll likely spend his life locked away with no mental health assistance. He couldn't find the words. It felt like judgment was just paperwork in this place. Simon was lost in the words of the stack that sat on somebody's desk. Davey wondered how many others were lost with him.

Simon kept his eyes on the empty jury box, nodded respectfully, and was led away. His vision shifted, and he noticed Davey behind him. The young man's feet stopped. Now, he blankly stared at Davey, who tried to smile at the defendant. There was no response as the bailiff forced him to keep walking. The quietness of the courtroom returned, but the weight of it all bore down on Davey. He eventually stood and left the cold court back to the warmth of the fall streets. He pulled out his phone and texted Rae.

Davey: All good?

Rae: No. I fell out of bed. I reopened my incision, and now I'm bleeding out on our carpet.

Rae: I'm fine.

Davey shook his head and chuckled, letting out a brief laugh before he called Cass. He walked down the road instead of heading for the train. He didn't want to risk losing signal underground.

"Davey, what's up?" He could hear typing in the background.

"Hey, Cass, just have a question for you if you have a minute."

"I don't, but I can multitask. Shoot."

Cass always sounded like someone juggling three cases and a lunch meeting. Davey could hear his fingers tapping keys, the tone calm but distant, the way people got when they were too used to bad news.

"You know the Simon Cribb case, right?"

"Yeah, sure. Wasn't the arraignment this week?"

"Yup, just leaving it actually. He took a guilty plea deal, but I'm beyond certain that he needs mental health assistance, too. Is there anything I can do for him?"

"Yes and no. Who was the judge?"

"Narra, I believe his name was. Old man."

"Yeah, old man is like 80% of judges, dude. But I know the name. If I recall, he can be pretty tough and generally doesn't see the use in mental health support. But you can try to write a letter to the court asking for mental health treatment during sentencing or an official pre-sentencing evaluation."

He continued, "Get that, and it would probably help a good deal. Most facilities tend to have at least some sort of rehabilitation program or assistance program. You can let him know that he should try to seek that out. You can tell him that avoiding trial might be the best thing for his mental health, given the pile of evidence. It's also important for him to know that even while he is behind bars, he doesn't have to lose his agency."

"There will be therapy, substance-abuse programs if he needs them, educational services, and counseling. He can still control some things." Davey thought that might be the key to making sure Simon might be able to manage prison.

"That's helpful. Thanks, Cass. Do you think that if I write a formal recommendation, it will be seen?"

"Almost definitely. You were supposed to be his therapist, right? I'd open with that and make sure to include as many of your conclusions as possible. I have to run. Text me if you need anything else. See you tonight."

"Sure, will do, see you later."

Cass hung up and left Davey, who was thankful for a short to-do list that might help Simon. He leaned back on the bench and thought about the first time he and Cass ever talked about anything that really mattered. It had been after midnight, sophomore year, both of them too broke to buy beer and too restless to sleep. Cass had been sitting on his dorm floor, eating dry cereal out of the box, talking about the woman who would become his wife.

"I don't know, man," Cass had said. "I feel like she's not into me, and I don't really have anything to offer."

"You've got plenty, Cass," he tried to reassure him, "and if she's the one, she won't care."

Cass had shrugged, then asked if he could borrow his notes for class.

Now, all these years later, Davey could still hear that same steady voice, more seasoned but still guarded. Cass had built walls for whatever reason. Davey tried to build his own walls out of care. The memory faded with the sound of passing traffic. Davey stood, brushed the dust from his coat, and started toward his office and his laptop.

The ride was consumed by what he might write to ensure that Simon would be treated correctly. He was all focused, but as he sat on the train, his mind started to drift. Am I actually trying to help a murderer? He settled on the belief that somebody had to. Davey knew he was a murderer, but to him, that didn't mean he shouldn't have access to the care that he needed.

He arrived at his office's street. To his surprise, though he realized it should have been common sense, Boris was at his stand. He climbed the steps to his quiet cube and opened his computer. For a moment, he didn't type. He just thought. He reflected, and he looked out of his smudged window at the mural of his wife. Then he began. He stared at the blinking cursor, wondering if compassion had a word count. The letter had to sound professional, detached, but he could feel the tremor in his fingers. Every sentence would be weighed by strangers who didn't care what Simon's silence meant.

"My name is David Karoll, an LCSW who has been in communication with Mr. Simon Cribb during his incarceration. I am respectfully requesting that the court consider a full and comprehensive mental health evaluation prior to sentencing, as well as petitioning that he receive adequate and appropriate mental health services during his incarceration. During my meetings with Mr. Cribb, he presented as anxious and withdrawn; he showed signs of PTSD, chronic guilt, and potential schizophrenia. I believe that the behaviors in our brief interactions displayed a trend of untreated mental health conditions that may have contributed to his circumstances."

"I would recommend that he be placed in a facility with intentional access to mental health services, continued counseling, and structured support. I believe that those services would greatly assist the presumed goal of rehabilitation. Mr. Cribb demonstrated a deep remorse for his actions. While the judicial system should strive to see justice for the individual who was murdered, I believe he should still be met with proper services. Thank you for your consideration."

He moved to print the letter, sign it, and mail it to Simon's defense attorney. He sealed it with Simon's case number. He let out a sigh of relief, at least trying to do something. His defense attorney didn't seem to be interested in what was best for Simon. At least he would see Davey's letter. It was out of his hands now. But he would still try to attend the sentencing. The stress of ensuring the letter would be done properly made him hungry. So, naturally, he took to the steps, walked across the street, and started for Central Sausage. Boris was there in what Davey assumed was his uniform. He wondered if the vendor owned anything else in his closet. He rose from his chair to greet his regular.

"David, my friend! Welcome! You work weekends now?"

"Just Davey, Boris, and just today. How's business?"

"Good, David, good. You try new dog?"

"Just the regular, Boris."

"I have Cluster Fluff dog. Extra big stuffed sausage deep-fried with surprise inside and melted marsh-a-mallow on top."

"Too extravagant for me, Boris."

"You like surprises, yes?"

"I think I'm actually good on surprises for now, but thank you."

"Two regulars?"

Davey nodded and paid in exact change. He was glad to have a little normalcy as he scarfed down the hot dogs, threw out his grease-filled wrapper, and headed for home. He dropped the letter in the blue USPS box. He had never been a religious man, but he said a prayer on Simon's behalf. Not for freedom, for assistance. The mailbox swallowed the letter, and he stood there for a while. The city moved around him, fast and loud. He stayed still, waiting for something to answer back.

Chapter 10: People First

Davey arrived back at his home and directly climbed the stairs to check on Rae. She was sitting up, watching a reality dating show on the TV in the bedroom, and snacking on a pint of chocolate chip cookie dough ice cream.

"Hey, babe."

There was no answer.

"Rae."

Silence.

Davey cupped his hands over his mouth.

"Earth to SolaRae! Will the real Rae Karoll please stand up?"

"Oh, hey," she replied.

"You look to be doing good."

"Great."

"Probably still shouldn't be going up and down the stairs yourself. You could trip."

"It's a good thing I didn't walk," she responded and had a bite of ice cream. "I floated."

Davey smiled, but the word stayed with him. Rae always used humor to hide the cracks, and he could see through it.

"Rae…"

"Davey, I'm fine, and you're interrupting my show. It just got dramatic."

"Right, because we need more drama in our lives."

She took another bite. "You wouldn't get it."

"Fair. Anyway, the group is supposed to be coming over tonight, but I can cancel if you want."

"No, go ahead, I'm good."

"Thanks." A shadow of a smile lightened his lips. "Okay if I tell them about the baby?"

"So their wives can gush over me?"

"Who's to say they would tell their wives?"

She gave him a look to suggest that there were no dumb questions, that one wasn't needed.

"So, yes or no?"

"Fine. It's a bit early, though; we have no idea how things will play out."

"That's fair. I'm just excited."

"Then share away, babe."

His smile couldn't be hidden.

"I'll go get set up. Holler if you need me."

"I won't!" She raised the volume of the TV so as not to be disturbed.

He left her in the bedroom with her ice cream and drama. He crept down the stairs and started the coffee before carefully circling the rusting chairs. He unlocked the door, poured himself a cup, and took his seat. Soon enough, he heard a car door close outside, and Eric entered the home unannounced. His rideshare drove off, and Davey wondered how much Eric typically tipped. He took his seat and slumped downward.

"How's she doing, dude?" Eric asked him.

"She's close to her old self. Glad that Election Day is over." He smirked, thinking about her bingeing on ice cream and reality shows. It was the closest to her old self he had seen her since she took up heroing.

"Nice."

After another moment, Cass and Jose walked in together.

"What's up, bro?" Jose patted Davey on the shoulder before taking his spot, while Cass went for a cup of coffee.

"Not much. How's it going?"

"Loving life, bro. Tired as heck… but loving life."

Cass sat down to join them and sipped on the coffee. He tried not to make a face at how bad it was. He failed. The same ritual every Thursday. Burnt coffee, tired jokes, the smell of men trying their best. It wasn't therapy, but it was close.

"Gentlemen, mind if I start things this week?" Cass asked. His voice was lighter than usual, but his eyes looked worn. The kind of tired that sleep couldn't fix. Davey had seen it before—on himself.

"Be my guest," Davey said, glad that he might be really starting to open up. Cass laughed, and it sounded almost natural. It wasn't that he was hiding sadness; it was that he'd learned how to sound fine. The sound didn't quite reach his eyes. Davey caught that and let it pass, the way friends sometimes do when they're scared to open up a different path. The laugh reminded him of his old apartment. Two broke guys arguing about ramen flavors, talking about the future like it was something they'd invented. Back then, Cass believed in everything.

"I just have to say," he started and paused, "I know we're all busy and dealing with our heroes, but I'm really glad we can find time for ourselves… like Davey…" He looked to Davey and gave him a smug smirk, "… and his jazzercise."

"Crap," Davey muttered. "She told you."

Cass grinned like the old dorm days, when he'd tease Davey about everything from ramen choices to dating philosophy majors. It felt good to laugh like that again.

"Of course she did, man! You didn't think you'd get out of that one, did you?"

"Hold on," Jose started. "Jazzercise? Jazzercise, bro?"

"Rae likes you to keep it tight, huh?" Eric added.

"No, dad bod before you become a dad?" Jose joked.

"You guys joke, but I feel like jazzercise would actually be a great workout," Davey responded. "But, I don't actually do it."

"Don't try to backtrack now, my guy. We're looking forward to your recital," Cass said.

"First, I don't think there are jazzercise recitals. Second, I'm being real. When I saw Echona, I almost called her by her real name. Jazzercise is just what I quickly switched to. It was the first thing that came to mind, alright. But, hey, if you want to do it, I'll bet you that I'm better."

"Ain't no way, Davey. I got music in my bones. You know, Jaz and I frequented the club in college before things got real. You know I used to be fun." The line was light, but something in his tone dimmed at the word real. Davey remembered those nights. The way Cass used to talk about Jaz like she was the whole horizon. Somewhere between graduation and responsibility, that shine had turned to duty.

"Yeah, yeah, I remember. Still think I got you."

"You're wrong, but I'm not about to prove it. Anyway, good save on the name thing. Appreciate it."

"Y'all would both lose to me. Be real. Mi gente might as well have made music, you feel me?"

"Not even a little, dude," Eric responded, and the other guys all laughed.

"If we're done with the dance contest bit of today's session, I actually have some news."

"You're coaching jazzercise?" Eric asked and earned some more laughter from Jose and Cass.

"No. But, somebody is going to be dancing for Rae."

"Bro, don't use a stripper to get your wife in the mood. Be creative." Jose jokingly moved his hands around his body.

"Ew. Also, wrong. Cass, care to take a guess?"

"How far along is she?"

"Dude, how are you so good at that?" Eric asked.

"Just good like that, man. Congrats, Davey."

"Wait… no joke? She's pregnant?" Jose asked.

"She sure is. Only a few weeks, we found out by accident. When she got stabbed, it was in her upper abdomen. They checked the lower bit just to be safe, and boom… baby. Well, not technically a baby, yet. The doctor said it was a gestational sac or something. I don't know the science."

"Sounds right," Cass said.

"Welcome to the club, bro. It's a wild time over here."

"Thanks, boys. Appreciate it. Does anybody else have any news?"

"Yeah! I'm starting up the stream this weekend. I'll send you guys the link if you want to check it out."

"Nice, I will absolutely do that. Way to go, Eric."

"Yeah, bro, same. I'll pull it up while I walk the kid."

"Walk the kid? Do you bring poop bags and a leash?" Cass asked.

"Good one, bro. Just a diaper bag. How about you? What's new in the world of law and endorsements?"

"Yeah, and how are you and Jaz?" Davey tried to pry without being too obvious.

"Same old, same old," Cass said.

"Really? That's it?"

"Work is work."

"Wasn't Echona at the same park that SolaRae got stabbed in?" Eric asked.

"Yeah, she was," Cass answered.

"And she's fine?" Davey questioned. "That could be pretty traumatizing to be a part of."

"Is this a support group for her or for us?"

"Just checking in, bro."

"She's fine. We're fine. Work is…"

"Fine?" Davey asked.

Cass nodded in agreement.

The word hung there too long. Davey had learned that "fine" was the easiest way to hide exhaustion. He wanted to ask more but knew Cass would just fold himself tighter if pressed.

"You know, guys, I don't know if I'm alone here, but when Rae got stabbed, it was a reality check for me. It was like, for a little bit, I forgot she was just human too. The heroes, our girls, are people first."

"I feel that," Jose replied. "The other day, Sara came home from a rough day out. It was maybe one or two a.m., and I just put the kid down again. She walked in shaking. I felt like I couldn't do enough for her. Or understand her trauma. I just hugged her and told her to try to get some rest. I don't think I slept that night. Cleaned the house, washed her suits. Everything but sleep until the kid woke up, and I tried to make sure he didn't wake her up, too."

"That sounds really tough, dude."

"It really does, Jose. How are you doing? That has to be a lot to handle. If you're burning out, we're here for you."

"Man, life is great. It really is. But I'm absolutely burning out. My mental is strong, but I don't know how much I can keep going on like this. My mom is only available so often, and I've never been able to nap when he does."

His words came out steady, but his face betrayed him. His jaw trembled like it was trying to hold the sentence together. Nobody interrupted. The silence stretched, the kind that demanded care but not words.

Davey leaned toward Jose.

"You're holding it down, helping her stay grounded, you're keeping things trucking. That's not anything to scoff at, Jose." He paused to make sure Jose heard him. "You also don't need to be everything. Sometimes just being stable is good enough. It's alright if the house doesn't get cleaned for a few days. Enjoy your time, don't just go through the motions. You're doing enough. You are more than enough."

Jose tried to stop himself, but broke down under the pressure.

"Yeah, dude." Eric started. "You gotta like recharge your dad battery pack and plug it back in." Davey and Jose both appreciated Eric trying to help and shared a chuckle.

"Seriously, Jose. You're not alone in feeling like you don't know how to help her or don't know how to keep going. But you're a good man and your feelings are valid."

Jose cleared his throat as an attempt to compose himself, while Cass stared on blankly.

"Thanks, bros." Davey and Eric smiled at him.

"How about you, Eric? How are things with Ava?" Davey asked.

Eric was moved by Jose's vulnerability. "Okay, I think. She wants me to be doing more, and I really hope the stream can show her that I can be something successful."

"I hear that," Jose said.

"It's like she believes in me, dude, but also I don't think she actually does. Like she wants me to have something stable, but doesn't think I can find that. Streaming is the first thing I've been excited for in a long time."

"She's worried about fluctuating income." Cass declared with his arms crossed.

"I guess. Probably? She said she doesn't think streaming is it, but is glad that I'm trying."

"She might not be wrong, but that doesn't make you wrong either. As the saying goes, sometimes you shoot for the moon and land in the stars. Anything is possible, Eric. You could be the next big thing." Davey added.

"You think?"

"Heck yeah, bro. You could go viral like tomorrow. Who knows?" Jose said.

"Just try to balance what you need to do for yourself with what you need to do for your relationship."

Jose looked at Davey. "That's good, bro."

He laughed. "Thanks, man. It's my job."

"So, who is the therapist's therapist?" Jose asked.

"Myself."

"Can't a therapist get a therapist?"

"Yeah, of course."

"But you don't have one?"

"Nope. I've tried. I compare their therapeutic techniques to my own too much, and don't get anywhere."

"I got you, bro. I'll be your therapist. What do I have to do?"

"Go get your master's degree, then get licensed, then do continuing education nonsense. Then, set up your private practice and insurance, or go work for a clinic or something."

"Dang, bro. You did all that?"

"Had to. Cass had to do similar stuff to get to be an attorney."

Jose looked to Cass, who nodded his head.

"The bar is something else," Cass grimaced. For a second, the mask slipped. They were all professionals in their own way, each carrying people who leaned on them. It was easy to forget that support had a weight of its own. He rubbed his thumb against his palm, a nervous tic that came out when he wanted to say more. Davey caught the movement and almost asked about it.

He didn't.

"I think that might be the most emotion we've gotten from Cass." Eric pointed out. Cass gave him a look to suggest he should stop talking.

"Yeah, I don't think I'll do all that. How about just being a friend?"

Jose asked.

"Good enough for me," Davey replied.

The room smelled of burnt coffee and emotional exhaustion. Jose wiped his face. Eric stared at the ceiling. Davey leaned back. Cass checked his phone.

"So, see you guys next Thursday?"

Jose and Eric both verbally agreed, while Cass nodded.

Cass stood first, his phone lighting his pocket again. He lingered at the door longer than the others. "Hey, Davey," he said quietly, "good talk tonight."

Then he left before Davey could answer. Davey wanted to tell him it didn't have to end there, that he could stay for another cup, another moment. But Cass had already turned toward the streetlight, his face caught between shadow and the glow of his phone.

They trickled out of the home, and Davey remained sitting down for another beat.

He eventually stood and put the chairs away. He locked the door, gave the rest of the dwelling a quick tidy, and went upstairs to his wife. She was finished with her pint. The empty container rested on the nightstand with a bit of condensation hovering around its base. She was still sitting up and watching her show. He paused in the doorway and observed her.

"I think this is the most I've sat still since I learned how to walk," she said without turning away from the TV.

"Probably true. You were always incredibly active."

She smiled. "How'd it go?"

"Good. Really good."

"Anything you want to talk about?"

"Nope. Thank you, though. Just going to try and get to bed soon."

She continued to watch her show as he prepared for bed. His chest began to feel tight as the emotional weight was heavy on him. Every story from downstairs still echoed. Jose's tears. Cass's silence. Eric's forced hope. The weight didn't belong to him, but it lived in him all the same.

He splashed his face with water in the bathroom and took a melatonin. The anxiety in him heightened. Rae was just outside waiting for him. She was safe, and he didn't know what he was panicking over. A bead of cold sweat gathered on his forehead. He started to leave the bathroom, then stopped himself. He turned around and paused before he grabbed an edible and self-medicated. He walked back to the bed where Rae had turned off the TV.

"You know I love you, right, babe?"

He didn't know what had compelled her to ask him.

"Of course, thankfully. I love you too." He said it softly.

He kissed her goodnight and tucked himself into their bed. Having her next to him, being able to touch her, started to help, along with the edible to calm his heart rate. He stared at the ceiling and watched headlights creep through their closed blinds, casting different shapes in their room. He could tell she fell asleep quickly as her breathing shifted and she began to quietly snore. Davey closed his eyes and let the soft hum of the street flow, paired with his wife's gentle snores, carry him into the night. The sound filled the room like a promise. For now, she was safe. For now, they both were.

Chapter 11: Electric Irritation

Within a few days, Davey received a return letter from Simon Cribb's defense attorney. It was a short note: "Mr. Karrol, thank you for your note. We will take it under consideration. Sentencing will be at the end of the week, 9:30 a.m." Davey studied the note, as if he hoped the longer he looked, the more words would appear. But none came up from the depths of the paper. He wondered if the incorrect spelling of his last name was a product of intention or carelessness. Davey felt like the latter would be worse than the former. He stared at it longer than he should have. The smallness of the mistake nearly stung worse than insult. If the attorney forgot who he was, what chance did Simon ever have of being seen as more than a case number? He also wondered if the wording of the sentencing hearing date was purposefully vague.

Was I too emotional? Too clinical or pushy? Davey thought back to his note and considered whether he had messed it up in some way. He brought the letter to show Rae. She had started to do significantly better but was still not in heroing shape.

"What do you think of this?"

She reviewed the note. "I wish I could say I wasn't surprised by the brevity."

Davey remembered when Rae used to write letters to victims' families she couldn't save, handwritten and heavy. She stopped after one came back unopened. It felt as if the world didn't care about an apology, only that she failed.

"But what about the vagueness for sentencing?"

"Honestly, I don't know if you need to read into it. You could try to call down there, but the end of the week could just really mean Friday."

"Yeah, but it could also mean Thursday."

"Definitely not Wednesday," she joked, but could see he was truly perturbed. "Babe, don't overthink it. If you're anxious about it, then call down. Why do you want to go to sentencing?"

"I just feel like I need to see this through, you know? Simon needs help."

"So does the family of the person he killed."

"I don't think he should be free, Rae."

"I understand that. But, babe, you probably did as much as you could to help him."

"I don't know. Maybe I should have tried to give the letter to the court directly. Or hand it to the public defender."

"Don't go down that rabbit hole, Davey."

Davey acknowledged the very real possibility that he might lose himself trying to help Simon.

"It feels impossible not to."

"Do you want me to go with you to the sentencing? I think I'm probably good enough to travel." There was a time he would have said yes but now he considered what it might be like if SolaRae, the arresting hero, was there too. Somewhere between then and now, they lost the quiet version of themselves that didn't need to ask permission to show up.

"Thanks, but probably not. Everybody will recognize you. You'll be the focus. Not making sure Simon gets help… not that you being the focus is a bad thing. It just might not be the best thing this time."

Rae looked disappointed but understood. Her notoriety would follow her wherever she went, regardless of whether she was in a suit or not. Davey's phone chimed. Eric texted the support group chat: A little behind, but here's the link for the stream! Starting tonight!!

Jose: Heck yeah, bro!

Davey: Nice.

There was no response from Cass. Cass never sent emojis. Never liked a message. He existed in read receipts and silence.

Davey felt like he should have given more encouragement. But his mind was elsewhere. He felt like he was being pulled in different directions. He had built his life around solving other people's chaos.

A mess of his own design.

For the remainder of the day, he sat with Rae as she alternated between reality TV and pregnancy literature. He was consumed by amateur legal research that was simultaneously impossible to understand and not helpful in the slightest. He took a break from his research and decided that there was no harm in trying to confirm when the sentencing hearing would be. He thought about calling Cass for help, just to make sense of the legal jargon, but didn't. Cass had enough on his plate, and Davey didn't want to look desperate. Still, he imagined Cass explaining it all, slow and calm, like he used to when they were broke students.

Davey made a few calls and spoke to a few less-than-enthusiastic legal secretaries. They weren't keen to help but eventually provided Davey with the knowledge that the hearing would be on Thursday morning, rather than Friday. He felt a small tinge of pride come forward. He was glad that his gut led him to the right decision rather than trust in the vagueness. Still, he hated how much pride he took in being right about something so small. Like if he kept finding minor victories, the larger failures might not notice him.

He returned to his research in an attempt to find any sort of precedent that might help Simon get the assistance that he needed in two days. The sun began to set on the November day. Davey preemptively took his cocktail of self-medication and sat with his wife before they both decided to try and sleep.

In the morning, Davey woke up to a few texts from the support group.

Eric: What do you guys think?? Only a few viewers, not bad, right?

Jose: It was great! I got to watch while the kid slept on me after their bottle. Loved it!

Eric: Thanks!

There was no response from Cass. Davey felt like he had failed his future brother-in-law. He assured the guys that he would be there for them, and he immediately let Eric down. He thought about texting back and lying to the young man.

"Crap," he said aloud.

"What's wrong?" Rae asked while still groggy.

"I forgot about Eric's thing last night." He used to pride himself on showing up for the people who needed him. That had been the whole point of the group. Lately, it felt like even his good intentions arrived late.

"The streaming? He actually did it? Don't those things usually have a way to watch it afterward? You could do that."

"I don't know that I have the time." He thought that he really didn't have much to do on a random Wednesday in November. "I'll tell him I can make sure to catch the next one."

"I'm sure he'll understand." She lay back down, and Davey did as he said he would.

The day met the tone of the others that had recently passed. Davey continued to care for Rae, even though she was at a point where she no longer required assistance. Her abilities came with an enhanced constitution, which apparently meant that she healed just slightly faster than someone without the H-gene. He tried to explore legal resources but routinely drew blanks. He didn't know what to do, but he knew that he had to try.

When dinner came, Davey ordered dumplings and brought them up to the bedroom. He set them down on the nightstand and began to open the containers.

"Dumplings?" Rae asked. "Are you trying to hint at something?"

"A guy can't just get some dumplings for his lady?"

"Hey, no complaints… either way…"

"I don't think you're well enough for that yet, Rae."

"What if I was?"

"What if I just wanted dumplings?"

"Did you? Did you just want dumplings?"

"Actually yes," he laughed. "My mind was only on dumplings, but I'm not mad that you went there."

"How about you come here?"

"Rae, I really don't know that that's a good idea." He started walking toward her as if his body acted against his mind.

"Then, be gentle." She pulled him in for a slow kiss. Rae moved the remote from the top of her bed sheet and turned off the TV. She moved the sheet entirely and motioned for Davey to join her. He didn't need to self-medicate that night.

In the morning, they woke, and he prepared to journey to the sentencing hearing.

He ordered a rideshare this time.

The ride was unexpectedly quiet; the hum of the electric vehicle's engine was borderline unsettling, as he was lost in thought. He remembered getting to the hospital the night Rae got stabbed: the same hum, the same stillness. The city always seemed quieter before bad news.

The car dropped him off at the steps of the courthouse. A small contingent of media had begun to gather. He slunk through the crowd of varying personalities and overheard some of them discussing how they might swing the mention of Simon's potential mental health concerns. Davey worked his way through the first doors and felt the buzz of the place. For whatever reason, hero-arrested defendants drew in a larger crowd in the gallery as some purveyors liked to see the results of their actions. He found a seat as close to Simon Cribb as possible. The buzz mellowed as the old judge took his spot. The courtroom felt mechanical with the rise and fall of the onlookers. The formality of it all seemed not to concern itself with the emotional state of the defendant.

Simon's eyes looked hazy, as if a thin veil covered them. Davey thought he seemed nearly vacant. Even in his brief responses to the therapist, there was a complex person behind the words. Now, it appeared like he was a shell. An overmedicated, under-cared-for shell of a human. A mix of anger and sadness overcame Davey. He did what he could to compose himself. Davey focused on the words of the judge, who he thought should have retired long ago. Then, it struck him like a freight train when the sentence was announced.

"The defendant, Simon Cribb, is hereby sentenced to life without the possibility of parole. The request for a comprehensive mental health assessment is denied."

Simon stared forward. Emotionless. For a moment, Davey thought

Simon might look at him. He wanted him to. Just one flicker of recognition that said, I'm still here. But Simon didn't turn.

The surrounding crowd was silent, and the scribbles of some media members filled the space.

Davey was deflated. He seemed to be the only one to care.

His sense of morality rushed forward, and his professionalism left him.

He rose like a tower from the gallery.

"Your Honor, this isn't rehabilitation! This isn't justice!"

"Sir, this man pleaded guilty to murder, among other charges. I am within my purview to sentence him. You are not his attorney. One more thing, and I will hold you in contempt and keep you here for the night!"

Davey was silent but remained standing as Simon started to be led out of the courtroom.

"This isn't right!"

"Bailiff." The judge ordered, and Davey was escorted out of the room.

He saw Simon; his lip quivered, but no words came.

Cameras snapped pictures of the therapist, anxious to include him in the next headline. He wondered what headline they'd use this time. "Therapist Outburst in Court. Hero's Husband Loses Control!" The story was never his to tell, but they would insert him into it anyway.

He looked back at Simon as he was being escorted out of the courtroom. There was no emotion. Blank.

He was put in a holding cell before being offered a phone call. His first call was to Cass. There was no answer. The ring felt longer than it should have. He didn't leave a voicemail. He never did. Cass never called back; not anymore.

He was permitted to try another number and was able to get hold of his wife. The superhero.

"Hello?" She answered. He expected a warm welcome, but of course, she didn't know the number. The fluorescent light and the stale air told him that this wasn't a place he wanted to spend much time.

"Rae, it's me."

"Davey? What's going on? What happened to your phone?"

"I messed up."

"What happened, Davey? Are you in trouble? Tell me where to go." He heard her shuffling over the phone and thought she might be trying to wiggle into her suit.

"I'm being held in contempt for the night."

"Davey… what the heck?"

"Just didn't want you to worry."

"Good attempt."

"Seriously, just leave me here, babe."

"Judge Narra is a piece of garbage. I'm coming."

"Rae…"

"Are you going to stop me from behind bars?"

"Please, Rae. Just text Eric that the group is canceled tonight and he can get word to the other guys."

"Fine. I'll let Eric know. I'll see you in a little bit… Dammit, David." She hung up.

Davey tried to get comfortable in the coldness of the cell.

At some point in his stay, as the late fall night broke through the few windows of the holding area, he started to hear a commotion. A few officers began to run past his cell. His curiosity piqued, "What's going on?" He yelled after one of the officers who was still within reach.

"It's SolaRae, she's back! She's outside!" The officer replied as he continued to follow his colleagues.

Davey was a mix of thankful, annoyed, and fearful of what might happen next. For a moment, he thought that the cold cell might be the better alternative than his wife, but she had been itching to get out of the house. His thoughts shifted to his outburst as an act of helping her get back to business, however untrue that might be. After a few minutes, the sound of serious boots announced themselves on the concrete hallway. They sounded terrifyingly rhythmic. They marched with purpose. Rae faced him from the other side of the cell. Her brightness overwhelmed the fluorescent lights. He could smell her perfume from the other side of the bars that held him. In his holding, he was awkwardly both terrified and aroused.

"I spoke to Narra. We're leaving." She didn't wait for an officer to open the cell. She placed her hand on the lock, channeled her heat from within, and melted it. Davey's eyes widened, and he quietly managed a note of gratitude laced with shock. "There are reporters outside waiting. You're going to have to talk to them." He nodded and accepted his fate.

She led him through the halls and to the steps of the courthouse, where the near-winter air forced a chill onto the crowd. Davey thought he would have rather waited inside. SolaRae walked toward the media. She was accustomed to the routine and faced the crowd as she had many times before. Questions started being shouted in her direction:

"SolaRae, are you back for good? Why this case? Is that your husband? How are you recovering?"

She controlled the chaos.

"Yes, I am back. I've recovered fine, thank you all for asking." Davey thought her superhero voice was even more impressive than normal. It was fierce, inspiring, and controlling. "You all know I haven't tried to hide my personal life. I believe in transparency and support the heroes who wish to keep their own lives a secret. Some of you who have cared to figure it out already know. It was never a secret. Yes. The man behind me is my husband." Davey subconsciously straightened his posture and widened himself to appear as if he was deserving of being Rae's spouse. "Why this case?" She looked back at Davey over her shoulder.

"Mental health matters. We can't expect a change in the system if those of us with a voice don't stand for something. Simon Cribb is a murderer and also a victim of falling through the cracks." It was the same argument he'd made in therapy notes, stripped of nuance but burning with truth. Hearing her say it out loud made something inside him settle.

"SolaRae, do you think he should be freed?" A media member shouted.

"No. Justice should be sought for the person he killed. But, not every situation is black and white."

There was a choir of furious scribbling and tapping.

"SolaRae, question for your husband?"

She motioned for Davey to stand next to her.

"Mr. SolaRae…"

"Just Davey." He cut off the reporter.

"Davey, is it true that you were held in contempt?"

He reached his hand to the nape of his neck and rubbed it anxiously.

"Yes, that's correct."

"Can you tell us more about what happened?"

"Um… sure. Well, I'm a therapist by trade, and I met with Simon a few times. It's clear to me that he needs mental health support. I wrote a letter suggesting a comprehensive mental health analysis, so that he might get the services necessary. It was denied… and I got mad."

"SolaRae, will you be championing any mental health initiatives?"

"I haven't gotten that far just yet, but I will at the very least be a voice in a subject that matters."

"Any thoughts on going into politics, Rae?"

"My thoughts are that's never going to happen."

That earned some laughs from the crowd.

"What's next for you, Rae? What's next for Simon Cribb?"

"I'll be getting back to watching over the city with the women who have been picking up my slack while I've been gone. I owe them all of the thanks in the world. As for Simon, unfortunately, I don't believe there's much we can do. I'm no legal expert, but I believe we might be able to assist him in an appeal of sorts."

"Welcome back, SolaRae!"

"Thank you all. I appreciate your support. If there are no other questions, we should be getting home."

There was silence before a final reporter began to ask a question. "Rae, last thing, what do you think of the new hero?"

"There's a new hero in the city? Sorry, I've been cooped up and haven't been made aware of it yet."

"They only just showed up this morning, so you're not too far behind."

"Good to know. Well, I look forward to meeting with her and working to help the city."

"Rae, the new hero is a man." Davey felt the words land like a strange confession. If men could have the H-gene, then the whole equation shifted. Power was no longer the women's alone. She was shocked and didn't know how to react. Davey tilted his head slightly in surprise.

"Thank you for letting me know. I look forward to meeting with him then. Until next time, friends."

Rae and Davey climbed into a waiting taxi; she had flagged one down before going to free Davey and told the driver to leave the meter running until they were done. They started for home.

"A man?" she asked Davey. "I thought the H-gene was only in women?"

"Apparently not," Davey replied. He started scrolling through his phone to see if any news of the hero had hit social media yet. "This is wild." He found a grainy video of a man walking the streets of the city in a leather jacket. "It looks like nobody knows his name yet. I can't believe this." The city outside blurred into a dripping watercolor painting whose artist hadn't taken the care it needed.

Chapter 12: More New Things, Good

"Could you tell where the video was shot?" Rae asked when they arrived home.

"It's pretty grainy, but I think I recognize Fort Wadsworth in the background."

"Staten Island?"

"Yeah, here, what do you think?"

Davey showed his wife the video.

He got close to her, and the perfume was intoxicating. The smells of the city, the holding cell, the train, could never compare to the smell of her. It was like the air lightened around her aura. She made him feel like he could float. He tried to return his focus to the video to watch with her. He loved moments like this, the quiet ones where the world felt small again. No heroes, no courts, no patients. Just the sound of her breathing beside him. It reminded him that the rest of it was temporary.

The video was incredibly grainy, like it had been shot on a 30x zoom camera, not built for clarity. There was a boat that seemed to have lost its engines in New York Harbor and was being carried directly toward Fort Wadsworth and the Verrazzano Bridge. A man in what looked to be a leather jacket stood on the edge of the sidewalk outside the Fort and over the water. The boat headed straight for him. He stretched out his arms to grab the bow of the lost boat. The momentum of the vessel began to slow as it pushed the man backward and broke part of the concrete beneath. Then the boat stopped entirely, and the man pushed it backward a bit. It was just off the sidewalk now, and the hero instructed the helpless crew to drop anchor.

"Wow. That's kind of incredible," Rae responded.

"Yep. But that's Fort Wadsworth, right?"

"Looks like it. Tomorrow I'll do some patrolling in Staten Island, see if I come across him, and make an introduction."

"How do you know he'll be there tomorrow?"

"Just a hunch. When Ava and I started heroing, we stuck to Queens at first. OwlHeart did the same in the Bronx and Echona in Brooklyn. It's natural to stick to what you know when you're starting. Maybe he's from Staten Island."

"Makes sense." Cass used to say that people never drift too far from the first place they were understood. He said it during one of those long college nights when they still thought the world was fixable. Davey missed that kind of certainty. He thought back to the night Rae first came to their dorm. Cass had already heard about her for months and was skeptical that Davey would ever be able to have somebody as great as he made her sound. Rae arrived carrying takeout and a dog-eared paperback she wanted him to read.

Cass sat at his desk pretending to study but actually attempting to observe her. She asked Cass about his major, his hobbies, his life, like she was already part of theirs. By the time she left, Cass was convinced of her quality, he said she was trouble in the way good people usually are. Davey remembered thinking that was the highest praise Cass was capable of giving. It was one of the first times in his young adult life that he let himself believe Rae would be around for a long time.

"Hey." Rae changed the subject. "Are you okay?"

"I'll be fine. Just wish I could have done more."

"It's not your fault, Davey. Sorry if I sounded upset earlier."

"You don't need to apologize, Rae. You didn't do anything wrong. I'm sorry that I didn't control myself. How are you feeling? You're really back into work shape?"

"Yeah, I'm a little stiff, but I feel good."

He went to hug his wife.

"Don't rush back, please. I don't need you hurting yourself by going too fast."

She embraced him.

"It's okay. I'm good. I had a great home nurse."

She kissed him and they prepared for bed. He lay awake longer than he meant to. Her breathing was soft, steady, but he couldn't shake the thought that healing demanded something in return.

In the morning, Rae readied herself for Staten Island and, as if she didn't miss a beat, asked Davey to zip her suit before she flew out of their bedroom window. The cool air cut across her face like a refreshing jolt. The city was back to being hers. By some odd happenstance, she didn't frequent Staten Island. It always made sense for Echona to cover Staten Island, given the proximity to Brooklyn.

As she closed the distance, she saw her opportunity. Sirens flew beneath her through the streets and looked to be going toward the Staten Island Zoo. She followed and began to see what the issue was. A mishap had led to some of the animals getting freed. She laughed before swooping down to help scared visitors and zookeepers. It was a job that she found to be more fun than troublesome. She chased an ostrich and an emu before she spotted an adult kangaroo. It charged toward a visitor. Rae yelled out for the visitor to move. A single man in a leather jacket stood still. He faced the kangaroo without flinching. Rae thought he was frozen in place and quickly tried to fly to the man to move him out of the way. The kangaroo jumped toward the man, feet first.

The animal beat her to him.

Its feet connected with his sternum.

Then, it fell backward and hit the pavement of the zoo walkway. It was dazed. The man picked up the kangaroo and threw it over his shoulder before he walked with it back toward its enclosure. Rae was bewildered. She followed the man. That has to be him, she thought. After he returned the kangaroo and safely sealed it, he turned to see Rae behind him.

"Oh, hey, SolaRae. Thanks for the help. Love your work," he said.

His voice was friendly but gruff. He was a small bit shorter than her, but that wasn't particularly uncommon. She was a tall woman. He wore a leather jacket, sunglasses, faded jeans, and well-loved Converse sneakers. He had a well-maintained mustache and medium-length hair. Under his leather jacket, he was shirtless. Rae could see a mix of what appeared to be scars and abs.

She continued to examine him, "Thanks. Happy to help. You're the new hero, if I'm guessing correctly?"

"Yup, that's me. Call me Rocker."

"Well, nice work stopping that boat, Rocker."

"You saw that?" He blushed. "Thanks, just doing what I can. My abilities just activated not too long ago. I've always had the H-gene. Just one of those people who haven't been fortunate enough to have powers until recently."

"Heck yeah, I saw it. Seriously, that was awesome. It'll be cool to see more research coming out surrounding the gene. I had no idea guys could be born with it, too."

"Oh," he paused. "They usually can't."

"But you have them?"

"Right."

"So, how?"

"One of those rare mutations. My doctor said my H-gene was dormant until recently. Guess it just needed a jump-start or something. But, it's obviously a cool change. What I was before the powers doesn't define me. I get to decide what kind of person I am now. You can spend your life stuck in what you were, or you can build something new."

"Interesting. Well, welcome to the team. What are your powers anyway?"

"Want to see?"

"Uhhh, yeah!"

He smirked. "Punch me. Full strength."

She gave him a puzzled look. "You sure about that?"

He nodded. She reared her arm and threw a punch toward Rocker. It connected with his sternum, and her arm vibrated. It sounded like she had just punched a metal beam. She looked at her fist; the knuckles had turned red. Pain rose from her fist to her shoulder.

"First, ouch. Second, that's sweet. Can you harden your body?"

"Yup," he said proudly. "I can make my skin tougher than a boulder, but that's not all. Watch this."

He squatted down and pushed himself off the ground. He leaped a hundred feet into the air before landing in a small crater that mimicked the city's other potholes.

"I'm also super strong."

"But can you fly?" she joked with him.

"I wish. I'll be stuck to the ground, unfortunately."

"That's alright, your abilities are super cool."

"I feel like you've been called a loser solely based on the puns you make. Am I right?"

"What can I say... I'm hilarious." She shrugged and laughed. "So, what made you take to heroing? I mean, I've heard of some people who have the active gene and just choose to stay on the sidelines."

"Guess we all get built a little differently. Maybe that's on purpose. Maybe we're all meant to find out what we're made for when the time's right."

Rae liked his thought process. She could get behind a world of people deciding what they could be for themselves.

"Yeah, I'm not so sure. Any chance I can meet the other heroes?"

"Of course, absolutely. Give me your number, I'll put something together." She handed him her phone, which discreetly fit into a hidden pocket along the side of her suit.

"Perfect," she said. "Oh, hey, are you in a relationship?"

Rocker paused for a minute. "Does that matter?"

"Oh, no, not at all. The rest of us are either married or engaged, and the husbands get together every once in a while. It's a superhero's husband support group."

"Nice. Yes, actually, I am. But, I'm not sure my wife would want to be in a husband support group."

"That's just what I'm calling it. It can be a spouse support group. Just let her know, and I'll talk to my husband too."

"Oh, right. The criminal therapist?" He laughed.

"The one and only." She smirked. "Well, there's probably more than one criminal therapist, but yes. Nice abs, by the way. I'm only a little jealous."

"I'm sure you have some underneath that suit."

"You're right, but I won't for long."

"Planning on going on a fast food-eating binge?"

"No, but that also sounds good. I'm pregnant."

He went wide-eyed. "No way. Congrats. So, the criminal therapist and the superhero got busy?"

"More than once." She playfully nudged him and thought that they would get along just fine. For a moment, she thought of Davey; he'd laugh at Rocker's confidence and immediately ask too many questions about his powers.

Meanwhile, across the river, Davey worked his way to his office. It felt like he hadn't been there for a lifetime. Once he arrived, it took him a few minutes to get back into the flow of things. His inbox was flooded with requests for initial appointments. Being married to SolaRae was now common knowledge rather than something that took a minimal amount of research. He worked on rescheduling with his clients who had been in the temporary care of another private practice colleague. Then, he made himself busy with new potential clients.

He had a new fire for mental health support, and he couldn't pretend to care without taking on as many clients as he could. He began to feel overwhelmed with anxiety. The feeling as if he couldn't do enough was ever-present. But his stomach had been conditioned to let him know when he needed a hot dog. So, at 12:15 p.m., he went to see his supplier of sustenance. Boris was in his usual spot on his lawn chair, but had traded his white shirt for a grease-stained gray hoodie. He rose from his chair as he saw Davey cross the street.

"David, my friend! Welcome back! I thought you found another stand."

"I could never leave you, Boris, and it's just Davey. How's business?"

"Good, David, good. You try new dog?"

"Just the regular, Boris."

"You like Thanksgiving, yes?"

"Yeah, sure."

"You try, Give Thanks Dog. Deep-fried turkey sausage on a potato bun with cranberry sauce on top."

"You know what, Boris? A regular and a Thanksgiving dog."

"Give Thanks Dog, David. It sounds better."

Davey chuckled. "Sure, Boris. One of each, please."

He paid Boris, and for a change, he had his lunch next to the stand instead of back in his office.

"Good, yes?"

Davey enjoyed the new hot dog and nodded his head while he ate.

"New things good, yes?"

"Very good, Boris. New things are very good." He meant it, but a small part of him still wanted the old things.

Chapter 13: Steam

"Everyone, thanks for coming. I hope you all have a great Thanksgiving coming up with any family you have. Next year we should try and do one of those Friendsgivings." Davey started the session. Snow had begun to fall outside the Kew Gardens home, and the steam of bad coffee warmed the room. There were five chairs in the room, rather than four. Rocker made his entry into the group of New York's heroes, and his wife had decided to see what the support group was about. "As you guys see, we have a new member."

"Woot woot!" Eric proclaimed, and Davey laughed.

"Want to introduce yourself, Laurel?"

"Gladly. Thank you for opening your home, Davey. My name is Laurel, and my husband is Rocker. The one and only male superhero. Really proud of him." She had long, dirty-blonde hair draped over her shoulders. Her feet just barely reached the floor. Eric noticed she was short, with porcelain skin and thicker thighs. He appreciated her beauty.

"Yo! Welcome!" Jose answered. "We have to get a new name like the Super Spouses Support Group or something."

"Or like the Powerless People," Eric suggested.

"The PPs? Bro... no."

"We'll workshop it, guys." Davey shook his head and laughed. "Laurel, thank you for coming. It's a pleasure to have you. It sounds like Rocker is fitting right in with the other heroes. Really happy to hear it. You know me, I'm Davey, and my wife is SolaRae. We have Eric over here with LunAva, then Jose with OwlHeart, and quiet Cass over here with Echona. How's it going, everyone?"

Eric interjected, "Question, if it's okay, but how does that work with the H-gene thing, since it's supposed to only show up in women?"

"Good question. It's actually not an issue for him. He's part of a small handful of rare mutations where the H-gene activates in men. I wasn't born with it, which I'm totally fine with. But Rocker's activation surprised the doctors and researchers. He's basically a walking study subject right now."

"Exactly. He's still our Rocker, wildly strong and all," Jose answered.

Eric nodded understandingly.

Rocker's story had the strange ring of grace about it; how something impossible could just happen, and everyone had to decide what to do with the miracle.

"Bro, how's Rae? Any pregnancy symptoms yet?" Jose asked.

"Nope. She's only just over two months. Seems to be pretty easy-going so far."

"Just wait. They'll come. Any kids, Laurel?" Jose asked.

"Nope. We don't want any. We love our life just the two of us." The words landed softer than she probably meant them to and Davey felt a faint ache of envy. The simplicity of "just the two of us" felt like a world he used to live in. He thought about the quiet mornings with Rae before headlines and before heroics.

"Totally fair. I have a kid. He's coming up on six months. Honestly, I get the idea of not wanting kids. It's not for everyone."

"That's true, Jose. But, you're doing great at the dad thing."

"It doesn't always feel like it."

"Is the dad-pack charged?" Eric asked.

"I'm getting there. I think I'm learning to let myself not do everything that needs to be done at the same time. Sara has been understanding. I think I've been trying to make sure everything is perfect for her, so she doesn't have to worry about it or ask me to do something. She does so much."

"Nobody is perfect, Jose. I'm glad you're giving yourself a break."

"It's hard to care for others when you don't take care of yourself," Laurel quietly added. "Also, Sara? Are we just using our spouses' names?"

"Exactly!" Davey excitedly agreed with her. "You're not a therapist, are you? And yeah, we all shared our spouses' names in the first session. No pressure to share Rocker's name."

"Ha. No way. I could never. I'm just well acquainted with them. I'll talk to him and see what he thinks."

"What do you do?" Cass asked.

"He talks!" Laurel joked, but Cass didn't seem amused. "I'm a software engineer."

"What's your favorite language?" he followed up.

"JavaScript holds a special place in my heart, but I've shifted to C++. I'm a sucker for complex syntax. Do you code?"

Cass gave her a nod of respect. "Nope. Never could."

"Yeah, it's not for everyone, that's for sure."

"How are you adjusting to him being in the spotlight now?"

"It's alright. I'm getting used to seeing his face go viral, but it hasn't made a huge impact yet."

"It'll get to be impactful, alright." Jose shared.

"Any endorsements yet?" Cass questioned. He was staring blankly out the front window, but he decided to participate again.

"Not yet, but fingers crossed."

"I'm sure he'll have plenty coming in soon. There will be some underwear company looking to use his face in their ads in no time."

"Oof. Don't like that." Laurel replied.

"Heh, protective?" Eric asked.

"I wouldn't say protective. If I can just have my husband not in a pair of tight undies, that would be my preference. It's weird. I'm incredibly proud of what he's doing. But, it's also… just a lot to process at once. I'm used to being the girl in the background. Not the one that's the spouse of a celebrity."

"Yeah, now just think about how we felt when they plastered a duo ad of LunAva and SolaRae in lingerie in Times Square."

"I remember hearing about that. Didn't it generate millions for the company? I heard it was one of the most successful ads in a long time."

"It sure did," Eric replied proudly.

"Yes. They're planning another one already." Davey was not quite as enthused. "Glad that it's starting well for you so far, Laurel."

"How about you and SolaRae? Can't thank her enough for being so welcoming to Rocker. And, you for being so inviting to me. Exciting that you guys are expecting. He filled me in on that, too."

"Yeah, it's exciting. Terrifying. But, exciting. You know what the worst part is?"

"It's the blowouts, bro."

"I'm sure it will be. I was actually thinking that the worst part is that just about everybody knows who Rae is. Recently, everybody knows who I am. That feels like it's no life for a kid. Or for any sort of privacy."

"Dude, privacy went out the window a long time ago. Honestly, I don't even know why Ava wears the mask. They literally do ads as sisters. It doesn't take too much energy to find out what Rae's family tree is, even for me. At least these guys have some form of privacy."

"That's true. I guess it doesn't make a ton of sense. But, it doesn't seem like people bother you guys."

"We're not really in public that much together. But, dude, imagine if people knew me. My stream would blow up!"

"You stream?" Laurel asked.

"I'm trying. It's been close to a month now, and I don't really have any viewers. I don't know if I made the right decision."

"A month is not nearly long enough. You should see some of the traffic patterns on regular high-profile streamers. Some of them bounce around like crazy. Stay with it, the rest will come."

"Thanks. I just don't know. I want to show Ava I can do it."

"Do it for yourself, Eric. Not for Ava," Davey replied.

"Yeah, bro, believe in yourself. Your last stream was great!"

"How are you and my sister-in-law, anyway?"

"I don't know. We don't really spend that much time together anymore. Texts are short. She's been away from the apartment for a while. Either on patrol or helping out her parents. I miss her."

Davey wondered if the talk he had with Ava long ago was still on her mind.

"I think I'm going to try and see what she's up to after this."

"That's a good idea. You should do that." Laurel encouraged him, and Davey wondered if she might be somewhat tuned into the disconnect in Eric's relationship.

Eric smiled at her, and there was a brief pause in the room before Davey took control of the quiet.

"So, Cass, anything going on? How are things with Echona?"

"We're good. Just work, really."

"What do you do?" Laurel asked.

"I'm an attorney and Echona's agent."

"Neat. You must be super busy. She's all over the place lately."

"Yes. Always busy. Just doing what I have to do."

"Hope you have time for yourself in there to take a breath every once in a while."

Cass crossed his arms and nodded at her. Davey flashed to their last real night of freedom before adulthood settled in. Cass had been sprawled on the dorm couch, law books open but ignored. Rae was visiting again, sitting cross-legged on the floor, challenging every argument Cass made just to see if she could win. They had laughed until campus security came by to quiet them down. Davey realized then that Cass needed someone who could disarm him the way Rae had disarmed him. Maybe that was why he'd fallen for Jazmine. The snow started to pick up, and the thickness of the early December snowflakes obscured the view of the night sky from the front window.

"Did any of your partners get asked to participate in the Rockefeller Center Christmas tree lighting? They want OwlHeart to act like she's putting the star on the top of the tree."

"Dude, why can't she just put up the tree herself?"

"Eric, bro, it's like 900 pounds. She can fly, and she's stealthy. That's it. She could maybe fly Rocker up there, but she can't lift that. I don't think anybody can carry it up there by themselves."

"900? No way."

"Bro, the thing is huge. It's a giant tree. They take it from Vermont or some rural state like that."

"It's actually usually from New York," Laurel said.

"Or Pennsylvania," Cass added.

"Have you guys actually been around Times Square lately? There are so many SolaRae plushies in those I Heart NYC stores. It's wild. It's like she literally is New York." Laurel asked. "Sorry if it has been asked already. I just saw them for the first time. I don't really go over there. It's wild."

"Hah. Yup. I forgot that might not be normal for most people. And don't apologize, you didn't do anything wrong. It's pretty crazy. I say that she belongs to the city more than she belongs to me."

"Well, she doesn't belong to anyone."

"You're right. I should probably adjust my wording."

"If anything, she owns you, dude," Eric joked.

Davey opened his mouth to rebut Eric's joke, but he couldn't; he wasn't entirely wrong. He didn't have a response, so he finished with, "Good group, everyone… will catch you all next time."

"You guys are alright, I think," Laurel shared.

Eric, Jose, and Laurel all moved from their chairs. Cass took a second longer to stand, and Davey noticed the delay.

Jose opened the door, and snowy air brushed past him. "Sheesh. I am so not ready for winter, bro. This sucks."

"Winter is great. You can always put on more layers. You only get to take off so many in summer, and we don't have an AC unit," Laurel responded.

"No way. I wish I could make heat like Rae. Can't stand winter," Jose answered.

The three of them, Cass following shortly, made their way out of the Kew Gardens home and headed back. Davey picked up the chairs with the same care he always did, as if mishandling them would cause them to simply shatter. He considered how normal the night felt. He was getting used to the support group, and suddenly it was as if he had a whole other family.

He was hopeful.

A smile crossed his face as he locked the door and ensured the coffee pot was turned off. He made his way up the creaking stairs. Not in a rush, but not with any particular attempt at being quiet. SolaRae wasn't home tonight. He reached the top, and it felt like the air got denser. A weight of dread fell upon his shoulders. There was the fate of Simon Cribb, fatherhood, Eric's relationship, and Cass's silence. He felt like he needed to do more. More than he was capable of. His vision blurred, and his chest started to tighten. The home itself felt like it was holding its breath.

After he found the bedroom, he leaned against the wall and slid down it to sit on the floor. His chest was pounding, and his forehead became tense. He knew he was having a panic attack, but the therapist felt helpless. He knew all the coping skills, the techniques, but he never focused on himself enough to know what would help him directly. He focused on what he could in the bedroom.

The bed was neatly made.

The blinds were closed.

The stained carpet.

The nightstand.

Home.

After a few minutes, he felt ready to get to bed. Rae wasn't home yet. He felt vulnerable. Lost. He didn't know what the next day might hold, and that worried him even more. He self-medicated and went to bed. The snow continued to fall outside his window. Before he fell asleep, he wondered if his wife was cold. She had warm suit options, but he didn't know which suit she wore today. He was back to worrying about Rae whenever she wasn't home. She was fine. He knew that. But, he couldn't make himself believe it. Not now. Not then. He hated it. It was comfortable.

Just moments ago, the house was filled with coffee steam and laughter. He thought of Cass again. The way his eyes stayed fixed on the window, the same way they used to when he was holding something too heavy to name. Davey made a note to check in. Then, like most of his good intentions, he filed it away under tomorrow. Now, it was just him, the silence, and all of the problems he couldn't solve.

Chapter 14: Head On BECSPK

"Can't you just lift it?" Rocker yelled to LunAva. They stood atop a building in the Diamond District.

"That's not how my powers work! I need to be able to lock onto it before I can alter its gravity."

"Alright. I have an idea."

The heroes had been alerted to a robbery at the Diamond Exchange. For a moment, Rae thought about how routine it all felt now. The call, the flight, the drop. Heroism had once been an act of courage. Lately, it felt more like clocking into a shift. She wondered if that was the cost of familiarity. Maybe awe was just the first thing to die when the new normal was accepted.

The thieves were driving recklessly up 6th Ave.

"The way these guys are driving, they'll take a detour through Central Park. We can't let that happen."

"You're right. So, what do you think?" OwlHeart responded.

"You and Rae get me to 59th. Just drop me from the air. Ava, you take Echona down there. When you're in the air, Echona, try to get the people to evacuate the area as loudly as you can. If we get there with enough time, I'll take the car head-on. Rae blinded the driver. It should crush the front end and bounce forward a bit. When that happens, Ava, lift the car into the air."

"Let's do it." Rae was proud of him for stepping into action and found it amusing. He had become so comfortable in such a short window. She thought of Davey and how long it had taken him to find comfort in his own skin at times. He had been quiet and deliberate. Rocker was the opposite, all instinct and no hesitation. Echona was quick to support his plan, while OwlHeart seemed pensive. As if she wasn't sure she appreciated the newest member becoming a leader. Comparatively, Ava typically opted to go with whatever sounded the most fun.

The heroes sprang off the rooftop and into action. They followed the car on its trajectory. It swerved through traffic, nearly sideswiping double-parked cars and clipping pedestrians. The tires slipped on the wintry roads and splashed slush onto the crowded sidewalks. They overtook it as Echona's voice filled the air and drowned out the chaotic noise below. The weather caused the heroes to move as fast as possible. A slip of the steering wheel could turn a heist into a mass casualty event.

Civilians started to clear the area. Some were slipping and sliding through the wet sidewalks. Others remained stationary as if the snow had frozen them in place to watch the spectacle that unfolded before them. With a small thud, Rocker was dropped from the sky and added a pothole to 6th Ave.

LunAva swooped in behind him and gently set Echona on the corner of W 59th Street. Her voice continued to fill the air like a loudspeaker on a loop. Then, LunAva took to the skies once more and positioned herself over Rocker, as SolaRae stood next to him. Brightness was already being channeled in her palm. The thieves approached.

NYPD cars arrived and blocked off W 59th to stop through traffic as the heroes worked. Rae extended her arms. The brightness that came forward rivaled the sun itself. Rocker had to look away and hope the car didn't swerve. Without a visual of the car, he wouldn't be able to adjust his position.

It hit him.

Rae dropped her brightness.

Echona thought ahead. As she heard the initial impact, she took the sound from the scene, so as not to frighten civilians more than they already were. It was a sharp sound that would have reminded any New Yorker of the screeching train brakes that were triggered a minute too late. The sound was immediately distorted and calmed. From the noise of brakes, it became a squawking baby bird before going entirely silent. The cold air filled with the smell of exhaust. The gray smoke fought with falling snow for spatial dominance. But neither won. Echona's abilities took precedence. There was something eerie about how easily power bent the world to her will. Rae often wondered what would happen if they all stopped holding back for the sake of the city.

She did not like the answer she imagined.

It nearly seemed like the air thickened with her control, and time slowed. The bright snow flattened to her will. The front end of the car collapsed into itself, and the rear shot upward as if it was trying to get away from the other half. LunAva, still floating above, locked onto the car and altered its gravity.

The lingering civilians were shocked by the silence. Some of them attempted to scream, but Echona's abilities extended to the closest ones. They opened their mouths, but nothing left their vocal cords as if they were stuck in a painting. The sound returned, and a few ending notes of terror broke the quietness. The noise of the city bent to Echona more literally than the air did. But the city was thick with anxiety. The tracks of the runaway car remained in the snow. The snow fell but didn't cover them, as if the marks on the pavement were a warning that the snow would not be so lenient with the criminals next time.

She had a bit too much fun with the car, as she toyed with it in the air like a yo-yo. The thieves, who had not thought of wearing seat belts, looked badly injured and nearly fell out of the broken windshield. She put the car down after SolaRae gave the word. She moved it as far out of the way as possible to ensure the officers waiting could properly apprehend the suspects.

The civilians who didn't take Echona's warning to heart began to applaud the heroes. Ava and OwlHeart landed next to the other heroes, while Echona took to speaking with the officers. Rocker dusted off his leather jacket. "Well, that was fun."

"Absolutely!" LunAva agreed with him.

OwlHeart looked at him like she couldn't believe he thought it was entertaining. Lives were almost lost. "I'm out of here, y'all. Holler if you need me." She gracefully took to the skies. The snow cleared a path for her, and a light frost breeze filled the area.

"Did I mess up?" he asked when he caught the look.

"You're good, dude," Ava reassured him. "She's like that sometimes."

"Yeah, she's... flighty," Rae joked.

"You're still not funny," he responded.

"Dude, I tell her that all the time." Ava threw her hands up as if she was exasperated.

"I'm hilarious, actually."

"She has her moments!" Echona yelled out as she walked back to the other heroes.

"How did you..." Rocker started.

"Super hearing, remember?"

"I actually didn't, but that's cool."

"It can be annoying. Anyway, reporters will probably be here soon. Cops are good with what I told them. Unless you guys want to have an impromptu press conference, I suggest we leave."

"Works for me." Rocker pointed up to a nearby rooftop and effortlessly jumped to it.

"Show off," Echona said with a grin. "Can I get an assist?"

Rae and Ava helped her to the roof, where Rocker was sitting, his feet dangling off the edge. They landed in the center, and he rose from his spot to join them.

"Nice plan, Rocker. Really. That was great, quick thinking," Rae complimented him as her cape flew in the winter breeze.

"Thanks. Just trying to help."

"Dude, are you really not hurt after that?" Ava asked.

"Nope. Not a scratch."

"That's so sick."

"Couldn't do it without you guys."

"I'm sure you could," Echona replied. "But we're happy you're here anyway."

"Same. Thank your husbands for me too. From what I've heard, they really welcomed Laurel at the support group."

"Glad to hear it. I'll tell Davey. How are things going for you guys with you being more in the spotlight now?"

"It's an adjustment. For sure. But I've been taking extra precautions. Got a new phone for endorsement calls. I go home discreetly. The sunglasses give me just enough cover, apparently."

"They'll figure out who you are eventually," Echona added. "I'm sure all our identities aren't so secret."

"At least most people tend to appreciate us and leave us alone. I mean, the whole city, maybe the country, knows who Davey and I are. It can't be too hard for somebody to find where we live, too."

"That's what I'm afraid of. Maybe I should've gone for a full face covering."

"Then people would think you're some villain or something. The media likes to try and play the guessing game. We let them, and they usually paint us in a decent light," Rae shared.

"It's a fun little game we all get to play," Echona responded.

"It sucks," Ava stated plainly.

There was a brief lull as they kept an eye on the streets below. Sure enough, the media came to paint their pictures.

"Hey!" Ava proclaimed. "We should get a team name!"

There was no answer.

"Guys, come on! It would be sweet!"

"On that note, I'm gonna head out. Catch y'all later." Echona headed for the fire escape and began to make her descent to the streets.

"See you later!" Rocker shouted.

"Ava… we're not getting a name," Rae responded to her sister.

"Rocker? Come on, dude. A name would be great. They always have them in the movies!"

Rocker looked to Rae. She tilted her head and gave him a look that begged him to side with her.

"I'm still getting used to this heroing thing. I think we table the team name for now."

"Dang. Fine. But don't be surprised when I start selling merch with our faces on it and some sick name attached. Like The Moon Rocks or something."

"We're not an indie pop band, sis."

"You guys are no fun. What about Heroes of New York?"

"That just sounds like an indie video game now."

Ava pouted and got lost in thought, trying to come up with a third team name.

"Oh, hey, Ava, how is Eric's stream going?" Rocker questioned.

She rolled her eyes. "Don't get me started. I really want him to find something to call his own, but I'm getting really tired of being so… supportive. I feel bad saying it, but his stream hasn't been getting viewers, and I don't know if it ever will. I've been sleeping at Mom and Dad's, so I don't have to be awake for his streams."

Rae wanted to tell her that distance was a warning sign, not a solution. She held it back.

"I checked out the last stream after Laurel told me about it. It feels like he's a natural, honestly. These things take time."

"I don't know how much more time I can give. Maybe I'll go back to the apartment for the next stream and be with him."

"Hey, do what's best for you," Rocker responded. "Not my pig, not my farm."

"Bacon sounds good." Rae was looking off into the distance as she added to the conversation.

"Pregnancy craving?" he questioned.

"What, a superhero can't want bacon after stopping a criminal?"

Rocker looked at her and raised his eyebrows. She could feel the look behind his glasses.

"Just for today, I'm blaming it on the baby. Fine."

He and Ava laughed.

"You're what, like, two or three months? I'm super not knowledge-able about baby development. Do symptoms happen yet?" he asked.

"I'm only ten weeks and we're going to say yes. Cravings definitely happen."

"When do I get to find out if I have a niece or a nephew to spoil?"

"When they're born. I don't think we're going to find out before-hand."

"Hey, I was going to buy gender-neutral baby clothes for Christmas anyway. Works for me," Rocker shared.

"Dude, it's way too early to be buying Christmas presents. We have time."

"Ava, Christmas is like three weeks away. Stores are going to start being picked over or become a madhouse."

"Wait, really? I thought we had like a month. Dang. Lost track of time again."

"Rocker, thank you, but no presents are necessary."

"If you think I'm not getting something for the heroes that have made my life so much more fun than it was... well, you are poorly mistaken."

"Should we do a Secret Santa?!" Ava asked excitedly.

"I don't think that's necessary."

"I'm with you, Ava. Secret Santas are a bunch of fun!" Rocker en-couraged her. "Should we do a price limit?"

"For us, maybe," Ava responded. "Have you seen how many en-dorsements Rae gets? The 'darling of the city', the 'light in the darkness!'" Ava mocked throwing up.

"First, don't be jealous. Second, babies are expensive! We can do the Secret Santa if Echona and OwlHeart are on board. But, we're definitely doing a price limit."

"You know I love you," Ava mentioned. Rae acknowledged her with a playful shove.

There was a peacefulness as the streets below seemed to return to a normal hum. Honking filled the space as it always had. Strollers ventured into Central Park that they had just saved from becoming a racetrack. Chilled visitors begged vendors for hot cups of coffee to keep them warm. The snow fell softly onto small piles that had avoided melting away into nonexistence. It felt like the clouds that released their snow were frozen in place. They wouldn't be content until the block was covered.

"So, what's next?" Rocker asked the other two heroes.

"There's usually a wait between when we're needed again. We can just chill or patrol a bit," Ava shared.

"I'm doing neither," Rae declared. "I'm going to get a nice bacon, egg, and cheese. Salt, pepper, ketchup. On an everything bagel." Bacon, bagel, egg, cheese; it reminded her she was still human.

"Baby craving?" he questioned.

"Rae craving."

"Have fun with that," her sister said. "I'm heading back to Queens. I think I'll try to be home for Eric's stream tonight."

"Good luck, Ava! Do what's best for you!"

"Thanks, Rocker." Ava floated off gracefully. There was no cool breeze that followed her like when OwlHeart flew away. Ava was able to control her own gravity, which meant she rarely flew particularly fast. When she did, it usually came at the cost of being fatigued.

"So, mind if I come with you for a bite?" Rocker asked Rae.

"Not at all. Come on. I'll fly you down. We can walk. There's a decent bodega not too far away."

They proceeded down to the sidewalk a few buildings down from where the media set themselves up. They ducked through alleys and corners to avoid being met with the full force of questions. They did not talk as much as they walked. The silence between them was not awkward. It carried something clean and weightless.

Chapter 15: Anchored

Davey and Rae lay with each other on their large sectional. The couch invited them in, and the fabric sank into itself. As the snow continued to pitter-patter against the windows of their home, it was particularly tempting. There were impressions of their bodies from the last time they found the opportunity to meander about by the TV. The room itself was enticing. They passed the blank TV and saw reflections of themselves in the nothingness of the black screen. It looked nearly like their alternate selves stuck in the television were motioning for them to take a seat on the couch.

The coffee table, layered in a thin dust, allowed them to find their spots of comfort with ease. The radiator in the front room could be heard beating to its own rhythm like an out-of-sync drum line. They gave in to the temptation and successfully planted themselves. There was plenty of room on the couch, but they nearly sat atop one anoth-er. They flickered on the television and bid farewell to their alternate selves. Davey put on a comforting but predictable Christmas romance movie, and the pair found themselves relaxing for what felt like the first time in weeks, if not months. Time began to feel as if it slipped away from them. The street lights flickered outside and illuminated the slowly falling snowflakes. Davey thought the neighborhood cat had managed to take up a dwelling somewhere for winter. It was a relief to him that it wasn't stuck outside. They wouldn't take it in, but they were glad somebody did.

Her hair nearly clouded his vision whenever she shifted about. She was half on her husband, half on the couch. When she moved, her perfume lofted like an incense mister. To Davey, it felt like a Realtor selling a house with the smell of warm chocolate chip cookies. But Rae didn't need to sell anything. He had bought into her long ago. They had become each other's comfort.

Davey remembered the first time they watched one of these movies together. Back in his first apartment, when the couch was second-hand and the walls were thin enough to hear their neighbors argue about groceries. He had fallen asleep halfway through the movie, and Rae had drawn a tiny heart on his arm with a permanent marker. He smiled at the memory and thought about how every small act of theirs had been stitched into something bigger, something they protected but never outright spoke of. It was more warm and comforting than any couch could ever match. The large blanket they draped on top of them had started to pill long ago, but like the chairs of the support group, Davey refused to throw it away. It warmed them even more to the point of forgetting it was even winter, lest they look outside or remember the comforting Christmas movies only came on during the winter season. His arm was wrapped around her. He didn't want to let go of the moment, of her. They were each other's anchor, the stationary object with no complaints about its position. They needed each other. They yearned for each other.

As the movie ended, she cozied into him more, like he was the couch that invited her to begin with. They sat in silence for a moment and appreciated what they were. He put his hand on her stomach. It was too early for any noticeable kicks from their child, but he felt like they still might be able to feel the warmth of his hand. He imagined they would recognize the lines that littered his hand and know that when they were ready to enter the world, they would do so to a mom and dad who loved them. He gently moved his hand upward. With his thumb, he traced the outline of the scar where she had been stabbed. There was no pain. Only a lingering scar from a person who felt scorned by the politics that governed them all. She healed. He did too. And their baby was fine.

He squeezed her and kissed the top of her head.

Davey grabbed the Smart-TV remote and decided to pull up Eric's stream after receiving a notification that he had gone live. There was a small window on the bottom of the screen beneath whichever game he decided to play. Davey didn't recognize it. Behind him was Ava, not in her suit. It was Ava the fiancé, not Ava the superhero. A small distinction, but one he knew all too well. Rae once told him that the hardest part of being extraordinary was remembering to be ordinary. Watching

Ava through the screen, Davey understood it for the first time. She looked like someone trying to remember how to rest. She didn't look unhappy, but something was off. It was similar to him realizing something was off with Cass during their last support group. Except, he knew what was going through Ava's mind. At least he thought he did. She sat with a cup of tea, steam still floating off into the room's cool air and dissipating. She barely supported his attempt to become a popular streamer. If he could tell, he wondered if Eric felt it too.

There was an array of disorganized books, trinkets, and memorabilia next to her. Davey never knew either of them to be big readers, so he wondered if Eric staged the background to give off a certain vibe to his stream. The viewer count climbed. It reached twenty-two before it plateaued. He looked at his wife, still bundled up with him. She had taken to looking at her phone, and he knew that she wasn't one of those nameless numbers. The stream started well. Eric seemed enthusiastic. Energetic and personable. It was clear that he was enjoying streaming. Or maybe he just enjoyed the excuse to play more of his game.

The snow began to stop falling outside. It had left the front window plastered in white, as if there was a curtain that magically appeared from the depths of the clouds above. The streetlights stood resolute as the dull brightness made it just visible enough to see the quiet street outside. Winter had a way of sending everybody inside who once preferred to hang around their stoops, walk their dogs, or go for a whimsical drive and honk their horns whenever they liked. The rattling of the train in the distance was a metronome of normality. Life persisted through winter. Goals continued to be lofty, almost as if in spite of the weather.

Davey thought Eric's dedication was admirable. He had been streaming for a while now. As the stream continued, the viewer number fluctuated a degree or two but never increased exponentially. At certain points, he would forget to speak after being sucked into the addictive game. He stumbled over his words as the night progressed, but persevered. As the night grew long, Ava, whose face had never changed from the look of questioning, left her spot.

She never returned. The radiator chimed a wordless tune of mourning for Eric. Ava had left her cup of tea behind, and now there was no steam left to warm the space. A tiny bit spilled out from the cup when she set it down next to her. No steam remained from the cup left to fight its way into the space.

His personality on stream began to dim. His excitement slowly declined, and he started to stream out of obligation. Not because he wanted to on the cold night anymore.

He texted Eric: Keep it up! You're doing great, love the stream.

He hesitated before sending it. Support was a language he understood but rarely practiced without feeling like a fraud.

In truth, he was indifferent. He was never much one for video games, nor was he one for watching streamers or internet personalities. But he could tell that Eric needed support. On stream, he saw Eric look toward his phone. He didn't pick it up but saw the message flash across the screen. A smirk found Eric's face, and his eyes lit up. Davey was glad he was able to help, and only wished he could do more. Rae yawned against him, and he took that as a cue to turn off the television. There was a flicker of the snow behind them that crossed the blackness of the TV. There was nothing but snow. No cat lazily stood guard as it once did, counting the passerby and waiting for its water. It was a blank winter neighborhood. It was inviting. It was cold.

"What do you think of Ava and Eric?" He asked. They remained on the couch, struggling to get up.

"What do I think about them?" The radiator answered for her as she answered the question with a question in the dimly lit room. The rhythmic ticking of the heat was just loud enough to be heard but was not intrusive.

"Yeah? She just seemed off in the stream. She didn't say a word. Didn't look happy."

"You're worried about her?"

"Well, yes, she's my family too. Eric is great. I just want to make sure she's not staying with him for the wrong reasons." Snowfall returned and lightly flickered in the blank space of the TV's reflection. They sat in silence for a moment.

Rae sighed. "She's been struggling recently, I think. She wants to be supportive of him. They'd had something special once. I think it's getting to her."

"Support can be hard. Especially when you don't really believe in it."

"I think it's becoming almost a feeling of resentment for her, honestly."

"That's a tricky spot." A train cut through the snow like softened cream cheese on a fresh bagel. "It can be hard to watch something die slowly."

"You think they should break up?"

"I think they should do whatever is best for each other. Some couples aren't meant to last." He squeezed her. "Some are." He kissed her head.

"I wonder how Eric would take it. It could be a wake-up call for him."

"I don't know that he needs one. I think he just needs to truly set his mind to something, believe in himself, and have someone who truly believes in him too."

"That's streaming?"

"It might not be. We'll see someday."

"I'll miss him, but I think you're right."

"Just because they break up doesn't mean we have to stop seeing him."

She nodded softly, encouraged by Davey's heart. They sat together for another moment and breathed in the need that their friends or loved ones might have in the coming days. He held her tight and watched the lingering snowflakes drip down the front window in the reflection of the television.

"We should get up," Rae suggested.

"Probably." He didn't move his arm from holding her.

The radiator spoke as if it were saying that it was time for bed.

"That's not getting up," she joked with him.

"Yeah, I'm just enjoying this for a moment."

She smiled at being loved so well.

He thought love was like this more often than not.

Not fireworks or declarations.

Just the quiet, unremarkable knowing that you are safe in another person's reach. "Can you help me with something?"

"Of course, what do you need?"

"Well, I need to shower before bed, but my scar is suddenly stiff, and I don't think I can wash myself properly. How about some help?"

He laughed. "Are you trying to be smooth?"

"Is it working?"

He tore the blanket off of them and helped her get up from the couch. "Apparently."

The radiator ticked louder than before, and the street remained un-nervingly quiet. They worked toward the stairs and saw their reflec-tions in the television once again. No snow. No cat. Just each other.

They climbed the stairs with the kind of tiredness that felt earned. The house hummed its approval as they passed the framed photos, the ones they always meant to update but never did. In the bathroom, the mirror fogged as the water turned warm. Rae's laughter echoed off the tile, a low, quiet sound that made the room feel alive. Davey helped her step in, his hands steady on her hips. The steam rose around them until the world disappeared. It was not passion that filled the space but something deeper. Gratitude. The simple relief of being seen and still chosen. When the water finally cooled, they stayed there, unmoving, the heat between them outlasting the shower.

Chapter 16: Weight of Something Small

In the morning, the snow fell in the December air, and they woke to a blanket covering the cars parked on the street. There was no distinguishable color difference between the road, the houses, and the small patches of dead grass that some were fortunate enough to have. Snowflakes covered the gaps in their bedroom blinds, and it looked like the soy sauce stain on the carpet from their historic night of dumplings was the only thing in the immediate vicinity that refused to be taken by the winter. They lay naked beside each other. The warmth of the several sheets atop them was an unnecessary addition to the heat that each other's body provided. A bit of light peered through the snow-streaked window and welcomed them to a new day. He turned over and put his arm around her after pulling the sheets over him.

"Let's just stay here all day."

"We have jobs, Davey," she muttered groggily.

Their breaths were muffled under the covers, and they could faintly hear the plows running through the streets.

"They'll be here tomorrow," he yawned. Rae smiled at how easily he could dismiss the world when he wanted to. It was something she both admired and envied. Her mind rarely stopped moving. Even now, part of her was checking the weather and thinking about the city's roads, about whether the other heroes would be coordinating snow rescues. Davey made her forget she had a second life.

Her hair formed against his neck as the sheets clung to them. The outline of the sheets on them appeared as if they were one organism. They moved harmoniously through life, complementing one another like a symbiotic relationship. They hardly knew life without one another. Davey remembered a night years back when they had slept on the floor of their first apartment after getting married. The movers lost their bed frame. They had used folded towels as pillows and laughed about how romantic poverty could be when shared. The house was still. It felt as if the building itself held its breath in an attempt not to disturb the married couple.

"We also have that appointment this morning." She was quickly approaching twelve weeks. Their child continued to grow, and they were determined to have nothing stop them. From seedling to rose, their flower would grow through winter unbothered. "Are we sure we don't have to know if it's a boy or a girl?"

"Honestly, babe, I don't care. The mystery is fun, but it's not like I'll be sad one way or the other."

He pulled her tight, as if they weren't already as close as possible. She yawned, and it broke the silence. They could hear the radiator downstairs struggling to kick in. It defied the rest of the quiet house and announced itself in the peaceful morning.

"I'm with you. I just don't know."

"There's no wrong decision, Rae. You don't have to make it now either."

"That's true." She wiggled against him beneath the sheets. The covers moved on top of them like a calm ocean current that crashed against a secluded shore that was somewhere warmer and all their own. "I think I'll ask if they can even tell. It might be too early. I'll make a decision after that."

"Sounds good to me." He closed his eyes on the cool pillow that formed to his head.

"Babe…"

He grunted in response.

"We have to get up."

There was silence filled by the distant rattle of the regular train.

"Seriously, the OB is in Manhattan." Her hair tickled his jaw when she spoke.

She tried to throw the sheets and his arm off of her and stand. He quickly reached back over and playfully tugged her back into the warm bed that didn't want her to leave, either. She giggled and turned to face him after collapsing back into the bed.

"Seriously." She kissed him. "We need to get ready." She kissed him again.

He thought about how strange it was that the smallest moments could hold the most permanence. A kiss like this would never end up in a photograph. No one would remember the sound of her sleepy laugh or the smell of her hair. Yet he would carry it with him forever.

Davey took a deep breath and exhaled. He soaked up the morning one last time, then let out an exaggerated sigh. Melted snow ran down the window as the morning sun strengthened in its position. He stood, begrudgingly, and started to make the bed. The soft sheets were still every bit as inviting as they were when he was lying underneath them. The house, creaking in the winter winds, finally stopped holding its breath. It was time to start the day.

They readied themselves and soon enough were prepared to descend the creaking steps toward the outside world. It was still an adjustment for Davey to see his wife leave the house in civilian clothing. Today, she wasn't SolaRae. She was Rae Karoll, and she was equally as powerful to him as any superhero ever was. He sometimes forgot that the world knew her differently. To the city, she was light incarnate. To him, she was the person who snored softly through allergy season and left coffee rings on his books. The contrast made him love her more.

"Train or car?" he asked her before they braced for the cool air. The radiator was already bidding them farewell, as if the house would be under its watch when they left.

"Car."

He pulled out his phone, and they waited in the warmth of their old home for a few minutes. The radiator would have to wait a moment to assume its watch. The car arrived and nearly slid past the home in the slush the plows left behind. The corners of its windshield that the wipers couldn't reach were still covered in the earth's white blanket, and the car wore a matching hat. Sludge built up near the wheels that would find themselves free with a hearty kick. Davey closed the warmth behind him with a soft click of the door. A train passed in the distance, and Davey began to regret not having them walk to one. It felt more apt to handle the winter than a car in traffic.

But it was too late to go back now. He opened the back door, confirmed the driver's identity, and motioned for his wife to go inside first. The heated seats and warm air in the car made the drive feel almost humid as it tore through the wet streets of Queens toward its neighbor. The force the car created with its heat pushed Rae's perfume around it and made the drive smell like a weird mixture of artificial sweetness. It was like a candy that tried too hard to nail the flavor and ended up being repulsive. But her perfume could never be repulsive to him. He had been around it long enough to be able to draw a figurative line in his mind between what was hers and what was made by the leak of the exhaust.

People in coats and wool hats navigated the poorly cleared sidewalks and stewed over empty dry seats on bus stop benches. The odd man or two walked backward so as not to have the wind beat against their freshly shaved chins. A woman extended her elaborate scarf to hide her face. Her eyes peered over it like binoculars looking into a world that was of her own design. It was a long drive that saw them pass over the East River on the Kennedy Bridge before making their initial arrival in Manhattan. The murky waters churned beneath them without any sensible pattern. The winter chill stirred them, and it seemed more uninviting than usual.

They crossed through Central Park, alive with a rhythm of its own. Nothing there cared about the snow. They adapted to it. The residents of New York were resilient, and the nature of it all matched the energy. The city blurred past them. Never slow enough to get a good look at anything worthwhile. Almost like nothing was worth seeing outside of their makeshift cocoon. At times, the outside was just a cacophony of chaos. One they didn't need to participate in.

The car arrived at the OB, and this time the driver was sure to brake in time not to skid past it. They were briefly double-parked but still met with the consistent honks of the impatient. Davey helped Rae out of the car and over a pile of gray watery slush. He started to feel his socks become dampened by the elements, but he didn't mind if it meant hers were dry. The car drove off as the driver lowered his window. Davey saw a cigarette show itself from the confines of the car. Slush splashed on the driver's sleeve as it protected the cigarette. How curious, Davey thought, to want a smoke that badly. The car vanished into the falling snow. The vapor of the cigarette silently disappeared among the giant structures that lined the streets of Manhattan.

They left the sidewalk for the waiting room. The chairs, the receptionist, and the posters on the wall were all remarkably unremarkable.

There was nearly nothing special that would signify the weight that a child would have on the world. Nonetheless, a child of a superhero. The first child of a superhero who was publicly known. OwlHeart had done a good enough job to hide her own pregnancy, her own name, and her own life with Jose. When she disappeared for a few months, there were speculations. None landed on the truth of her having welcomed a child. She was in the clear, at least for now.

But that wasn't going to be an option for Rae. Her quest for transparency suddenly weighed on her in the bland waiting room. She quietly exhaled as she took a seat after checking in. The typical chair was both inviting and mildly disconcerting. Her husband could feel something was off with her, and he started to rub her back. Her light breaths whisked away into the quiet vent system of the office. A weathered toy bobble-head of Derek Jeter sat on the receptionist's desk, unshaken and stationary. Its fake eyes stared at the couple. It felt like it was watching her just as intently as the media did when she tried to save the city. She felt judged by the inanimate object. Yet, it watched over them until their name was called and seemed prepared to keep an eye on whatever couple found themselves in the terribly mundane waiting room.

They were welcomed into an equally normal room by a nurse and sat together with the model of a uterus sitting idly by on the small counter next to the ultrasound screen. The room was cool, like the people who controlled the ventilation of the building refused to switch it to heat. A light breeze came from the air duct and wafted Rae's perfume to mix with the sterility of the environment. Davey thought if her smell had to be altered in one way or another, he'd prefer it to be sterile rather than exhaustive. The walls themselves felt clean. Davey believed that if the treatment of the room was any indication of patient care, then Rae had chosen the right place after all. The all-time Mets rival that stared him down in the lobby could be forgiven in his eyes.

He offered Rae his faded hoodie as an extra layer of warmth.

She very matter-of-factly decided to lie on the reclined bench with her shirt up, awaiting the cool gel that would envelop her stomach. She was determined not to be affected by the air conditioning that needlessly filled the room. She declined his offer, and he tried to zip it before remembering that it had broken off long ago. After a few more minutes, Davey noticed that goosebumps started to crawl across Rae's skin. He offered to step into the hall to see if a visitor was coming when there was a soft knock on the door.

A young technician entered and introduced herself. She was friend-ly but moved about and spoke in a mechanical rhythm that let them know she would likely be out of their lives as quickly as she entered. She warned of the gel before spreading it across her lower abdomen. The scar of Rae's wound peeked through the bottom of the shirt she'd rolled upwards. The technician pressed the scanner gently against her stomach, and in an instant, the parents-to-be looked toward the mon-itor in an almost rehearsed synchronization.

Davey was lost. Rae tried not to be, but was. It was a blur of black and white, and Rae thought she might never get used to seeing the depths of her insides.

"Do you guys want to know the sex of the babies?" the technician asked.

"You can tell already?" Rae asked.

"It's a little fuzzy but relatively clear. If you want to know, I can tell you, and we can reconfirm at your next appointment."

"Then, I think I would like to know," Rae spoke with a tinge of excitement in her voice.

"Hang on…" Davey chimed in. "Flip it and reverse it for just a second."

"What's up, babe?" She turned her head to look at him.

"Did… did you say, babies?"

Rae turned back to the technician. Her mouth was slightly open, eyes wide, and eyebrows raised.

"That's correct. As far as I can tell, it looks like you're having twins."

"You're saying there are two… like… I'm growing two people?"

"Neither of us has twins in our families. How is that even possible?" Davey added to the questions.

"Correct, and it's entirely possible. I'm not getting an incredibly clear picture, but it seems to be two, and it seems to be a boy and a girl."

The walls of the small room felt as if they began to constrain the couple. The sterilization became an anxiety. The coolness of the air conditioning felt to increase, and for a moment, it seemed like Davey couldn't hear anything. The sound of the woman talking was muted for a moment, and he started to sweat. He took off his trusted hoodie and sat next to Rae. She touched his arm, but he barely felt it. His vision blurred, and he collapsed his head into his hand, resting his elbow on his knee. Rae fixed her shirt and sat up. She turned to face him.

"Davey?" she called out to him.

Silence.

"David," she tried again, and the muted sound returned to full capacity. He heard his name being called again.

"We're going to need a bigger house," he said plainly and with a small bit of remorse in his voice. He couldn't wait to be a dad. It was something they had discussed many times. Something they both felt they were as ready as possible to take on. He just hated the idea of leaving his home, though his home had long since been wherever Rae was. He laughed, a breath that was slightly too heavy to be anxiety-free joy, and pulled her hand into his. She squeezed once and didn't let go. The hum of the machine continued beside them, indifferent to the way their world had doubled.

Chapter 17: Rattle

The tension in the small, well-lived-in Woodside apartment was palpable. Unopened books clung to one wall in fear that they might be knocked over and accidentally spread in the chaos, for all of their secrets to be known. Random trinkets shook in their positions as the jury of it all. Eric was preparing for another attempt at streaming when Ava entered the studio. In the dead of winter, it felt like steam visibly rose from her head and dampened the ceiling of the apartment. Her day as one of the saviors of the city proved to be a tough one.

The plow that crossed down 44th Street shot a chunk of snow upward that smacked the wall next to their window. A bit of blackened snow found itself lodged against the windowsill. It joined the trinkets and books as onlookers as the show commenced. The radiator of the apartment rattled as if it were a bell cueing up the next fight of the night.

"You're streaming… again?"

Eric hadn't noticed her come in.

"Hey, you're home! Yup, just getting things set up. Have to stay consistent if I want to grow my viewers. How was your day?"

She scoffed. "Long. I just want to sleep. Do you have to stream tonight?"

"Sorry… I already sent out a notification that I was going live. How about I cap it at an hour and make it a short one tonight? Hungry? Let's order whatever you want."

"I just want to sleep, Eric," she said in a harsh tone that stung him. She started to change out of her hero suit.

"Sorry, I'll be quiet. Did I do something wrong?"

She took off her mask and threw it down. He used to love watching her unmask. It was a ritual that made her human again. Tonight, it felt like she was shedding the last layer that connected them. The snow on the windowsill started to fall back onto the street as if it had to shield its eyes from the happenings of the studio apartment.

"Eric, just stop," she said flatly, and a brief moment of silence filled the small dwelling. "Why do you keep doing this?"

"Doing what, Ava?" he asked with a gentleness to his voice.

"Streaming!"

"Oh…"

"Or whatever other idea you think you will be good at because you don't want to actually work!"

"I think I can be good at streaming."

"How many viewers have you had, Eric? How much money has your stream made? Nothing is happening."

"It takes time, A."

"Or maybe it's just not for you."

He didn't say anything.

"Eric, I think we need to take a break."

"You don't want to get married anymore?" His voice shook, and his eyes misted over.

"I… I don't know. I'm going to my parents. I just… I need you to figure something out. We were fun. We both had goals. Something just changed."

"You became a hero." He hadn't meant for it to sound bitter, but it did. The words hung between them, heavy, undeniable. For the first time, she didn't try to correct him. Maybe because he was right. Maybe because she no longer felt like the same person she'd been when they dreamed of simple things.

The radiator had nothing left to say after it let out a pitiful jingle.

She considered his words. His emotional state. The relationship they used to have. A picture of the two of them that he had playfully put in a handmade macaroni frame sat on his desk. It loomed over the room as if they were actually on the Empire State Building, not just there in some time and space trapped in glue and carbs. She stared past him at the picture. She flicked her wrist, and the picture landed face forward on the desk. She took a breath that lingered. There was a time when that breath would have been followed by a compromise, a small laugh, a gentle touch. Now it was just air moving through a space that felt too small for both of them to inhabit.

"I think I just need space, Eric."

The room fell quiet. Indistinguishable chatter from walkers below their apartment could be heard inside. But the inhabitants of the room didn't make a sound. They stared at each other. Eric's eyes were watery, longing. Ava's eyes were resolute, piercing. It felt as if they were at a negotiation table in the Financial District, where whoever spoke first lost. She cut through it.

"You're not going to say anything?"

There was no response.

Sirens blasted down their street, followed by a chorus line of cars honking and people shouting.

"Fine." She started packing up a bag of her things. To Eric, every crinkle of the duffel bag felt like a wasp sting that couldn't be sated in its displeasure with him.

The particularly heavy-footed neighbor upstairs began to stomp around above them as they could hear the echoes of music. It vibrated through their walls. The books grasped onto one another, careful not to be shaken at just the right decibel to be moved from their positions. The trinkets looked on, judging.

"I… I just don't know what to say, Ava. I'm sorry. I'm trying. I love you."

She froze at the words. She wanted to believe him. That love was enough. That it could still anchor them. But love without direction felt as if it had no gravity. She felt as if she had spent too long holding them down to see when they might rise together.

He sat on the edge of his chair, his hands shook in his lap, he was unsure of what to do with them. The air in the apartment had turned heavy, the kind that made it hard to breathe. He wanted to stand, go to her and close the distance. They had fights before. He wanted to hold her in the same way he used to when she came home battered and exhausted. But she wasn't tired tonight. He could tell that she was finished. He looked around the room for something to hold onto. Anything that still belonged to both of them. His eyes landed on her mug that found its way onto his desk, half full of cold tea still, the ring it left beneath spread like a stain that wouldn't come out.

He whispered, barely audible, "I'm still here, Ava."

She didn't answer.

The radiator popped, once, like a single tear from the building itself.

The sound broke him. He pressed his palms together, pressing so hard his knuckles went white, as if he could hold himself from falling apart.

A t-shirt collapsed mid-air into the bag below. The bass from the music upstairs got louder. She finished packing the bag and zipped it shut with finality. There was a toothbrush, a charger, a few changes of clothes, a few suits, and the blanket she couldn't sleep without. All willing participants in her departure. Eric watched her pack the blanket and thought of all the nights it had wrapped around them on that same couch. Every thread had seen them through both laughter and silence. It wasn't just fabric leaving with her. It was history.

"We'll see if I need to come back for the rest."

"At least come back for your Christmas present. I can't return it anymore." He tried to smile at her, but he couldn't force it.

She opened the studio door. As if it were the straw that broke them, a few books began to fall from their shelf. Eric watched her leave and immediately picked up the macaroni frame from its spot. He placed it back in its upright position. She closed the door gently behind her. She didn't feel a need to slam it closed. The message had been delivered. Before she left the confines of the building, she texted her sister.

Heads up, I'm going to mom's. Eric and I are on a break.

Meanwhile, in Kew Gardens, Rae showed Davey the phone as they sat with each other on the couch, watching another of their predictable movies.

"Guess she decided what was best for herself," Rae said. "I'll give her a call."

"Probably a good idea. I'll check in on Eric, too."

"You're a good friend, babe." She kissed him on the cheek before heading to another room to talk to her sister.

He turned off the television when she walked away and watched her reflection disappear from the blank slate it had become. He picked up his own phone and could hear every step Rae took to go upstairs. Each stair whined as it creaked, unwilling to become accustomed to its purpose. Then silence. He texted Eric first.

Hey, man, I heard from Ava. Just checking in with you. Here, if you want to talk. He stared at the screen before sending it. There was a strange guilt to reaching out through a device, like tossing a rope to someone already half underwater. He hoped Eric would grab it anyway.

After a few minutes, there was no reply.

He tried calling, but it went straight to voicemail. He presumed that Eric might just want to be left alone and thought it was an understandable ask.

Then, his phone alerted him.

Eric had started streaming.

He tuned in as quickly as possible. But something was off. Davey only saw the game. There was no Eric. No staged apartment in the bottom corner. The game and the viewer count inhabited the screen as if they had shared custody of it. Some viewers began to send messages to him. He seldom replied. His viewer count plateaued in his typical low-twenty range.

Then, it reached thirty.

He started to respond to more of the incoming messages. It felt like watching someone relearn how to breathe. Every new viewer, every small ping of attention, was a breath back into his lungs.

Thirty-five.

His voice turned from flat to borderline excitable.

Forty.

He turned his face camera back on.

His eyes were puffy and red. The apartment looked the same behind him, but a few of the books were missing from their previous spots. There was no figure in the background. Just Eric. Davey exhaled slowly. It was not directly a sigh of relief, but something close to it.

He could hear Eric's radiator rattle in the background, an ending bell of sorts. Eric looked to be in a groove now. Smiling. Addressing chat. Losing himself in the game. His eyes flickered to the corner of his desk, and a light smile crossed his face. Davey's chest tightened. Not with anxiety, but with something between pity and pride, something closer to hope. Eric laughed at a comment that came through his chat. It didn't sound like the laugh he knew from the support group, but maybe it was the laugh that Eric had left. The radiator rattled again, quieter, more distant, but still present.

Chapter 18: Where the Snow Watches

After OwlHeart begrudgingly posed with the star atop the Rockefeller Center Christmas tree, she whipped through the cold air and joined the other heroes, who all ceremoniously lit the tree. She wasn't a fan of the obligations that heroics led her to take on, but she was good at them. Rae did these events because she felt forced to in a way. OwlHeart did them because of her natural charisma. She had no bad side. Her thick thighs stood strong and were anchored in the weight of her sheer likability.

Rae was a star to the media, but her distaste for them had started to become noticeable. OwlHeart was becoming an icon. Her dark tan complexion stood out from the snow that fell around them, and the lights of the bright tree highlighted her beauty. She spread her arms to show the decorative wings and frills. She was owning her name as the owl and being the overwatch of the city.

Cameras flashed around them, not to be outshone by the lights on the egregiously large tree. There were a few dull words that somebody in some unnecessary position of power shared. Snow, as if on cue, began to whimsically fall around the crowd as merry carolers attempted to hoist their voices to the top of the buildings that surrounded them. From the slush on the streets to the warm high-rises above the crowd, only a select few of them would ever get to appreciate the differences. The vacant penthouses watched them below from their high towers and proceeded to be speechless at the sounds of the city.

Off in a corner somewhere, the advertisements on a digital city billboard swiped from one Christmas-themed picture to the next. They encouraged a year full of opportunities ahead, or a way to get a good night's rest before Santa came to town. Each was as hollow as the last and only held its position for a fleeting second to capitalize on the attention span of the travelers below.

Spectators struggled to get a decent view of the tree and the heroes after being blocked by barricades and vendors selling absurdly priced plush dolls of the heroes in festive hats. Rae's feet were sore from standing in her fixed position for the whole ceremony. She smiled and posed for the onlookers, as was required of her and other popular figures in December. It was a tradition for most people, but for her, it was just another commercial advertisement.

When the festivities were finishing, the heroes fielded some questions from the reporters who cared to attend. Some were line drives to first; others caught the corner of the foul pole in the opposite direction. They received a final question from a tabloid columnist who asked if the group of heroes might be adopting a team name. LunAva excitedly stepped forward to attempt to answer with whatever name she thought was cool at that time, but was stopped by Echona. Her voice playfully overpowered LunAva's, and she undoubtedly stated, "No." Ava looked at Jazmine and pouted.

If any of the heroes possessed the capability of reading minds, they would have heard a slew of harsh language intended for the hero of sound. Her enthusiasm for a group name contrasted with the annoyance of Rae and the resounding answer of Echona. The crowd dispersed to the trails of old Christmas songs, and the heroes flew off to a nearby rooftop. A red velvet bag waited for them. It was sealed, but the snow that fell had started to make the outside of it damp.

"Ladies and gentleman!" OwlHeart said excitedly. "I present you with the first Hero Secret Santa. Thanks for giving me your gifts ahead of time, so I could work out where to keep them."

A child's cries broke through the air from beneath them after they hadn't been able to purchase the plush that would end up torn or stained by the time it got home.

"Sorry, there's one missing..." Echona hung her head in disappointment. "I forgot about it, and Cass has been working nonstop. I couldn't ask him to grab one for me."

"All good, Jaz. No biggie." Rocker reassured her. "Who'd you have?"

"Ava... sorry, girl."

"What Rocker said, it's all good. I'm not feeling super festive this year. I got something for one of you guys still," Ava added.

"Still on the fence about Eric?" Her sister received a nod.

"Well, shoot, y'all, I want a gift," OwlHeart laughed. Rae and Rocker both declared, "Same" in unison and shared a giggle of their own. They exchanged their gifts. OwlHeart gifted SolaRae a onesie with a cape attached. Rae also drew OwlHeart's name and had a similar idea. She gave her friend a slightly larger bit of kid clothing with an emboldened owl across the front of it. Rocker gladly gave his gift to Echona, and LunAva gave hers to Rocker.

The city below them continued to hum about. There was no break for the needlessly rushed. Laughter filled the air. Echona came down from her guilt, and LunAva allowed some joy to enter the air. As they began a tradition of their own, they heard the screech of sliding tires and the crash of a car into another. The consecutive sounds tore through the laughter and dropped on it like an icicle crashing to the pavement. But the team that formed didn't shatter; it only temporarily froze. They weren't afforded the same pause that was expected of them when the media was around. And that would have to be something they all continued to live with.

The city never lingered in tragedy for too long. By the next evening, there were new problems to concern itself with. Rae wasn't home when Davey stood up the everlasting rusted chairs. He filled the first floor with the warm smell of instant coffee as the chimes of the radiator helped cue him when the time for the other men to arrive was approaching. The cool breeze brought in a few wandering snowflakes when Jose hurriedly opened the door and hopped inside with a shiver.

"Bro, this sucks." He walked to his normal seat and softly patted

Davey on the shoulder as he passed. "You catch the tree lighting last night?"

"Yep. Rae hated it."

"Yeah? Sara wasn't a big fan either."

"I guess it's one of the many duties of the city's heroes. The great enemy of public relations." Davey's phone chimed as he spoke. He pulled it out of his pocket to see a text from Eric: Okay if I still come to the group?

Davey: Absolutely.

Within a few seconds of sending the text, Eric walked in slowly with a slight grin. The cold air came in once again to let the men know that winter was not going anywhere.

"Did you suddenly get super speed?" Davey joked with him.

"That would be nice," he responded. "Maybe I could go back in time if I did." He tried to smile at his own joke, but the light didn't quite reach his eyes. Davey caught it. The flicker that used to be joy had dimmed. It was replaced with something raw. Eric had always been the first to joke, first to fill silence. But now his laugh was smaller, thinner, like it had to squeeze through something inside him just to get out.

"Glad you're here, Eric."

"Yeah, bro. Wouldn't be the same without you."

"Thanks, guys," he took his chair and slumped in it.

"Stream seems to be doing pretty well. How do you feel about it?" Davey asked.

Eric's face brightened, and his shoulders relaxed. "Really good. It feels like I'm starting to take off a little."

"That's awesome. I'm glad you're sticking with it."

"Way to not let the man get you down," Jose joked with him.

"I mean, she's not wrong. We were together for a while, and I could never find something that lasted long and wasn't some soul-sucking job in a cube in a tall office somewhere."

"Just because she wasn't wrong doesn't mean that you were wrong," Davey encouraged him.

"I guess that's true," Eric considered the idea that they could both be right. "Anyway, I think I'm going to see this one through. Do it for myself, you know."

"Heck yeah, bro. That's what's up."

"Really admirable, Eric. Glad to hear it. Don't lose that drive."

"Thanks, guys. How's the pregnancy, Davey? Any news?"

"Oh, yeah, get a load of this…" he leaned forward, elbows on his knees, and hands clasped together. "Twins."

"No joke?" Jose was shocked.

"I kid you not. Twins."

"Actually, it sounds like you'll have two kids," Eric joked.

Davey laughed and acknowledged the joke.

"Boy and a girl by the looks of it."

"Congrats, bro."

"It should be interesting to say the least. But otherwise, she's doing great. I think I'm more worried about it all than she is."

"Nah. She's worried, bro. Trust me. She's probably just good at hiding it. It's natural. Sara was anxious but wouldn't say it until I asked her directly."

"That's fair. I mean, I know she's anxious. We don't usually hide much from each other. I feel like I'm just internally freaking out way too much. Kids in the sociopolitical climate that just led to their mother getting stabbed…"

The weight of their decision to welcome children crashed onto his shoulders like a head-on collision. And he was pinned between both cars. Snow fell outside and slid down the front window that was warm from the inside. The flakes wiped away so quickly that it looked as if it were raining rather than snowing. A streetlight began to flicker like it had had enough of the cold and decided that it didn't possess the will to continue on with its sole duty. The chime of the washing machine finishing from the small laundry room broke the silence before Eric did.

"There's not, like, an instruction manual, dude."

"Facts, bro. One day at a time, one leap at a time. It's hard, fun, tiring, and rewarding." Jose agreed with Eric's point. He looked at his phone and checked the time. "Hey, Davey, is Cass or Laurel coming today?"

Davey checked his own phone. "I'm really not sure. I texted them this morning, but never got a reply. I'll try to call them real quick and see what's going on." Davey hit the call button for Cass and waited for an answer.

It rang.

And kept ringing.

No answer.

"He didn't pick up. Must be stuck at the office."

"Man, he just loves to work," Jose commented.

"I don't think that's it," Davey responded. "I think he probably feels like he can't stop working. If I know him like I used to in college, he's afraid of messing up once and losing his position in life. He doesn't stop, because to him, he can't."

It hit Davey harder than he expected.

Cass buried himself in work to forget.

Eric streamed through heartbreak to stay afloat.

He wondered what he himself was doing to keep from sinking. The group had become their shared life raft, coffee-stained and creaky, but afloat.

"Dude needs a balance," Eric said.

The front door opened again as the cool breeze found its way in. They all waited to see who would enter. Then, the blonde hair announced itself first before she did.

"Sorry, I'm late, guys." Laurel walked in and grabbed a cup of coffee. "Cass is late, too?" Her question lingered longer than it should have. Cass's empty chair felt heavier than the rest, as if the room itself knew something they didn't.

"Might not be coming tonight," Davey replied. "I can't seem to get a hold of him."

"Interesting," she responded as she took her seat. "Miss anything?"

"Eric's a champ, Davey's having twins, and I'm still tired as heck."

"Still mushy?" Eric joked.

Jose gave him a look to question if he was seriously asking him, but responded anyway. "It's starting to turn solid." He hung his head.

"That's only a little gross," Laurel said. "Twins, huh? Exciting? Terrifying? Both?"

"Both," Davey shared. "Definitely both. What's new with you, Laurel?"

"Not much really. I'm under a tight deadline at work, which is stressful, but I'm trying not to let it impact my home life. Rocker's schedule has been pretty full. Some early endorsements are coming in. We're just trying to spend as much time together as we can."

"Cheers to you guys. We know how hard finding time for our relationships can be." Davey encouraged her. Eric and Jose both nodded in agreement. "Props to you for drawing a hard line in the sand for work-life balance. Maybe you should try to share your methods with Cass."

"Maybe. Do you think he'll actually be receptive? I mean, I barely know him, but the guy seems to be all business."

"Never know. He might take it better from you than from somebody he's actually close to. I think he just needs a break."

Another note of silence took the room. They all contemplated how they might be able to help Cass. His absence was both noteworthy and jarring. Davey thought it might be more meaningful than he let on. He had clients hit a downward spiral and stop coming to therapy. This wasn't therapy; it was a friend-driven support group, and he felt like his friend needed him. If only he would answer the phone.

The quietness was soon filled with the religious whine of the old steps. Rae, in a baggy t-shirt and shorts, walked down them.

"I'm home!" She announced herself loudly before seeing the spouses in the front room. "Oh, sorry, I didn't realize it was group night. I'll be upstairs."

"All good, babe, thanks!"

"Wait… did she just fly inside through one of the windows upstairs?" Laurel asked.

"Yeah, they do that sometimes," Jose shared nonchalantly.

"I'm kinda glad Rocker can't fly if that's the case. I feel like it would scare me whenever he just randomly appeared back at home."

"It does, but you eventually get used to it," Davey replied.

Rae was halfway up the stairs when she turned and went back down. "Aren't you short one?" She took a quick inventory. "Cass?"

"He couldn't make it."

"Sorry to hear that." Rae started back up the stairs. "Have a good session, everyone!"

The room got warmer as the four of them laughed through the anxiety surrounding their fifth member. The streetlight outside began to flicker once again, and tried to rejoin the conversation. The attempt was one of futility after the winter had its say and the light entirely dissipated into the flurries that surrounded it. As the group concluded, Eric, Jose, and Laurel all started for the train together, bonded through the necessity of support. Their conversation continued and heated the chill of the air with their breath. Davey closed the door behind them with a soft click that created a comforting barrier between real-world problems and his home. He gently put the old chairs away, ensured the coffee pot was turned off, and climbed the steps to his wife. The warmth upstairs was waiting for him, but his thoughts lagged behind in the front room. The scent of old coffee and laughter still hung in the air, the kind that tried its best to cover worry. He thought of Eric's tired smile and Cass's silence and hoped both would find their way back next week.

Chapter 19: Quiet Bullhorns

A few weeks after the support group session, the sun's late rising allowed them the luxury of staying in bed for longer than they normally would have. Christmas passed, and what was left was the dreariness of the season. There was no more spectacular joy to look forward to beyond life's normalities. It was New Year's Eve, and they weren't entirely sure they even wanted to stay awake until midnight. They weren't sure they would be together at midnight. But that was the life of a hero and her spouse. Eventually, a plow loudly passed and scraped along the pavement. It was only doing its job, but it served as a harsh awakening.

No birds were chirping, and there was no vibrant blue sky that welcomed the watchers below. Congealed grayness filled the atmosphere as the clouds stretched across New York City and released thick clumps of snow. It fell quickly and felt like the clouds refused to move along in their journey to whatever destination seemed to need a refresher on the power of Mother Nature. This sort of morning, Davey clung to the makeshift cocoon that the couple called their home. The hours of sleep were never enough compared to how he longed to have a lazy day with Rae.

His bladder called upon him as if he were the one who was growing two children and already constantly needed to use the bathroom. He ran out of bed. Rae was unflinching but groggy. He maneuvered from the fluff of the carpet to the coolness of the tiled bathroom floor and shivered as he relieved himself. It was cool mornings like these, when the radiator didn't feel quite strong enough, that he contemplated not sleeping naked. But, he considered what fun it was to do so next to his wife and dismissed the concept of pajamas.

After an unusually long stream, he returned to the bed, and the covers welcomed him back like they never wanted him to leave. Rae shifted her body to be up against Davey's. Her hair tickled his jaw like it did before, and he did not attempt to swoop it out of his face. She wiggled against him, which they both knew he loved, but it was not something they discussed. She reached for her phone and dropped the charger onto the floor. It lay as an indent in the soy sauce stain on the white carpet and looked like it nearly formed a keyhole of sorts in the darkness that would continue to not be cleaned.

Davey's eyes were closed as his head was smothered by the pillow, the blankets, and her hair. He wouldn't have had it any other way. He heard her phone unlock. She always left the sound on at night in case of some grand emergency that only SolaRae could handle. She yawned as she scrolled through the day's headlines and social media happenings. Her eyes were still attempting to adjust to the requirement that they should be open. The sound of a faint shovel chipping at the frozen piles of snow next door served as a dull alarm clock. He was sure that it would be the cue for some neighbors to keep up with their own shoveling and rush outside to compare shovels. Davey's eyes wanted to open, but he fought them and held them tight. If he opened them, the day was real.

"Babe…" Rae started.

He answered with a low grunt.

"You need to see this."

He yawned and took a moment. She didn't speak again, and the silence was taken by the crinkling of sheets and the cracking of stiff joints.

"What's up?" Davey finally responded with curiosity.

"Here." She handed him her phone.

It was a news article from an online outlet posted overnight. It was a pain to read with an advertisement for some medication or product he would never need after every other paragraph. But then he got to the meat of it all.

There was a death.

An expletive was shouted from outside after a winter walker slipped on a patch of black ice and landed in a pile of hard snow.

The death of an inmate at a local correctional facility.

Rae sat up in bed with him without the cracking of joints. She was flexible as ever, even while around three months pregnant.

Davey reread the lines.

An inmate at a New York State correctional facility was killed at the hands of another inmate. Davey wondered why this was news. He heard it happened, unfortunately, too often. He kept scrolling down the needlessly long article. Then, he found a picture of himself. He paused. In his groggy state, he wondered if he had a twin who was a convicted criminal, and his parents hid from him. It would all make sense now, why Rae had twins in her.

He read some more.

Then, he saw the inmate's name who had paid the ultimate price for whatever crime he had committed.

Rae grabbed his arm and squeezed it, acknowledging what he read and seeing a flinch of pain cross his face. She deeply inhaled and exhaled. It clicked for him. His groggy eyes woke and widened. It felt like he started his day with a blow to the gut that took the wind out of him and made his heart race. Dang, he thought. He didn't have the mental capacity to contribute any meaningful words or plans of action. He could barely wrap his head around the news. It wasn't just an inmate who had lost his life behind bars.

It was Simon Cribb.

For a moment he forgot how to breathe. He remembered Simon's eyes in the courtroom, the way they landed between rage and confusion like someone trying to claw their way back to reason. He remembered the silence after the verdict.

Davey felt like a failure.

A private guilt that came with believing he might have been the last person who could have made a difference and didn't. The snow continued to fall outside their window. Davey considered pleading with whatever celestial being controlled the weather and asking for time to rewind. To take the snow away and let him try to live through fall all over again. Maybe then he could save Simon. He moved the sheets off him. The house was still weirdly cold, but he started to sweat. Not Simon. Not yet, he thought to himself. Rae felt helpless. She didn't know how to help her husband. If she could even help. He shifted and whipped his legs to the side of the bed. He set them down on the carpet and hung his head. His arms grasped the back of his head.

The breaks in the blinds allowed some early light to paint a picture of Davey's distraught shadow on the wall behind him. Rae moved from the covers. She wrapped her arms around Davey and rested her head on his shoulder. He wanted to collapse into her, to let her hold every ounce of the weight he carried, but it didn't feel fair.

The guilt was his to bear.

The bed that had felt like safety a moment ago now felt like punishment.

"I'm here for you," she told him quietly.

He moved one of his arms to hold onto hers to keep steady.

Grounded.

Present.

"Yeah, I know." He kissed her hand.

He gave her back her phone and retrieved his own. He started to see more popular outlets pick up the Simon Cribb story. Some included his picture in court as he stood against the judge. Others didn't. He thought the most pertinent detail, whether he was included or not, was Simon's struggles with mental health and the lack of support he was offered. There was an outcry from mental health and justice reform advocates alike. There was a similar outcry from individuals who thought his death was beneficial to society. As if the old justice of an eye-for-an-eye had somehow begun to ring across the boroughs as modern law.

An email crossed his screen from a therapist colleague. The Simon Cribb case was picking up steam. Unfortunately, more than it did when he was being sentenced. There was a demonstration being organized in front of the courthouse to start a fight for mental health and justice reform. It was short notice, but they asked Davey if he would appear and say some words through a bullhorn.

They also asked if SolaRae or any other heroes would come and support the demonstration. Davey wasn't sure he even wanted to ask Rae after her incident at the last heated public exchange. But she was reading over his shoulder and jumped at the chance to support him.

"It's a good thing I still fit into my normal suit. My maternity one's still being made. I'm going to get ready and we're going to make some noise." She kissed him on the cheek and left the bed. When she left the room, he sat for another minute in the quiet. The news alert still glowed on the phone screen beside him. His reflection in it looked like someone else entirely. Someone older. Someone already worn out by trying to fix what kept breaking.

They got ready quietly. Together but separate. Davey didn't feel like talking. He was thinking about what he might say. How might he be able to effectively communicate the need that was so drastically shown through the life of Simon Cribb? She spritzed her perfume that momentarily took his mind somewhere more pleasant. Not New Year's Eve. Not now. He helped her zip her suit, and they embraced. He draped her coat over both her shoulders and her cape. It created some weird combination of hero and civilian.

He threw on his hoodie, the same one as always, and followed his wife down the stairs. His footsteps were heavy on the steps that felt quiet for the first time. He had already decided to take a car. He ordered it on his phone before they descended away from the cocoon that he desperately wanted to hide back inside. The house creaked in the winter breeze as if it were issuing them a farewell. It felt lukewarm.

It wasn't of any comfort to him this time. He opened the door for his wife and sealed the barrier behind himself with a loud click. He hoped the driver of their temporary transportation would think Rae was a cosplayer for some convention rather than the actual hero. He didn't have the patience for a fan.

The car ride was uneventful. The city that at one point blurred past them seemed to move in slow-motion around them. The snow fell so slowly it felt to almost be rising back to the heavens and flowing in reverse. The car tore through the muck and dropped them at the nearest intersection. Preemptive NYPD cars had blocked off the streets. Davey and Rae arrived just before the crowd gathered. He thought it might give him space to feel the area. That it might give him inspiration on what to say. The colleague who sent him the email was there with a few others.

They were all on their phones spreading the word as if crowd size equated to life value. He noticed Davey, told the couple where to stand, then handed him the bullhorn.

The crowd started to pile into the cordoned-off area. Walkers turned corners, riders disembarked from confused rideshare drivers, and loaded buses let people off at the nearest stop. Coats, wool hats, mittens, scarves, and impromptu posters in support of mental health lined the street. Simple chants were declared in unison to make sure that, even though the court was on holiday, the message would be heard. Then, as if a curtain dropped and a fight night introduction song began to play, the organizer prompted Davey and Rae to stand center ring. He turned on his bullhorn with a screech that silenced the crowd. Then lifted it to his mouth.

A quiet moment remained before he began.

"I..." he hung his head, and Rae moved a step closer to him. She was assuming the superhero pose, and unlike other events, she wanted to be there. She needed to be. He needed her. "Some of you may know me as Mr. SolaRae or the man who got himself a night in jail." There were some laughs throughout. He joined them with his own chuckle.

"Simon Cribb... was not a headline. He was a person, and a son, and a neighbor who found himself at the wrong place at the wrong time. I do not excuse what he did, but he needed help and only got handcuffs. The system didn't try to help him. I wrote a letter myself asking for a comprehensive mental health analysis. It was promptly denied."

A harmony of boos filled the cold air.

"I wish I could say that Simon was an outlier in the way that the system lets people with mental health struggles down. But, it's nearly a guarantee that dozens of others remain invisible to the headlines and the system. Jails are full of people who need support, not cages, and I don't think justice has to mean being forgotten. There isn't justice in sending our most vulnerable away without any measures of assistance."

He paused as another bus of demonstrators seemed to unload at the end of the street.

"I'm tired. I'm tired of seeing the system fail. There's a real lack of access for people who need it long before they ever have to enter the judicial system. First responders aren't always trained for the Simon Cribbs of the world. If he only had support when he found himself living on the street, maybe his life could have turned around. But the systemic inequalities that marginalized groups face daily did not allow that to happen. Both his life and his death cannot be ignored."

"Inmate crime has been around for as long as I can remember, with virtually no accountability. I'm sure some of the wildly atrocious conditions don't help the situation either. There needs to be programs, mental health response teams, safety and mental health oversight, and alternatives for the nonviolent. Unfortunately, Simon wouldn't have fit into that category. But if he had the support he needed, we might not even be having that conversation. We're all neighbors, families," he looked at his wife.

"Heroes and civilians. We need to do better for one another, and I encourage you all to stay vocal. The fire you all have for reform can't end because another story comes out in the morning about…" he lost his thought.

"…about a new animal at the zoo, or a new pop-up shop. Thank you all for showing up for Simon. I only wish there were people to do that before he lost his life."

A voracious round of applause supported Davey and seemed to go on for a good deal of time. He found himself in a mix of discomfort and pride before handing the bullhorn to Rae.

"I can't add onto what my husband has shared, but as a hero, I support this cause and his calls for reform. A lot is expected of me. To show up. To save people and stop criminals. I think it's about time that our judicial system starts showing up for people, too. Thank you all for coming out. I know it's a holiday, I know this was impromptu. I hope you all have a safe night and a better tomorrow."

She turned off the bullhorn and embraced her husband in front of the crowd. "We should have gotten you a platform a long time ago," she whispered in his ear. "They listened to you."

The crowd continued to cheer on the couple. The applause blurred into a low hum in his ears. He didn't smile, not right away. He just stared at the crowd and wondered if Simon would have believed any of it, if the words meant anything to the man who had once sat across from him asking for help without any words.

For a moment, Davey almost saw him there, just another face in the snow.

Then the vision was gone, and the city returned to its steady rhythm of moving forward without permission. Davey was not entirely sure of what he actually said, but he was glad it was effective. He was glad to see that his words apparently carried some weight. The sun broke through the darkness while the snow continued to fall. The sounds of the city were muted by the crowd. There was no honking, no rattling of a nearby train, or the screeching of its brakes. Just a crowd. And a cause. Davey realized that change didn't only have to come from the capes.

Chapter 20: Echoes of Soy

The crowd began to disperse back to whatever warm establishment they came from. It was strange how a bullhorn seemed to echo when it was off. Some people thanked Davey for his words; others left, but with a strengthened resolve. One in attendance approached the couple as the night grew long.

"Hi, Mr. and Mrs. Karoll," Davey was surprised to hear their legal last name. "My name is Josephine Chandra. I'm a political advisor, and your words moved... well, everybody here. Have you ever considered running for office, Mr. Karoll?"

Davey blinked. For a second, he thought she was joking. He'd spent his career helping people who already felt unseen, not standing on podiums trying to be seen himself. The idea sounded both absurd and dangerous, but it also stirred something deep that he couldn't quite name.

He laughed. "Davey is fine, Ms. Chandra. I can't say I really have. I have no desire to be in public office. I don't really know how well I'd do. Or how much change I'd really be able to implement."

Davey studied her face; she was serious.

"Well, you'll never know until you try." She handed him a business card. If you ever want to sit down and talk, give me a call. There's a special election coming up for the city council. I think you could have a real shot and be a valuable voice. Don't get me wrong. I know it's a hard choice between trying to be the helper in the room versus the leader of the movement. Sometimes, it's worth it. At least consider it. Talk it over, think about the kind of world you want your kids to grow up in."

"I…" Davey paused. "Wait, how did you know we're having kids?"

"It's my job to know Mr. Karoll." She was a young woman. Dark brown skin with darker hair and eyes to match. A pleasant smile and an impressive intellect.

"I don't like to leave people hanging, Josephine. We'll talk it over, and I'll let you know either way. But if it means I'll have to lose my hoodie, then I'm not so sure." He tried to joke with her.

"I don't think you should anyway. New voters like casual more than they like a man in a suit. As long as you stick to your mission and what you promise to try and enact, I think a hoodie would be great for your image. You're personable. Likable. A hero in your own regard."

"She's good, babe. Really good." Rae added to the conversation. "Thanks for talking with us, Josephine. We'll talk on the way home."

"It's my pleasure. Really. Thanks again for your words, Mr. Karoll."

The advisor left the couple. Her footprints created a path in the fresh snow that looked to be uninterrupted. It sat in front of him, ever-present. They were nearly alone now in front of the courthouse as Davey ordered a rideshare home. When it skidded to a stop in front of them, they climbed into the car. Davey stared out the window, not paying attention to the weather or the late-night vendors and walkers. He was lost in thought and being transported around the boroughs. He imagined all the faces from the rally, the way their breath rose together like smoke signals against the night. Ordinary people, angry and tired but still showing up. Maybe that was what leadership really looked like. Not perfection, but persistence. Mentally, he was still at the courthouse. The air from the vent blew a pleasant heat into the car that wafted Rae's perfume. No exhaust joined it this time.

It was only her, and she addressed him, "You should do it."

Davey laughed in the car. "I really don't know that I can. I mean, a campaign can be stressful, I'm sure. What if people don't like what I have to say and start getting violent like the one who stabbed you? I can't have that on my conscience. Plus, what about logistics with kids? You have an unpredictable work life. I would have one too."

"Davey," she cupped his hand in her own. "We'll figure it out. Don't look for excuses not to do this. I love you and I'm with you. Whatever happens from here, over the next six months, or over the next sixty years. I'm with you."

He felt like he loved her more every day. "I'll sleep on it." He smiled at her and returned to looking out the window. Rae let go of his hand and started to scroll through her phone. Davey's speech had started to go viral. Commenters praised, twisted, and mocked his words. She chose not to show him yet. Not to deflate any goal that he might be developing. She knew he was capable of taking on the city council. What worried her wasn't his ability. It was how much of himself he gave away when he believed in something. Davey carried burdens like solemn vows. Rae knew once he said yes, there would be no halfway. He just had to believe it himself first, and seeing negativity off the bat would do the opposite. She told herself that the negative voices were often the loudest and kept scrolling. Rae was unwaveringly proud of him, while he was uneasy. As they arrived home, he kicked the snow from their stoop. His sock was getting a bit damp in the process, but he made sure no lingering ice might try and take down his hero.

He unlocked the door and let his wife in first. As he gave the door a soft click behind him, he let out a long sigh of relief. He was home again, one of the few places he felt able to think and process. As he removed his hoodie, his phone beeped. Then beeped again. And again. Emails and texts were coming in from reporters and outlets trying to see if they would be able to have a few words from him on the state of mental health. One called him the "Champion of the Crisis," which he naturally hated. He decided they could wait and creaked up the stairs to his wife. She was undressing in the room and wiggled the suit down her body. He went to hug her from behind and wrap his arms around her shoulders.

"I love you, SolaRae."

"I love you too, Councilman Karoll." She giggled at the thought.

Not a giggle of mock or jest. One of inevitability.

They kissed, and kissed again.

"Wait…" Rae said. "I'm actually hungry."

"Dumplings?" he joked.

"Absolutely." She kissed him a third time and then retrieved her phone from where she had set it on the bed and ordered some dumplings. "The restaurant is packed, it looks like. Delivery isn't for another hour yet."

"That works for me. Oh, hey, happy new year." Davey said with a smirk as she finished ordering it and tossed the phone onto the dresser. He kissed her and didn't think about whether or not they would be awake for midnight. He didn't care; it didn't matter. For the first time in months, his thoughts stopped reaching backward. They weren't at the courthouse, or with Simon, or buried in guilt. Just two people who had survived another year and decided to love anyway. He playfully pushed her onto the bed and kissed her more.

In the morning, the smell of soy sauce and perfume filled the bedroom. The sheets lazily covered them like an abstract painting that had brush strokes going in every direction. A new dawn welcomed them through the cracks in their blinds, and it stopped snowing at some point overnight. He turned to put his arm around her, as was morning tradition. She was already awake but stayed in bed.

"Morning," she said not quite as groggy as he was.

He responded with a happy grunt and welcomed her to slide next to him.

The open dumpling container sat on the nightstand again. There was one remaining. A twin for the one from last time. This morning, Davey snatched it when he was awake enough to spot it. In his attempt to have breakfast, he knocked over the container and spilled the remnants of the soy sauce. He added to the old stain.

"Crap," he said.

"No biggie, babe. We're just repainting the carpet, one night at a time." She laughed with a bit of tiredness still in her voice, and he kissed her cheek after swallowing the dumpling. He reached for his phone and was met with more inquiries for advocacy quotes.

"Babe?" he asked. "I think I'm going to do it."

Rae clumsily turned to face him.

"Really?" she said excitedly.

"Yeah, I think so. But if it ever becomes too much for us, or you, or for the kids." He touched her growing belly. "Then, I'm out."

"That's good enough for me." She kissed him. "It's time to build the room instead of being the helper in it. I'm with you, babe."

"I know." He kissed her back.

He held onto his phone and studied it slowly as if waiting for it to give him a nod of encouragement to proceed with his intention. Instead, the radiator rattled below in tune with the train that passed.

He texted Josephine: It's Davey, I'm in. The moment after he sent it, his pulse quickened. It was the same feeling he had the night he first stood before a crowd to speak. A mix of terror and hope that maybe he could still make something better out of what was left.

A response came nearly immediately: I already have your number saved. Glad to hear it. Come by the office when you have a chance. I'm there almost every day, and we can get started.

"Wow, she's good," Davey said aloud. He looked at her business card a little closer and saw a Brooklyn address. He thought it would be a perfect opportunity to visit one of the other boroughs he actually liked, launch the next phase of his career, and check in on Cass if he was working from home again.

Chapter 21: A Different Room

The air of Brooklyn landed somewhere between Manhattan and Queens. Close to home, but it was becoming more like the central borough than he cared for. He didn't have any clients who were scheduled to meet on New Year's Day, so he ventured to meet Josephine. Rae had her own heroing to do and wasn't able to join him in the endeavor, but he promised that he would fill her in on the details. She asked him if he would call her into the meeting, which he politely declined. He was awestruck when he approached the address in Brooklyn Heights. He had seen upscale modern places before, but the office put those all to shame. Every aspect he could see through the thick glass seemed carefully curated.

The walls competed with the decorations in general sleekness. From the street, still covered in snow, it looked like the office had seen no winter. There were no boots lined up by the door. No puddle gathered from the melted slush. He lived in winter, as did the rest of the city. The office seemed to exist in a perpetual state of late spring. He wondered what kind of heat source could hold off winter this way. Maybe this was what power looked like up close. Warmth that never had to fight to exist. It was the first time he realized how much effort it took for real life to stay livable. The flowers and plants bloomed.

It seemed warm, but not hot. Comfortable and inviting, a large decorative fan that seemed worth more than everything in his own therapeutic Queens Plaza office circulated the air on the vaulted ceiling. The people, the desks, the decor, the logo on the door, the walls and doors themselves all seemed to want to be there. Why would they want to leave such a perfectly designed spot? It reminded him of his bed. He wondered if people made life-changing decisions here, too.

He pulled the door open in a hard, difficult motion. Not out of displeasure, but because it was oddly heavy. It fought against his attempt to enter the office space. When he managed to take the loaded step into the office, he was immediately greeted by a chipper young woman whose desk faced the door. Close enough to notice but not close enough to clutter the entry. Perfectly placed.

"Welcome, Mr. Karoll." She addressed him with a smile. "I'll let Ms. Chandra know you're here. Can I get you some water or a coffee while you wait?"

He felt like he was an understudy who never bothered to learn the script. Everyone here seemed to know their lines. The receptionist smiled on cue. The hum of conversation sat just below the music. Even the faint citrus scent in the air felt rehearsed. Davey adjusted his sleeves and half expected someone to hand him a cue card.

"Um… water. The water is fine. Thanks."

"Not a problem. Sparkling or spring?"

"Uh, sparkling." He started to look around the office without taking another step inside.

"Regular, lemon, or peach?"

He slowly blinked. "Coffee, actually, black."

"Right away, Mr. Karoll." The smile never left her face as she walked methodically toward the rear of the office. It was an open concept with a tidy kitchen in the back and lofted office space above the ground level. She returned with a quality mug that rivaled his typical Styrofoam. The coffee was good. And he wasn't sure he liked it.

"Ms. Chandra will be right down. You're welcome to take a seat or a look around if you'd like."

"She knows I'm here?"

"Yes, she does."

"But you only went to get coffee."

"I sent her a message from my phone when I saw you approaching the door. We run a tight ship here, Mr. Karoll."

He opted to walk the office floor a bit and never felt more out of place. There were no faded hoodies or rusted chairs. Only perfectly minimalist desks with the occasional family picture or bobblehead, reminding visitors that personality was still valued here.

A quiet staffer on the floor thanked him for his remarks at the rally when Josephine descended the thin steps from her lofted office. It felt as though the world froze around her. But it wasn't winter here; it was spring, and her company had clearly flourished. She moved like she owned the place and it was hers to belong in, which he thought she probably did. He thought of Rae for a moment and how she could command a room without trying. Josephine had that same gravity, but hers came from control. She drew people in through precision, not warmth. She didn't soften a room. She organized it. He wasn't sure that he belonged in her world.

"Welcome, Mr. Karoll. I'm glad you came. I think you made the right choice. Why don't you follow me?" She motioned for him to follow her up the steps she had just descended. She led him to a large desk that seemed to be a fixture in the space. Another woman sat at the desk behind a small laptop and in front of a larger curved monitor. A folder was placed at the seat he figured was his, as Josephine walked to the other side of the desk. "Mr. Karoll…"

He interrupted her. "Please, just Davey, I don't need the formalities."

She smiled. "Absolutely, Davey, and that's why I think people will love you. This is one of my partners here at the company, Shira."

"Pleasure, Shira."

"Welcome, Mr… Davey. The pleasure is ours."

"So, we have plenty of time, but I wanted to run you through some things. We set up an email for you and are sending you the details now. Any press appearances, political memos, or requests for quotes are going to be directed there. We'll have access and a consultant constantly monitoring it. We'll develop some talking points together and can handle most of the emails. If there's anything we're unsure of, we will always reach out to you first before responding."

He heard staffers below moving about. He wondered if they had more than one aspiring politician or if they were already working quickly for him.

"During the race, there will almost definitely be scrutiny or harsh words. We'll take care of that for you. Your job will primarily be press appearances, policy work for us to elaborate on, and time to show yourself across the boroughs. We think we can sell you as somebody striving for reform for the people by the people. A neighbor looking out for a neighbor." She leaned forward over the desk. "So, what do you think?"

He didn't have an answer. Outside, a plow splashed snow onto the parked cars, but none dared fall outside the door of the office. He was excited for the future, but he felt his chest tighten. It reminded him of the first time he led a therapy group. The pressure of knowing people might actually listen. Back then one wrong word meant a tense session. Now one wrong word could become a headline. He rubbed his eyes and rested his hands on the desk in front of him. He took a few deep breaths.

"I'm… I'm not sure. It feels like a lot."

"A lot that you are capable of by the looks of it," Shira said. She clicked a button on her laptop. On the screen behind her played a video of his speech at the rally.

"Davey," Josephine started. "People don't walk into this office because they are unsure. They walk in because they've decided. Because they know what they believe in and know they can do something about it. I know that you can do it. We can't guarantee a win, but we'll do everything in our power to make it happen. It wasn't happenstance that I was at the rally. It was fate. So, are you with us? Do you want to do this thing and make a change?"

He was quiet. Both Josephine and Shira waited for an answer. They didn't interject or say another word. They were good at what they did. They were selling him on the idea. He thought that they might be just as good at selling him to the city.

"Let's do it," he said quietly. "I'm in," he affirmed more loudly.

"Let's do it, Davey." He shook hands with Josephine and Shira. It seemed as if their portion of the meeting was over as he was guided back downstairs to some of her staffers. They started to take high-definition pictures of him in his faded hoodie. Questions were asked about basic talking points and opinions, and his responses would become the benchmark of his campaign.

He started to feel more like he belonged the longer he stayed. He was on his way to becoming a member of a club he previously had no interest in joining. By the time he was done, he opened the door to the street and braced for winter. The door was easier to exit than it was to enter. Spring left him, if only for a moment. He would be back.

His steps down the cold street were lighter than they had been. As he walked, he pulled out his phone for the first time in hours. He wondered if Josephine's office was actually some magical world that let the outside time slip away while he sat in perfection. He checked the clock again to be sure. Barely two hours had passed, yet it felt like an entire day. The place seemed to work like a spell that traded time for conviction. He unlocked the phone and tried to call Cass. Unlike the last time he tried to call, it went straight to voicemail.

He heard from Rae through Echona that he ended up working too late the night of the last support group. But now, it didn't even ring. He called a taxi to take him to Flatbush. The city had started to thaw, but the streets felt hollow. Snowmelt mirrored the shop lights and made the borough look half asleep. He wasn't answering, so he was determined to drop in. Even if Cass didn't feel like talking, he thought it might be good for his friend to know that he was around.

Chapter 22: A House

He arrived on Cass's street, where the slush had totally taken over. It clung to curbs, stoops, and underneath cars, to gutters, windows, and roofs. It was a bright wintry day, but the street in Flatbush was gray. He climbed the unshoveled stoop to his house and saw a light on in the front window. He knocked on the wooden door, and it answered with an empty thud. He knocked a second time. The door seemed to be the only one at home. He tried to call Cass again, but it echoed the first attempt and went straight to voicemail.

He was compelled to try the door handle, even though Cass habitually locked his door ever since one of his roommates had stolen a signed Patrick Ewing basketball from his college dorm. The handle made a gentle click as it twisted further in its cycle than expected. It surprised Davey, but he thought that Cass might have just been working too hard and had forgotten to lock it. He slowly entered the home as if he would be caught somewhere he shouldn't be, in the middle of a comical heist. The air inside felt wrong. Not heavy, not light, just still.

He hadn't been to Cass and Jazmine's house in a long time, but it still had an aura of familiar territory.

There was no sound inside. No TV left on or music softly filling the space. There was no shuffling of papers or slamming of keys on the laptop. The house was minimally decorated. Cass had never taken to interior decorating, and neither had Jazmine. But it didn't feel purposeful. It felt empty. He walked to the living room and saw Cass's hand stretched over the top of the couch.

"Cass!" he yelled. "It's the best therapist and future councilman this side of the Hudson! Where have you been, man?"

There was no response.

He approached the couch and saw Cass with his eyes closed. He felt glad that he had taken a nap and given himself time to breathe. He began to walk away and let his friend sleep. As he turned, he got a closer look at the situation.

The coffee table was in front of the couch.

An empty prescription pill bottle.

A half-empty beer.

A few stray pills, three or four, rolled away from the bottle.

They were scattered like survivors of something horrid.

He wanted to believe there was another explanation.

That Cass had dropped the bottle or spilled them while half asleep. He wanted to believe it so badly that he said it out loud. "You just dropped them, right?"

His voice cracked on the last word.

They moved against the grain of the coffee table.

The air felt stale in the bland house.

He walked to the other side of the couch and knelt next to his friend.

"Cass?"

Nothing.

He shook him gently.

"Buddy?"

The radiator growled in the other room. Davey's heartbeat quickened, his breathing grew shallow, and his shoulders tensed.

"Cassius?"

He noticed the faintest rise and fall of his friend's chest.

For a second, he froze. He didn't want to touch him. He didn't want to know how cold his skin might be.

He held his breath until his lungs burned, as if he could bargain his own air to keep Cass breathing.

Too shallow.

Too slow.

Too still.

Davey pulled out his phone. His hand shook violently, and tears started to well in his eyes. The phone slipped from his grasp. A tear hit the floor. It took longer than he liked to dial the emergency number.

"Cass…" he cried out softly.

A small "9-1-1, what is your emergency?" was muffled over Davey's cries.

Chapter 23: A Room With No Sound

The ambulance arrived with lights and sirens to welcome the new year as if they were something celebratory. The paramedics took Cass, and rather than leave him alone again, Davey rode in the back. They cut through the slush that covered Flatbush. He called Rae. He thought it was better than calling Jazmine directly. He knew there was a version of this story where she was the one to find him. He couldn't let that exist. Not if he could carry the image instead.

"Hey, babe, how'd it go?" she asked.

He was silent until he realized that she was referring to his meeting with Josephine. It was only earlier in the day, but he struggled to remember.

"Good," he had cleared his throat over the phone. "Listen, Rae, there had been an accident."

She could hear the sirens over the phone, cluttering her husband's words.

"What's going on, Davey?"

"It's Cass."

He thought about how he had failed his friend. He had noticed something was wrong but hadn't acted until it was too late. He could've talked to him. Talked to Jazmine. He remembered Cass's laugh, the one that used to fill the support group and turn discomfort into something human. He couldn't remember the last time he'd heard it. The absence hit him like a physical sound. He had seen something, but he hadn't said anything. Davey filled her in on the details.

"I'm so sorry, Davey. You're going to King's County Hospital?"

"Sounds right."

"Okay. I'm in the Bronx just finishing up some work with Owl-Heart and Echona. I'll grab her before she gets too far down the street and bring her there. I'll see you soon."

"Thank you."

"Davey… I love you."

"I love you, Rae."

He hung up the phone and stared at the unconscious body of his friend in the cramped enclosure they had found themselves in. He was sure they were speeding as efficiently as possible, but it didn't feel fast enough. From the back of the ambulance, he couldn't see any walkers blurring by or snow being kicked up by the tires. His hands started to change color, not from the wintry chill, but from his strong grip on the side of the gurney. The noise of the sirens above him vibrated the interior, and the air smelled broken. He thought that maybe he had left Josephine's office too late. Knocked on Cass's door too softly. Called his name too quietly. The world around him carried on with ambition while it felt like he was more frozen than the ice that clung to the sidewalks of the city. The sirens didn't sound like rescue anymore.

They sounded like regret.

He counted their rise and fall like breaths, willing them to sync with Cass's chest.

They arrived at the hospital, and Cass was whisked away faster than Davey could keep up with. His friend was out of his hands. He put his arms behind his head and interlocked his fingers. He stared, unblinking, at the gurney that was surrounded by figures in white coats and scrubs. He continued to look onward as if to issue a prayer to some deity he wasn't quite sure would hear him. He took a seat in the waiting area, and his legs bounced frantically. The hospital was constantly active.

He felt like another fixture in its fluorescently lit hallways, watching the dutiful nurses, doctors, and technicians go about their business without a second thought. The place carried an aura of sterile hopelessness. He slumped over as far as he could and attempted to bury his head between his legs. He hoped that when he lifted it, he might wake up from whatever nightmare he had found himself in. He wondered how many people had sat in that exact chair hoping for the same thing.

The thought didn't comfort him.

It only made him feel less singular in his pain.

His request was never answered by the time the heroes walked in.

A cough.

The click of a vending machine and the clicks of a keyboard.

He felt a hand on his shoulder. God? he thought.

It was Rae.

Her cape swooshed over him like a comforting blanket. She rubbed his back and offered a smile. He touched her arm as a way of saying thank you.

He looked toward the rest of the waiting room. Echona stood at the information desk, still in her superhero outfit. She slowly lowered her hood, then removed her mask. Her secret identity didn't matter. Not anymore. She was just a person. A worried wife. A hurting heart. Jazmine slowly walked toward Rae and Davey. Tears welled in her eyes. He stood to greet her, and she moved to hug him. She looked smaller than he remembered. Heroes weren't supposed to shrink, but grief did that. It folded people inward, made them occupy less space in the world.

"Thank you," she said quietly. "I'm sorry."

"You don't have any reason to apologize, Jaz."

The embrace between friends lasted as long as it needed to.

"I should've been there more," she spoke through the tears. "He needed me, and I didn't know it."

"I should be the one to apologize. I thought something was wrong, but I didn't do enough to help him talk through it. I thought the support group would be enough, but he never opened up. He never said anything was wrong."

"That's just Cass, Davey. His work, the expectations, it all broke him. The firm started denying some of his billable work, so he had to work extra to make up for it. The endorsements kept flooding in. The city broke him and ran the meter while it happened."

She spoke with a saddened fury. Her skin went paler than normal. Fragile. Other patients shuffled around them, waiting to be seen. A sleeping family member propped himself up in an uncomfortable chair, his neck crooked as the silent TV in the waiting room aired some insignificant headline.

"It's neither of your faults," Rae encouraged them both. "The medical staff is good. We don't know anything yet. But if… when he wakes up, we'll all be there for him."

Jazmine bit the inside of her cheek and hugged Rae. Her hands were shaking. "Thank you both for being here."

"I'm glad it was me," Davey said as he wiped a tear from his cheek. "I'm glad it didn't have to be you."

She thought about how she agreed with him. She considered that she might have panicked instead of acting, like he had, if she were the one who found him on the couch. They sat together in silence and waited for news. Mechanical beeps conversed with the hospital's ventilation and vending machines, all having some unusual conversation as if they weren't benchmarks in the halls of life and death.

Another ambulance arrived outside and wheeled in a patient who at least seemed to be conscious. Staff rushed to the new gurney as effective cogs that triggered one another into motion. Every doctor who walked into or through the waiting room earned the stares of Davey,

Jazmine, and Rae. But it took a disconcertingly long time before one arrived to address them. Davey started to believe that if he stared hard enough, he could summon good news. Like true focus might be a kind of prayer in itself.

"I'm sorry."

The stony doctor addressed the three of them. The sounds of the hospital dispersed. They could only hear the practitioner.

"We were too late. The opioids were too fast-acting, and we couldn't bring him back in time. If you'd like to see Cassius, you can come with me."

"I didn't get to him in time?" Davey asked, his eyebrows fluctuating with the sadness in his voice.

"I assure you, this is not your fault."

Davey heard the doctor's words but didn't believe them. He was too late to start the support group. Too late to arrive at Cass's house. Too late to the couch, the phone, and the ambulance. He was too late for his friend.

The doctor turned to walk back into the fake brightness of the hospital. Rae and Davey followed. Their footsteps echoed a slowing heartbeat. Jazmine was still. She couldn't fathom not having him in her life. The sound of the entire hospital disappeared. Rae noticed it first when the automatic doors to the back room made no noise. She looked back at Jazmine. Frozen. Scorned.

She had taken the sound from the hospital.

Rae ran to her. Her heavy boots didn't make a sound against the linoleum floors. She grabbed her shoulders and looked her in the eyes. Jazmine's tear ducts unleashed like a broken dam that had collapsed under the pressure behind it. Rae put her hands on her friend's cheeks. She could tell that, had there been sound, Jazmine would have been unleashing the terrors of a truly broken heart.

She wrapped Jazmine in her arms and held her head. The doctor and Davey stood idly by in patience. Davey attempted to hold back his own tears for his friend and failed.

The automatic doors held open for them to walk into a new tomorrow. A world they all didn't want to wake up in. Davey stared at the room that had just been filled with sounds but was now empty. He was too late. The words echoed inside him without sound. Too late for his friend. Too late for Cass. The sentence rewrote every breath he took until it felt carved into his ribs.

Chapter 24: The Breathless Snow

The wintry air blew fiercely outside the funeral home near his final resting place. It clashed against the double doors that had to be forced open and pulled tightly shut. The gray sky made the world feel small around the place. They weren't in a large city. They were in a place much worse. A place they had no desire to be. Jazmine sat front and center, as close to her husband's open casket as she could be. She wore a long black-sleeved gown. The thought crossed her mind about making it a celebration of life, but she decided that there was nothing to celebrate. There was only something to be missed. She kept waiting for the room to fill with sound. For someone to laugh by accident. For proof that life could still exist beside death.

But it stayed still. Even the air seemed unwilling to move. Davey sat next to her, followed by Rae, Ava, Sara, Jose, Laurel, and Rocker. All in a uniform, unlike the ones they wore to save the city, uniforms they hoped not to wear again for a length of time. Cass had no parents or siblings to mourn his loss with them. No uncles, aunts, or cousins.

Jazmine was his family. At one point, Davey was, too. He wanted to reach for her hand, but grief had rearranged all the rules of touch. He didn't know what comfort looked like anymore. The front row all wore small ribbons pinned to their tops in shades of purple and blue. A few rows behind them, in the mix of colleagues and associates that claimed to have known him, was Eric. He wore a similar pin. He and Ava had not spoken or rectified any wrongdoing, and he knew that this was not the place to do so.

A minister, who didn't know him, gave a few stale words that meant as much to Jazmine as finding a loose penny in her dryer. He opened the floor to anyone who would like to say a few words on Cass's behalf. The mix of relative strangers remained quiet. The front row did as well, albeit for a very different reason. Then, a voice rose from the gallery.

"I'd like to say something." It was Eric.

He shuffled out of his row and took the long walk to the podium. He paid his respects to Cass as he passed and placed a folded piece of paper atop his body.

Eric adjusted the microphone a bit and cleared his throat. "I... I didn't know Cass for very long, but I knew he was a special man. We were very different, but in a way, we couldn't be more similar. Both of us were looking for a way through life with loved ones." He glanced at Ava. "Trying to figure things out the best way we know how to. He didn't feel like he was capable of opening up. I just want to encourage anybody who needs a friend or an ear to reach out to somebody. Reach out to me, even if you don't know me. Your life is valuable. You are important."

He started to cry. Silence filled the room, broken only by the occasional audible sniffles of the heartbroken. A tissue was being used. Chairs shifted as some wiped their eyes. The wind crashed against the building, making it creak. Jazmine didn't cry this time. Her body felt like it had already emptied itself days ago. What remained was something quieter, an ache that lived in her and refused to leave.

"We all have somebody to talk to, whether we realize it or not. Just... take the step. Miss you, Cass."

He took the walk back to his seat. The crowd hung on to the sound of his shoes clicking down the center aisle.

The minister retook the podium.

"Is there anyone else who would like to say a few words?"

There was nobody.

"If that is all, we invite his loved ones to say a final goodbye before transport to his lot in the back. The rest of you, should you wish to stay, can meet us there."

He moved away, and the building began to empty. The front row remained until it was just them, and Eric, who sat still in a sea of open chairs. Rocker and Laurel rose first. They silently maneuvered to the casket, stared at the lifeless man, and continued outside.

As if it were a predetermined order, Jose, Sara, and Ava stood next. The women bent and each offered Jazmine a crouched hug, while Jose patted Davey on the shoulder firmly. Both men's eyes misted over as they looked at each other. The three of them moved to leave the building after paying their respects. The door opened to the cold air and sounded louder than anything the minister had said. The winter outside felt honest in a way words never could. On the way out, Ava decided to sit next to Eric for a moment. She hugged him, said a brief word or two, and then left for the outside. He remained in his chair.

Davey and Rae rose next. She let him take the lead. They paid their respects, and Davey parted with, "I'll see you again, brother."

Then, the room grew empty. Eric walked out with Davey and Rae. Only Jazmine remained, with a few workers standing to the side. Not rushing her, but ready to take him away from her forever. After a few more minutes, she stood. Her black gown trailed behind her. She placed her hand on his chest, and a tear fell onto his cheek.

A parting gift.

A wishful thought.

A broken heart.

She wondered if he'd hear it wherever he was now. Or if silence was all that waited for both of them. She touched the piece of paper that Eric had placed on him and opened it. She thought it to be as much hers as it was his. There was no expansive note or outburst. The note simply read: "Thank you."

She folded it again, put it back on him, and took it upon herself to close the casket. She was the last pair of eyes that would see him. She walked out of the room as her heels clicked on the ground. They slowly faded out like a heart that had given up beating.

Outside, she joined the group of people who remained—the ones, she thought, that truly cared, or cared about their own image enough to show up.

They lowered him into the ground as snow fell around them. There were no last words. Even the harsh wind stopped and seemed to pay reverence. It felt like the world paused and held its breath. Snow fell onto the casket. Jazmine had no tears left to give, but gasped for air as she couldn't take it any longer. Jose stepped forward and removed his pinned ribbon. He gently tossed it onto the casket and stepped back in line.

They placed the dirt onto him, and it was real.

Her husband was gone.

The sky was a heavy gray as Ava left. Snow whispered down around her, and the world felt strangely hushed. Moments ago inside, she had slid into the empty chair beside Eric, wrapped her arms around him, murmured something soft and broken into his shoulder. Now she stood a few feet away, pulling at the edge of her gloves, staring at Cass's grave as the last shovelfuls of snow-dusted earth were settled.

Eric remained seated a moment longer, head bowed. Then quietly he rose. He found her alone with the snow. "Ava..." he began, voice low against the cold wind. She looked up at him. For a beat there was nothing but the distant sounds of the dirt and the soft fall of snow.

"I didn't know what to say in there," Eric admitted finally, reaching for her hand. His fingers were cold beneath her gloves.

Her eyes closed as a few tears broke free. She squeezed his hand without speaking. After a moment, she managed, "You did great."

It was almost a whisper.

Eric gave a small nod. "Thank you."

She drew a breath, steadying herself against the ache in her chest. "I've been thinking a lot about… about us," Ava said quietly. Her voice trembled on the last word.

He looked down, thumb stroking her hand. "I'm sorry, Ava. I was always just scared to disappoint you."

Ava's heart clenched.

The old hurt flared, but this time there was also understanding there.

"I love you, Eric. I always have." Her gaze swept the bare trees dusted white. "But, I've been angry at you. Angry because I thought you didn't care about anything, not your own dreams, not me."

He swallowed.

The snow crackled lightly under their feet as he took a step closer.

"I cared. I do care. I've just… I didn't know how to be what you needed."

"Watching you in there, I saw something change," she said. "You spoke for Cass. You looked at me differently." Her voice grew firmer, tinged with the old fierceness she had as LunAva. "I know you could do more than just stream games. You just need something to believe in. Somebody to believe in you."

Eric's eyes met hers, steady and soft. "I think you might be right." He squeezed her hand. "I want to be better, Ava. For you. For me. For Cass."

She squeezed back, tears finally slipping past her composure. "I want that too someday, I think." A brittle smile touched her lips.

In the silence that followed, all she could hear was the whisper of snow and his steady, quiet breathing. At last she exhaled. "So… what do we do now?"

Eric smiled faintly. "Maybe being a part for a while would be good for both of us. We take it one day at a time. I'll try harder to be someone you're proud of. But you don't have to fix me all at once."

She nodded, eyes bright. "Thank you, Eric. For coming today. For saying those things. But you don't have to be someone I'm proud of. I've always only wanted you to be somebody that you can be proud of." He leaned his forehead against hers.

"Thank you for everything, Ava."

They stood together in the cold twilight, the space between them filled with all the unspoken things: love, regret, hope. For a moment, after burying their friend, Ava and Eric were exactly where they needed to be, together in the silence and attempting to forge a new understanding. The snow caught a faint glow in her eyes, like the memory of a dim light. It faded as she blinked. She was only Ava for now. She didn't need to be a hero.

Chapter 25: Five

A few weeks later, the white snow turned into hard gray slush. The sort that lingered on street corners or vacant parking lots long after the turn to spring. But it wasn't spring. It had just become February. Snowfall had become infrequent, but the air didn't feel warmer. It felt emptier. Thinner. He walked through the motions of setting up for the evening and was slightly less gentle than usual when he set up the old chairs.

They clanged together as he whipped them to the typical spots. Four chairs became five a few months ago. Davey kept it at five. Out of stubbornness or a refusal to believe in what he knew. He moved to set up the pot of coffee and poured slightly fewer grounds into the filter. There was one less person drinking coffee now. He moved to take his normal seat.

The front window appeared damp, and the streetlight that once flickered had since been fixed. Dusk hadn't come yet. The days were starting to grow longer and sometimes felt never-ending to him. He looked outside for a beat and spotted the neighborhood cat back on its stoop. The February chill apparently was not too cold for it. He wondered if the cat would notice the missing person, or if it would assume that they had grown out their hair, dyed it blonde, changed skin complexions, and become shorter. The door swung open forcefully, and Jose, Laurel, and Eric all entered the residence in succession. Jose and Eric took their spots, while Laurel helped herself to a cup of coffee.

Cass's chair remained open, as it would for as long as the group met.

Rae came down from the stairs; her steps announced her presence before she did so herself. Her long hair was tied into a bun. She wore a loose tank top and stretchy leggings that supported her growing belly, which had just begun to show more than it had.

"Mind if I join you guys tonight?" she asked curiously. "It's okay if you want to keep it just spouses."

There was no answer.

Davey would have loved to have her, to spend more time with her, but he wasn't going to make that call.

"Sure," Eric spoke up.

"Good with me," Laurel added.

"Same," Jose said.

She fully entered the room and stood behind Davey. She put her arms on his shoulders. He moved quickly and, though she didn't ask for it, gave his wife his chair. He switched spots with her and rested his hands on her.

Nobody knew how to start.

Nobody wanted it to.

If it started, that meant Cass would really not be joining them. Not because he was working late or didn't want to. Because he couldn't.

Davey drank some of the coffee that didn't feel quite right going down. "Thanks for coming, everyone."

Silence.

"He'd be complaining about the coffee right about now."

There was no response until a half-laugh from Eric broke through, and Davey continued.

"I just want you all to know that I'm here for you. Please talk before something happens that you can't reverse."

"Love y'all," Jose shared as he stared at the ceiling, as if angling his head upward would make the tears that began to form retreat inside the ducts. Eric patted him on the shoulder.

"So, you're really running for city council?" Laurel asked Davey.

"He sure is," Rae responded for him with a smile as she looked up at him with a proud smirk.

"That's great, bro. I'm glad you're seeing it through," Jose said.

"I feel like… I feel like it's what Cass would've wanted. I can't drop out. For him. For Simon. For anybody who is struggling but can't find the words to talk to somebody right next to them. Things need to change. I'll start with things here if I can."

"Dude, you're talking like you're already a politician. You got this in the bag," Eric responded.

Davey blushed and rubbed the nape of his neck. "Thanks, Eric.

I can't say that I've ever wanted to be a politician, but I feel like this might be the right track for me."

"We're all in your corner, Davey," Laurel shared.

Rae squeezed his hand that landed softly back on her shoulder.

"I have some news…" Eric started and then paused.

"Go ahead, Eric. Share whatever is on your heart," Davey encouraged him.

"My stream got its first sponsor."

"That's awesome, bro. Way to go."

"Told you building takes time. Way to pull in the traffic," Laurel and Jose supported his endeavor.

"Thanks, sorry. I didn't know if sharing good news would be okay."

"Eric, I think we could all use some good news," Davey reassured him. "What's the sponsorship?"

"I'm not allowed to share before the stream happens, but it's a big tech manufacturer that likes my stuff. I'm really excited." He smiled before attempting to hide it.

"It's okay to smile, Eric," Rae added. "I'm glad you're still here, by the way. I don't care what happens between you and my sister. You're a great guy, Eric."

He looked at the floor.

"Thanks, Rae. I don't think we'll be getting back together, but maybe her next guy can join the group, too. We can share notes." Eric chuckled.

Rae shook her head with a smile.

"We have some news too."

The air started to feel fresh again as the ice machine in the kitchen announced that Rae's newest snack obsession was refreshed.

"We're definitely having twins and definitely having a boy and a girl."

"Are they going to be separated at birth, only to find each other decades later and join a rebellion together?" Eric questioned.

"Ideally, not," Davey said flatly. "But, nice."

"When are you due again?" Laurel asked.

Rae put her hand on her belly and looked down with a smile. "Around the middle of June."

"Names?"

"Not even close."

"Yeah," Davey added. "I was Baby Karoll for like the first week of my life. Born premature, spent time in the NICU, parents couldn't agree… but I feel as long as we beat that, then there's no rush to pick a name. Did you and Sara have a name picked out, Jose?"

"Bro, she had a name picked out before she got pregnant. I was just along for the ride." He laughed. "If it was something I hated, I would've said something. But it was fine, so I rolled with it. Now, little Rio Ruiz is growing up every day, giving me an attitude, and he makes life fun."

"Solid?" Eric asked, making sure the inflection suggested it was a question rather than a compliment.

Jose laughed again. "Yeah, bro, solid."

Davey left from behind his wife's chair to get a refill of coffee. He bumped past the empty chair on the way back. It rocked lightly in its place, not being held down by any anchor.

"It's still wild to me how she's able to pump on top of buildings," Laurel said.

"Same, girl. I have to get some notes from her when it's my turn."

"You guys can be the Pumping Heroes," Eric suggested. It made Rae remember the instances of Ava trying to add a team name to the heroes. She thought of her sister, considering that she and Eric might be meant for each other. But it wasn't her place to suggest that.

"Yeah, she's my hero. I'm just happy to be the sidekick."

"Jose, you're a hero in your own regard. You're a hero to Rio. He gets to spend his days with you. I'm guessing that's all a kid can ask for," Davey comforted him.

"Yeah, dude. How's the dadpack?"

"Honestly, bro, nearly fully charged. I've been allowing myself to rest. Allowing the home to get into a functional mess, and that's okay. Sara and I talked a while ago; we're connecting in a way that hasn't felt like it happened in a while."

"That's great, dude. Just don't have another kid yet," Eric joked.

"Hey, bro, no promises." He pushed Eric in jest. "Still not planning on kids, Laurel?"

"Nope!" she responded. "We are so, so good without them!"

"That's totally fair. Whatever is best for your relationship is best, and only you guys know that," Davey responded.

A February breeze pushed against the door. The group looked at it in unison. They expected somebody to walk through it. A missing friend. Nobody ever did.

The session finished with an array of ups and downs, solace and chagrin.

Eric and Jose left together, as Laurel stayed back for a beat.

"I just want to thank you both," she addressed Rae and Davey. "You've both been so welcoming to Miles and me. We just… we can't thank you enough."

Davey was caught off guard by the mention of Rocker's real name.

"We're glad you guys are here," Rae answered. "If either of you ever needs anything, we're here."

Laurel hugged them both and opened the door.

"See you guys next week."

The meow of the stoop cat across the street filled the quiet air, as if it were signaling that the visitors had all left.

Rae kissed her husband, and together they tidied the house. He attended to the five chairs and lingered at one in particular. Locked the door to protect any accidental intruder from his wife and ensured the coffee pot was off. She went up the stairs first, and he shortly followed. When he entered the room, Rae was sitting on the bed, crying. Her head was buried in her hands. He didn't say anything or ask if she was okay. He stood in front of her, let her collapse into him, and rubbed her hair.

He exhaled. Together, he thought. Always together. He realized grief never really left a room. It only sat quieter with time, waiting for the next silence to fill.

He could still hear a faint cry from the cat outside that had retaken its faithful position. He wondered if it was meowing on guard, as he assumed that was its purpose, or if it meowed out of sadness and realized the tall, well-dressed, dark-skinned man would not be returning. Not tonight. Not ever.

Chapter 26: Moonlit Playlist

He walked in circles at the small Bathgate Park track in Belmont until the kid fell asleep. It wasn't large, but it was his. His community, his family, his park. The Valentine's Day air was lukewarm. Not wintry, not spring, but a sign of things to come. It was a rare day for the time of year. He was thankful for it. Thankful to get out of the house and not be frostbitten immediately by the weather. Every winter, he questioned his parents' decision to move from Puerto Rico. Although deep down he knew why. Realistically, he couldn't imagine living anywhere else. Belmont was dense, and at times it felt overpopulated.

For Jose, it was the kind of space where you knew your neighbors and knew when to mind your own business. He tried to keep in his triathlete shape by walking the track or around the neighborhood. He determined not to embrace the gut that was growing as his wife was losing the baby weight. At times, it didn't feel like he had all that much of a choice. It was headed for him like a slow crossing train, and he was tied to the tracks with a knot that could easily be slipped but hadn't been yet. After his son fell asleep, he did an extra lap to make sure it stuck. Then, he walked down Bassford until he reached a small gated alley. The lock on the metal gate was open but remained in place, signaling that although security was lackluster, it still wasn't a place for visitors.

He moved the lock slowly, opened the gate, making sure it didn't hiss at him and wake the child. Jose pushed the stroller through it before walking down the alley and turning a corner behind a building. The alley was dirty. Signs of people less fortunate than him. Or less caring. He wondered how many people the city forgot before they ever became a headline. He leaned against a building and pushed the stroller back and forth in slow motion.

He checked his phone and felt a light breeze from in front of him. His eyes raised, and in front of him, his wife appeared. She was in a full OwlHeart suit. Face covered, lower half covered in gentle frills to appear as feathers, but comfortable enough not to chafe her larger thighs when she was busy hunting down criminals and keeping the city safe. A tank top that matched her lower half, which made pumping on rooftops an easier task. Sleeves on her forearms with a drape of sorts attached that made it look as if she had wings when her arms were stretched.

"Fear not, citizen!" she said in an attempted gruff voice. Her suit brushed against some of the brick wall of the building at her side.

He laughed.

"Hey, amor."

"Not convincing? Dammit," she said quietly, not to wake her child, before she approached Jose and kissed him through the mask. It smelled like a mix of sweat, milk, and cocoa butter.

"So… you got the goods?" he asked.

"You know it." She looked around slyly.

A siren drove past the alley.

She lowered the zipper of a side pocket on her thigh and retrieved a bottle of milk.

She held it in her hands, looked around again, and then gave him the bottle. "Ten ounces of liquid gold."

He held it up to the sun and looked into the bottle. "Looks pure. I'll be in touch."

She couldn't keep her composure and started to laugh louder before managing to stop and say, "Yo, we're funny."

"Heck yeah, we are. See you at home tonight?"

"Yeah, should be good. I'm not sure how late, but I'll try to keep you updated."

"Got it, amor. Be safe."

"Will do."

She turned and started to walk away, to take to the skies again. He stopped her and asked the question that had been on his heart. The one he was nearly afraid to ask his wife. Not because he was fearful of her. Because he was fearful of the answer. Of the fallout.

"Have you heard from Jazmine, by the way?"

She looked at him as the nearby heating unit of the apartment they stood behind turned on with a rattle and clang.

"Yeah… I think she's done."

He didn't answer for a moment. A honk from the street next door brought him back to reality from his temporary state of avoidance.

"I don't blame her," he said.

"Nobody does. Doesn't make it easier to see her go, though."

"Maybe we can make a larger support group or something. Keep her involved, you know?"

"I'm not sure she wants to be around anybody still, but that's a good idea. I'll talk to the other heroes."

"And I'll talk to the guys."

She smiled at him and approached her husband again.

"Happy Valentine's Day," she said.

They kissed again, which prompted her to fly off quietly and create a small breeze that felt like a fan on her son's face. Jose put the bottle into the diaper bag and left the alley as quietly as possible. He walked down the street and wondered if Cass had his type of love. He hoped so. Everyone deserved at least one person who could make the weight of the world feel lighter, even if just for a night. The type that jokes, supports, and feels together.

The wheel of the stroller crunched along the sidewalk. He walked through the Bronx for a bit until his kid woke up. Then they headed home. It was late afternoon, and they stopped at his mom's along the way. Jose's dad had never been in his life, and he was determined to be a man who broke the cycle. His mom was cooking an unnecessarily large dinner just for herself. Perfectly fluffed white rice, aromatic beans with little bits of pumpkin, fried pork chops that assaulted your taste buds with how full of love they were. She always cooked for her son and grandson, although he wasn't eating fried pork yet. All served with a large, perfectly ripe avocado, a glass of pineapple soda, and the desire to never stand from his chair again.

It had been a long time since Jose had to cook dinner for Sara. But when he ate at his mom's, he always brought a plate back with him. After energy returned to his body, he realized why he had been chasing after his triathlete physique. Mom's cooking wasn't making it easy. They returned to the short walk home as darkness fell over the city. On the way, he stopped at a vendor on the street selling small bouquets. He bought one for Sara. Even if he didn't end up seeing her tonight, he would still get her flowers that she would come home to. They smelled like a mix of nature, rain, and exhaust as he carried them down the street. When he reached his building, he was thankful that only the pure aromatics of sweet florals remained.

He lifted the stroller up the steps of his stoop and propped open the door with his foot while maneuvering the stroller inside. It was a difficult task, but one that he was all too familiar with. When he got into his first-floor apartment, he parked the stroller and took out his son to let him explore the floor, Rio's favorite pastime. The apartment was quiet, but not empty. Jose would always prefer to spend evenings with his wife, but this was perfectly agreeable to him. As the night grew long, he put Rio down in his crib. They had just opted to move him from the bassinet to the crib in the small spare room. It was a leap. Not one he thought he was ready for. Rio told them in the way that he was able that he was ready for the change, which was reassuring to his dad.

Jose stayed awake, watching a show he had little interest in but hoping his wife would walk through the door. The house was lived in, but it wasn't the night he would prioritize cleaning. It was the night he hoped to prioritize his wife.

He grew tired of the nonsensical show that filled the quietness of the home and decided to turn it off. Instead, he opted to play some soft music that filled the apartment with enough noise to be noticeable but not enough to wake up Rio. A playlist he and Sara made long ago. He listened to it when he missed her. It was a lengthy playlist and one he was in no trouble of repeating songs when he listened to it. He snacked on some of the leftovers from his mom's place, then realized that she might not entirely be to blame for his diminishing physique. As the music faded and the moon worked toward its peak, Sara walked through the door. She wore civilian clothing after she had taken to landing on a nearby rooftop, changing clothes, and climbing down a fire escape. All in an attempt to keep her identity a true secret.

His face lit up as if it wasn't the dead of night.

He moved to embrace her, but she put up her hand to stop him. "I am way too sweaty, babe. Let me shower before you touch me."

Jose swatted her hand down gently. "I'm sorry... do you think I care?" He slid on the hardwood in his socks toward her and wrapped his hand around her curves.

She blushed and giggled while he kissed her cheek.

"He's down?" she asked.

"Sure is."

They listened to the music in the background as he touched his forehead to hers.

"You're a great dad, Jose Ruiz." She gave him a peck on the lips.

"And you're our hero." He returned and pulled her tight. He reached for the flowers that he had left by the front door. After bringing them to his side, he said, "For our mom of the year."

Then, he kissed her again.

Noises from the outside started to come into the apartment.

Walkers.

Honking.

A train screeching at its station.

The song switched to "Best Part (feat. H.E.R.)."

"Is this our playlist?" she asked after noticing it.

He smiled at her. "Of course."

The sound from outside began to dissipate, while the activity remained the same. He took her hand and walked her from the entryway into the living room. The space opened up a bit, and Jose turned to face her again. His hand was back around her waist. He held her. He never wanted to let go. They kissed slowly to the music. She put her arms underneath his and rested her hands on his shoulder blades. The music continued.

It was just them.

There was no noise, no disturbances, no crying from a baby, or loss of a friend.

She lifted them slowly off the ground.

They hovered in the air and kissed.

They felt light and airy, as if they were made for one another.

The moonlight broke through their window. It felt like they floated in the atmosphere, and the moon was theirs alone. The only spectator to their love.

"Thank you for loving me," she whispered to him. She had been self-conscious for as long as he could remember. It persisted when she became a hero.

"Loving you is something I choose to do. It's something I am. In every bit of who I am, love for you is there." They kissed again.

"I don't just love you, Sara. I need you. I choose you. Over everything. All the noise, all the competitions, I choose you. I choose him." He pointed to the baby's room.

"I choose you, too," she responded softly.

Outside, the city didn't stop because it couldn't. Inside, it didn't stop because they didn't want it to. The world fell away. In the small apartment in the Bronx, love was louder than the noise.

Chapter 27: Detours

The dreariness of March came to the city as Rae embraced her six-month belly and the growing twins. A carjacking in Midwood led some of the heroes to action. Rocker and Rae stopped it faster than it started. They had become an increasingly cohesive unit, but a civilian was struck in the crime, and an ambulance couldn't get through a traffic jam caused by a separate accident that blocked the road in both directions. The yelling and honking didn't allow the emergency sirens to break through. It was a city where everyone wanted to be heard, and nobody wanted to listen. They tried to yell for people to clear the way. A person needed real help, and nobody listened.

Rocker could have lifted them, but he didn't want to risk hurting them more accidentally. They needed a paramedic examination, and they couldn't get one. Time was running out. They needed Echona to break through the situation, make it quiet, to control the space. But she wasn't there. She hadn't been spotted anywhere for months. Horns overlapped in nonsensical attempts to be louder than the others. Rae felt nauseous and lost some of her faith in the city. She was about to welcome children into a world that only cared for itself. How brutally harsh, she thought. She fell silent in the mayhem. The noise filled her so completely it felt like quiet.

Rocker took it upon himself to fix the situation and started simply moving cars out of the way. He was prepared to take on any issues from the NYPD, insurance companies, or drivers head-on. He had become a hero to help, but nobody else seemed to want to in this moment. The ambulance broke through and rushed to the hospital.

"Up for a detour?" Rae asked him.

Rocker shrugged. "I have nothing going on."

They traveled from Midwood to Flatbush.

Rae needed to check on Jazmine. She had been disconnected. Absent. Not returning calls or texts. She occasionally responded to a message in a group chat with an automated emoji reaction, but nothing more.

They made it through the wet streets of slush that had been refusing to melt into spring. The sidewalks started to get more crowded, and the brave bicyclists decided they wouldn't wait any longer. Rae was thankful for the ones who wore helmets and mentally scolded the ones who didn't. The air began to warm but felt dense as they approached Jazmine's house.

The door was open. Something Rae had heard Cass would never do.

They climbed the stoop and knocked on the door frame.

There was no answer.

"Do we…" Rocker started before seeing Rae enter the house.

There was no television on or music playing in the background.

They entered the living room and saw her hand hanging over the couch.

Rae peered over the couch and saw Jazmine lying down. Her eyes were closed.

"Jaz?" she asked quietly.

No response.

"Oh no," Rocker said.

"Jazmine!" Rae yelled as loud as she possibly could.

She jumped up from the couch. Her eyes shot open. "What. The. Heck."

"Whoops," Rae said and chuckled.

Jazmine's hair was knotted. She was wearing one of Cass's old baggy hoodies that he had stopped wearing a long time ago. Dark bags were under her puffy eyes.

"What do you want, Rae? Miles?"

"Just checking in," he responded.

"I'm good. You can leave and let me nap again."

"I… I don't think that's true."

"Listen, I appreciate it, dude, but don't act like you know me. It's been like four months or whatever." Jazmine lay back down.

He didn't answer, but he took a step back.

"And in those months, he has been an amazing addition and good friend."

"Rae. I'm fine."

"No. You're not," she replied. "I can't begin to imagine what you're going through, but I'm not letting you slip into a hole you can't pull yourself out of. If you want me to leave, fine. I'll leave. But I'm coming back tomorrow. And the day after that. And every day until I pop. Then Ava will come, or Sara, or Miles. But you don't get to dismiss yourself."

Jazmine thought hard about those words.

Then, she broke down.

"Was he that unhappy? I loved him! He had to know that. I always tried to talk to him about what was going on, but he never opened up. I was here for him… I was here." She buried her face in her hands and wept. Rae watched her and thought of the couch where Davey had found him. The same silence. The same weight.

Rae moved to the couch and sat next to her. She put her arm around her, and Jazmine sank into her. "It was never about you, and it's not your fault."

"How could it not be?! I didn't pay enough attention. I could've… I could've done more."

A neighbor outside began hammering his shovel into a chunk of frozen slush. The metal on the ice reverberated through the air.

"Jazmine. It's not your fault."

A dog walker with an untrained pet walked down the road. The dog began barking loudly at the man with the shovel.

"It is, though. I have to live with knowing that."

"It's not," Rocker moved closer and tried to comfort her. "When I was younger, I tried to take my own life. I didn't know how to make things feel better. I didn't know how to make myself feel purposeful. It was nobody's fault but my own. I didn't talk to anyone. Tell anyone my struggles. Thankfully, my attempt failed, and I was able to get help. It's not your fault, Jazmine. He lost his fight. He didn't have the words and didn't think he could say what was going on."

"You did nothing wrong," Rae reassured her.

She continued to weep until the noise of her sobbing took over the clang of the shovel. Her tears began to make Rae's suit damp.

"Why don't you come back to heroing? Be with us. We will be your support. We will always be your friends. Whatever you need. My kids need more than one aunt. Maybe one that thinks our team doesn't need a name." Rae tried to joke with her. A bit of a smile crossed Jazmine's face and challenged the tears.

"We could use you out there, Jaz," Rocker said.

"I don't think that Cass would have wanted you to quit. He loved you. He loved what you stood for."

"You think so?" she asked.

"Absolutely."

Jazmine cleared her throat. "Okay... I'll do it for him. I'll go back out there."

Rae hugged her. "I'm looking forward to it."

"Can I... can I ask something?" Jazmine started. "Do you think somebody might have a spare room I can stay in for a bit? I don't want to be here alone anymore. I think I'm just going to sell it and try to start over. I think that's what he'd want me to do."

"Dude," Rocker said, "Staten Island is beautiful this time of year. Come on over. Laurel would be fine with it."

"Really?"

"No doubt."

They helped Jazmine clean the house a bit and pack a bag before locking her past behind her. She took a good supply of Cass's things that held sentimental value.

He would never leave her. But she had to try and move on. One step at a time. Rae smiled as they left the house. The air felt lighter. She felt like helping her friend was just as important as helping the city. The man with the shovel gave up on his task when he realized the hard slush wouldn't budge.

He returned to his house as the heroes left for a new day. The city didn't soften, but for at least one day, Rae felt like she had helped somebody return from the ledge, and that was plenty. Some days, saving one person felt like saving the whole world.

Chapter 28: Shatter

In the middle of April, the heroes patrolled in the Bronx. One unit, one team. A family. Rae had turned the corner and was well into being seven months pregnant. The golden stripes on her maternity suit stretched from her side downward over her belly. It nearly made the twins who grew inside of her appear like a sun that matched the one on her chest and her cape. She had begun to take the role of verbal leader rather than participatory fighter.

Outside of the occasional ball of sun-rivaling energy that she threw at something, she was happy to float a few inches above the ground and get off her feet when she had the chance. The warmer spring weather started to bring out more residents who liked to question their luck with an odd crime here or there. The heroes walked past a dive bar that seemed a tad too rowdy for the late afternoon, but nothing seemed to be criminal in nature. As the group walked by, the drunkards stared at them. The heroes did not attempt to engage with them.

Then, a glass bottle landed at Echona's feet. She was still getting back into the groove, and it didn't seem like the city would allow her an extended grace period. It shattered on the sidewalk, and a bit of beer splashed onto her feet. She turned toward the men slowly. The alcohol-infused laughter of the men filled the street. They rivaled the clicks of bicyclists and the constant rattle of trains that could be heard nearby. Rae stuck out her hand to grab Echona by the arm. They didn't need to engage them. There was no reason to. Echona felt the message and turned around to keep walking. For a moment, Rae wondered when stepping back had started to feel heavier than stepping in.

"Guess you're not so special after all, huh?" the man who threw the bottle yelled out.

"Heroes… more like zeroes," another man said, which caused the drunks to laugh loudly.

Then, Echona stopped walking again and faced them. Her sneaker screeched on the beer-soaked sidewalk. "Real original, idiot"

"Jaz," Rocker whispered. "We don't need to do this."

"Go back to your drinks!" OwlHeart yelled out. "Surely, there's nothing better for you to do at 3:30 in the middle of the week."

"Guys, are they trying to boss us around? Do they know they have no actual power?" said the third drunkard who was wearing an untucked button-down shirt.

"They ain't strong. They just have fancy clothes," the drunk who threw the glass said. He took a step towards the heroes.

"Here," Ava said. She mentally picked up a large piece of shattered glass and dropped it gently on the man's head. "You dropped something. No need to thank us for helping you get it back."

"Neat trick, little girl!" the man with the button-down yelled out.

Echona tilted her head and squinted. "What the heck?"

"Guys… come on…" Rocker pleaded. The man who stepped forward heard him and replied.

"Yeah, listen to your token guy and leave. We don't need you or your fake guy friend. No man lets a girl control him."

Rae stepped forward now. "He is more of a man than you will ever be. Go back to your drinks. Now."

"Oh, is he?" the man responded. "How about you let me take you into the bathroom, and I can show you what a real man is like." He grabbed his crotch.

"I'm good," Rae asserted. "I've had the best there ever will be and can't quit it." She rubbed her belly. It stuck out beyond the rest of the group. "I don't need to see your toothpick."

"Little Miss Sunlight is a comedian now." The man repositioned the piece of glass in his hand.

"I'm only here to serve." She took an ironic bow as far as her belly allowed. She nearly stumbled but caught herself and stood firmly in front of the other heroes. The first hero of New York. The darling of the city. The light of the boroughs.

Her suit stretched taut over her belly. She had been worried that she might need a bigger maternity suit before her children entered the world. She stuck out her arms after her bow. Both palms began to emit a bright light. "The Heroes of New York hope you have a good night."

LunAva got excited for a moment. "Wait," she whispered. "Do we have a team name now?"

OwlHeart gave her a sideways look. "Girl, what?" LunAva looked at her feet. The spilled beer moved to her boots.

"You don't get to leave so fast. Tell me another joke!" the man insisted.

The two other men walked forward, each with a beer in their hand. In quick succession, they both swallowed the rest of their drink and threw their bottles on the ground. The shatter echoed like a warning, and the street grew quiet.

The laughter stopped.

A boot scraped over a glass shard with a crunch.

The three drunks stood within whispering distance of Rae and the other heroes.

"Rae…" Rocker was continuing to try and de-escalate the situation. He clenched his jaw and feared that his attempt would be futile.

"Guys, I gotta be honest. I'm tired of heroes," the front man said. "Taking all the glory and not doing anything worthwhile."

The two men in the back agreed with him.

The bar door opened to allow another patron inside who was not involved. A tiny bell dinged at the top of the door when it swung. Rocker swore the ding could be heard avenues over through the silence of the unnecessary face-off.

"Your breath stinks. How much have you had to drink? What would your mother say?" Rae responded.

The street felt too narrow for the drunks on the sidewalk.

"There's the comedian," the man growled.

In an instant, the man gripped the large shard of glass. A bit of his own hand was cut in the process.

He swiped forward and sliced at the space in front of him.

At Rae.

A car flew by the people on the sidewalk and splashed a bit of water from the April rainfall that chose to linger in the Bronx.

Her suit was cut.

Her hand went to her stomach before her mind caught up, instinct moved faster than pain.

Blood began to fall from the cut on her stomach and mixed with the spilled beer on the floor. It created an unfortunate concoction of fluids that she was shocked to see. She placed her hand on her belly and looked at the blood on it.

The world seemed to slow down to her as a train sped by in the distance.

She stumbled backward.

Echona and OwlHeart stopped her from falling and helped her find her footing.

The three drunkards laughed.

"Not so heroic now, huh?" the leader stated.

Rocker stepped forward. His eyes glazed over.

He pulled back his hardened arm and approached the man with the glass shard.

His knuckles turned white from the tightness of his fist.

LunAva squinted her eyes with a fiercely protective look and stared intently at the man.

In a swift motion, which nearly appeared rehearsed, Rocker punched the man across his jaw. The power he held was beyond any the drunkard expected. The man flew off his feet backward down the sidewalk. Before he crashed down on the pavement, LunAva mentally picked him up, lifted him off the ground a few more feet, and dropped him.

The two other men froze.

They had no words. No ability to counter what they had just seen.

Echona altered her voice for assertiveness. "Leave!" she yelled.

The men stared at her blankly.

"Now!"

They stumbled and ran to their friend.

He was unconscious, so they left him.

The heroes turned toward Rae.

She was continuing to lose blood.

Her deep breaths filled the silence.

"It's happening," she muttered through her breaths. "The babies… are coming."

The incident incited premature labor, and she began to feel contractions.

"Crap," Ava and Jazmine said in unison.

"Do we call for an ambulance?" Rocker asked.

"I don't think we have time. It's about to be rush hour. There might be too much traffic," OwlHeart responded.

"Alright… okay… um…" Rocker was trying to come up with an idea. He ran his hands through his hair. "Can I pick her up and run her to the hospital? If we make some sort of bandage or something?"

"That could work."

Echona thought for a minute. "Take off her cape and tie it around the cut. That could at least help manage the bleeding."

Rae's chest rose and fell rapidly.

Traffic had begun to clutter the street as the heroes attempted to help her.

It felt as if the eyes of drivers who were forced to idle had been forced not to pay attention to them, lest they be asked for help.

The heroes helped Rae into Rocker's arms. She lay across them like a baby in her own regard.

"Um… can you guys carry Echona in the air? Maybe it would be helpful if you called out to people clogging the sidewalk to make a path? Or let me know which would be fastest?"

The women nodded.

They got ready to carry Echona through the air.

"Wait!" Rocker called out. "Somebody needs to get a hold of Davey."

"I got it!" Ava yelled back. With one arm, she held onto a side of Echona; with the other, she grabbed her phone.

He sprinted through the streets. He wasn't running like a hero. He was running like a friend who couldn't lose another.

It felt like he was in a race with every train, bus, or car that he passed.

From above, he heard the distinctive yells from Echona. She was attempting to get people who lingered on the sidewalk to move for Rocker. But the people weren't moving fast enough. He zigged and zagged through the crowd when necessary. They were nearly at the hospital when Davey finally answered. He was in Brooklyn, working on his campaign with Josephine's team.

"Davey, move your behind."

"What? Why? Where? What happened?" he asked on the other side of the phone.

"Rae went into labor, we're taking her to NewYork-Presbyterian on Broadway near the Bronx. Closest one to us."

"How? It's too soon."

"Just get here, Davey." She hung up and decided not to tell him about the attack.

They arrived at the hospital, and Rocker ran her inside.

Medical staff took her from his arms and swarmed her.

His heart was pounding, filled with adrenaline.

Drops of blood fell onto the fluorescently lit sterile floor.

He heard a nurse call a Code OB.

Through double doors, they whisked her away on a stretcher. The beeps of monitors, coordinated shouting, and the running of a faucet added to the chaos. Rae was disoriented. Unable to make out the words of her attendants. She couldn't tell if she was okay. And her babies?

She began to be prepped for preterm childbirth.

A doctor said the cut from the glass caused a small partial placental separation. But it seemed to be minor. They strapped an oxygen mask on her.

Rae was lost in the confines of the bed. The railings closed in on her.

They rushed her from a delivery room to an operating room, where she felt a numbing agent enter her body.

She couldn't speak through the mask that added to the barrier of medical terminology and technological chimes. Alarms beeped. The medical staff feared fetal distress after detecting minimal dips in the twins' heart rates. There was a rush around her, as she remained unaware of what they were doing to her.

Her blood pressure began to drop, and her vision faded.

Other doctors stabilized her and put her to sleep.

Meanwhile, Davey ran through the doors of the hospital. The heroes all waited for him at the entrance.

"What's going on? What happened?"

Echona stepped forward.

"There was an accident. She got attacked, and it sent her into preterm labor. The doctors are working on her now."

Davey's forehead scrunched together.

He left them and walked toward the double doors.

A nurse called out to him, "Sir! You can't go back there."

He looked at the nurse. His hand was on the button to open the doors.

"Watch me."

Not again, he thought. Not her.

He opened the doors and ran down the hall.

Searching.

Looking for his wife.

His love.

The nurse tried to run after him before deciding it wasn't that big of a deal this time. For the heroes. For SolaRae.

He found an operating room and could barely peek through the window on the door. He saw her. She lay still on the bed.

Then, he heard it.

A cry.

A small yelp of a child who didn't want to leave the warmth of their mother.

He saw the child transferred from one doctor to another. The cries were weak but distinct.

Alarms started to beep.

His anxiety spiked.

The tubes, monitors, and tiny hats he barely saw all started to create more questions than he would get answered.

The second child was coming, but something was wrong.

Their oxygen was too low.

Davey's chest pounded enough for them all.

There was no crying. The second baby disappeared from his view after barely seeing it. A nurse looked up and saw him outside the room. She walked over to the door and talked to him through the thick glass pane.

She was muffled, "You're dad?" the nurse asked.

Davey took a second to comprehend her question and then nodded.

"Your family is okay. They all need some help, but they'll be okay." The nurse walked away.

He slowly blinked as he tried to wrap his head around the situation.

He broke down. The fear, the relief, it all came rushing out; they all competed for priority.

After a few moments, the nurse left the room to speak with him. "They are small. Just under four pounds. Premature labor happens often. A couple of weeks in the NICU to help them grow, and they'll be alright. They're small, but they're fighters. Children of heroes, after all."

Davey was crying. "Thank you. Can I see them? Can I see her?"

"They are still just finishing up your wife. An emergency C-section was necessary. But, if you follow me, I can take you to the babies."

He nodded. After looking through the small window to see his wife again, he followed the nurse. Every step felt as if it elongated the hallway. The bright lights seemed to never end. He arrived at the room to see his children through the NICU nursery glass. Their eyes were both closed.

He pressed his forehead against the glass and sank into it. He whispered to them even though they couldn't hear, a promise that he'd never let them feel alone.

Close enough to see them, but not close enough to hold them.

To feel their tangibility.

Their chests rose and fell like small, gentle tides crashing on a pristine beach.

After a while standing by the glass, he received a call from the post-anesthesia unit.

Rae was waking up.

He marched through the labyrinth as quickly as possible, frustrated by the sheer lack of accessibility that the hospital seemed to have. It's never just easy, Davey thought as his heart raced and he wished he could be in two places at the same time.

He eventually found her and ran to her side.

"Rae… you're okay." He kissed her hand.

"The babies?" she said tiredly. Weakly. "They won't tell me what happened."

He paused and held her hand for a second, just appreciating that his family was okay.

"They had to do an emergency C-section. But they both will be fine. Just have to stay in the NICU for a bit until they grow. They're tiny… they're strong."

Rae attempted to smile but barely could manage one.

"So, they're okay?"

He smiled at her.

"Perfect."

"I guess…" she cleared her throat and tried to take a sip of water. "I guess you'd better be ready to be a dad."

He kissed her hand again.

"More than ready."

In that moment, he saw her groggy and pale but knew that together they would be able to do anything.

A nurse opened the curtain near Rae's bed. "Excuse me, sorry, I just got word that they were able to move the twins into their own room. If you'd like, I can get a wheelchair and you can wheel your wife to them."

"Yes," Rae said, not giving Davey a chance to answer.

The walk back to the babies didn't feel as long for him, but she grew anxious, as if she had to impress somebody who already innately adored her.

They rolled down the halls; each door opened with a slow click and shut behind them. They left their anxieties behind the metal barriers. His pace quickened as his excitement grew until they arrived at the room.

Two babies.

Two tiny isolettes.

Warm light shone down on them.

Rae started to cry at seeing them.

"Hey, babies…" she started. "It's your mom."

"And your dad," he added.

"We're here, and we always will be."

"You're already taking after your mom by working to your own schedule… she's pretty great. You'll see."

They clasped hands and stared at their creations.

"You're going to love your aunts and uncles, too. You have a bunch, but don't let fun Aunt Ava hear that. She can get jealous." Rae chuckled as some of her strength started to return.

Davey picked up his phone. In a group chat, he sent: They're here.

He put his phone back in his pocket, ignoring the flood of tones. He focused on the only sounds that mattered. The interconnected thump of four heartbeats. The monitors clicked in time, a mechanical lullaby that carried their new rhythm into the night.

Chapter 29: New Grounds

The twins continued to strengthen over a few days in the NICU, and it looked like they might be able to leave sooner than expected. The room was becoming their own. Their friends had given them an unnecessary amount of flowers, stuffed animals, and food. Rae appreciated the food the most. She did her best to limit herself to the generally accepted pregnancy foods, which is why she devoured a tray of sushi, a large cold-cut-filled sandwich, and a swig of artificial caffeine. Her colostrum had begun to turn to milk, and she was prepared to ensure her babies got all the nutrients necessary. She knew fully well that some babies and mothers don't take to breastfeeding, and she was okay with that. It was their journey, and she couldn't wait to see how it unfolded. She thought about how little in life went as planned, and how grace came from learning to love what did.

There wasn't enough room for both of them in the hospital, so Davey came as often as possible. Daily. He arrived as soon as possible and didn't leave until he was told to do so.

"You're sure you don't mind?" he asked Rae. "I can have Josephine push the event." He had scheduled a campaign event weeks earlier. Now that his family had grown, he wasn't sure if he should be leaving them.

"Babe, I'm good. And if I'm not… there's like twenty people just in this hall who will run to help. Do your thing." She was sitting in her chair, shirt off, holding one of her babies for skin-to-skin contact. A blanket draped over the two of them.

Davey's phone chimed, and he checked it quickly. He was nearly hoping that it was a message from Josephine saying the event was rescheduled. Instead, it was a notification that Eric had started streaming. He clicked on it out of curiosity. For a brief moment, he forgot about politics, the hospital smell, everything but his friend's voice breaking through the noise.

"Holy crap," he said.

"Language," she responded jokingly, "there are children present."

"Check this out." He walked the phone to her and raised the volume.

"Welcome in everyone, thanks for stopping by!" Eric was enthusiastic. "I know a lot of you have been loyal over the last few months, but I just have one request."

The viewer count on his stream climbed to seventy-five.

"There's a family that just had two kids unexpectedly."

One hundred.

"I mean, it was expected. They knew she was pregnant. It was purposeful."

One hundred and fifty.

"But they came early,"

Two hundred.

"So, if anybody has anything they feel called to give…"

Three hundred.

"Any donations from this stream will be given to that family."

Four hundred.

"To support my niece and nephew."

Rae widened her eyes and blinked hard, caught between laughter and tears. The small screen on Davey's phone felt like it was holding the whole world.

"Looks like you're friends with a celebrity," she said.

"I've been married to one. No biggie." He smiled at her and kissed her head before he started to leave the room. "Bye, kids."

Davey proceeded down the hall. He glanced at his phone and started to see donations coming through the stream. He locked his phone, tucked it away, and felt happy. For the first time in a while, he didn't feel anxious about leaving his wife and kids. He felt safe. It was the first time in months that he didn't mistake calm for something pejorative. He felt like his world had shrunken and grown simultaneously.

He left for his event, an additional next step in his life.

It was at a café in Manhattan, a small Q&A with potential supporters to get to know him. He was thankful that it was at least relatively close to the hospital.

He took the train down and met Josephine and Shira. The rhythm of the train felt like a heartbeat, steady and mechanical, a metronome for the life he was trying to balance. The late spring air was refreshing as it brushed against his face.

The women both greeted him with a firm handshake.

"Thanks for getting here early," Josephine remarked. "There's a small staged area in the back, past the counter. We'll sit you down with a coffee and a small microphone just so you don't have to strain your voice. We don't exactly know what questions anybody will ask or what the turnout will end up being. Just play it cool and stick to your brand."

"Easy enough." Davey yawned afterward.

"How's the family?" Shira asked.

"Amazing. Really amazing."

"Pick names yet?"

"Nope." He shrugged. "We think we have a few more days before discharge. We'll pick before then."

He opened the door for the women and followed them inside. The peppy receptionist from the office was at the counter and picking up his coffee.

"One black coffee for the future councilman!"

"Ha, thank you."

The smell of freshly ground coffee beans filled the café. The dim lights were enough for him to want to fall asleep, so he thought he'd best work on the coffee. Soon enough, city residents started to enter the café. Josephine's team had picked the place to be quaint and welcoming, but they had evidently underestimated the crowd that would show up. The café was nearly packed by the time they had to shut the doors and cut off people outside.

He took a sip of his coffee, then took a step toward his future.

"Thank you all for coming," he said into the microphone. "I'm sure you all know already, but my name is Davey Karoll. I'm running for city council, and my platform can really help change the city for the better. If anybody has any questions, I'd love this to be a discussion instead of a speech."

He laughed, and a member of the audience raised their hand. A middle-aged man. He was called on by a member of Josephine's team and stood at his chair.

"I don't think you know me, Mr. Karoll. My wife was killed last year. An intruder broke into our house, stole our food, and stabbed her. She bled out on our kitchen floor."

"I'm sorry to hear that."

"Are you?"

There was silence filled by the crunch of coffee beans in the background and the vibration of pots.

The man continued, "Because it seems like it has worked out in your best interest. That murderer is who launched your campaign. Isn't it?"

Davey gulped.

Simon Cribb. This was the survivor of his robbery. The night that changed his life.

"I am. Truly and deeply sorry."

"I don't buy it!" He sat down.

The words hurt Davey like ripping off a stuck bandage.

"Nothing can bring your wife back, and I wish I had met Simon before he did what he did."

He considered his words.

"Whether you believe it or not, I am irrevocably sorry. You're right."

He stood from his chair. His pulse quickened, not from fear but from memory. Simon's face still haunted him in flashes in the form of a trembling hand, or a voice asking for help that nobody heard. An NYPD car sped by the café and illuminated the inside with its lights.

"Simon's case is what spurred me to consider running for city council. But it's because I saw all of the things that were wrong that surrounded it. He had deep mental health issues and should never have been discharged from the inpatient program he was in. If they had hung onto him, maybe they would have had a breakthrough instead of freeing up a bed.

Too many times in this city, things are done for financial interest rather than human interest. Simon paid the price for his crime with his life. I never wanted to be a politician. I wanted to be a therapist. But the need for change surrounding mental health advocacy and judicial reform is too great. I can't just sit by anymore." For a second, he thought of Cass. Of all the people who didn't make it to the help they needed. This was his penance.

The coffee grinder stopped.

There were no claps or boos. Just the hum of the espresso machine. Another hand rose and was called on by the staff.

"What will you do for the normal people? The people who don't have mental health issues?" A large man in a flannel stood and asked the question before sitting back down with his arms crossed.

"Thank you for your question. Honestly, sir, I think everybody could benefit from having a therapist. We all could use somebody to talk to, and part of my message is encouraging you to find somebody before it's too late."

He paused to gather his thoughts. A cough and a screech of a stool on the tiled floor broke through the silence. His voice steadied even though his hand softly trembled.

"It's almost guaranteed that somebody you love has been or will be affected by some mental health problem. Anxiety, depression, PTSD, OCD, schizophrenia, ODD, there are so many that don't get acknowledged. So many people who need help but can't get it. Mental health doesn't just affect criminals. It affects everyone. My goal is to make help available and make mental health not be criminalized."

There was a light applause now, and Davey smiled. He thought that now he might be able to win. He didn't know if winning would fix anything, but it felt like just trying might be enough. To make a change for his friends. For Cass. His wife. His kids. To do something that mattered.

Chapter 30: The Beginning

A few weeks passed, and the couple became comfortable. They began to feel accustomed to their new life back in Kew Gardens. The bassinets were put together, the bottles had been prepared for when they needed them, and the cat across the street kept watch on their home. An extra layer of neighborhood security that Davey never realized would be his own. The world had finally slowed enough for him to notice small things again. The hum of the fridge. The weight of morning light. The sound of soft steady breaths that hadn't been there a year ago.

Rae sat with the babies on the large sectional and began to feed one of the twins. The other hadn't taken to breastfeeding and preferred a bottle. That usually made mealtimes a little more difficult, but she couldn't blame her daughter for being particular. It was only a slight annoyance when the boy wanted milk, which spurred the girl to want some too. She hadn't yet figured out how to make a bottle while holding a baby if Davey had gone for groceries or needed to make a campaign call.

He was in the front room, setting up as many chairs as he could.

The circle would be tighter, but they were both thankful for it. All of the heroes were coming to the support group. To be with each other. To meet their newest additions.

When the chairs were set and the coffee brewed, Davey went to make a bottle for his daughter, who started to get antsy. He held her in his arms. Any time he had done so since they were born, he felt his problems and anxieties disappear. There was no looming election. There was only his family. He sat with her in his usual chair and fed her the bottle. Her tiny fingers curled around one of his, and for a second the whole world seemed to rest inside that grip. The chair creaked under them, but held. They persisted.

Shortly after, Jose and Sara entered the home and let in the warm, pleasant early summer air. They left Rio at his grandmother's, so as not to overwhelm them with a third child. Jose took his normal seat and motioned for his wife to sit next to him, ensuring she didn't accidentally take Eric's chair. They both looked at the baby in Davey's arms with a loving glance. Jose felt that familiar ache of joy, the kind that reminds you every good thing comes with the fear of losing it.

"Want another?" Jose asked, only half joking.

"With whose body?" Sara joked in response, and he kissed her cheek.

"Where's the other one?" she asked Davey.

"Having his own dinner." He nodded toward the couch where Rae sat with her back to them.

She could see their reflections in the television. The faint presence of their family flickered in the screen's reflection, half real, half dream. "We'll be over there in a minute!"

"Take your time, girl," Sara reassured her.

After a moment, Eric entered by himself.

"If it isn't the streamer extraordinaire!" Jose welcomed him in. "What's up, bro?!"

"How's everybody doin'?"

"Pretty good. Can't thank you enough for those donations, Eric. Really. We appreciate it more than you know."

"Hey, what's family for?" he asked rhetorically and took his seat next to Jose.

From his chair, Davey could see Rae start to get up from the couch when Ava walked in.

"What's up, sis?" Davey asked her.

"Shush. I'm only here for my niece and nephew. Let me see!"

Ava walked over to Davey and stared at the girl over his shoulder. Rae managed to stand from the couch that never seemed to want to let her leave. The boy was still feeding, and she entered the room with her shirt partly off. Her son hated being covered as he ate.

"Ew, put it away," Ava joked with her sister.

"Hush. He's just having dinner," Rae responded.

"I know, I know. Only messing." Ava walked over to Rae to look at her nephew. "So, is there like a seating order or something?" she asked the larger group.

"Yes," Jose and Eric answered in unison.

Rae nodded for her sister to follow her. "You sit here."

She picked a seat three down from Eric and two down from Davey. Before, she took her seat between Sara and her husband.

After a moment, Miles, Laurel, and Jazmine entered the house. Davey wondered if the number of people coming caught the cat security off guard. Surely, the pet wasn't used to this number of visitors at once. Did the cat think something was wrong? Or was it glad that the support group had grown?

Laurel helped herself to coffee and told Miles to sit next to Ava. She moved to sit next to Eric. Laurel noticed the way his hands twitched when he laughed. The weight of the last few months had aged them all, but laughter still found its way through the cracks.

As Rocker stepped further in, Jose grinned and cracked his knuckles.

"Alright, bro, I've been waiting for this."

"For what?" Rocker asked.

"You stopping boats and tossing kangaroos is cool and all, but let's see how that strength holds up against a former triathlete."

Rocker couldn't tell if he was joking or testing him.

"You want to arm wrestle me?"

"You scared?" Jose teased.

"Not even a little."

Rocker pulled over an empty chair, and the group started cheering before the match even began. Eric yelled out, "I feel like we should be putting bets on this. Let's go, Jose!" Sara rolled her eyes but smiled.

While Laurel responded, "My life savings on my man!"

Their hands locked, muscles tensed, and the chair creaked dangerously as if it was on its last leg. Jose held his ground for a moment before Rocker gently pushed his arm down like a dad playing with his kid.

"Man, that's messed up," Jose laughed, rubbing his wrist. "I swear I had you for a second."

"Sure you did," Rocker said with a smirk. "Good form, though. You should go pro."

"In losing?"

"Nah. In trying."

The sound of laughter mingled with the smell of cheap coffee and the summer air sneaked through the doorway.

"So, what's up, everybody?" Miles asked. "Do we have names yet?"

"You all have waited this long. Let everybody get situated, and maybe we'll tell you," Rae said.

"Man, that's some garbage, we have to know!" Jose called out. "I'm taking up quilting and was gonna try and do their names on a blanket or some crap that will just get throw up on it."

"Quilting, dude?" Eric joked.

"No joke. Quilting is relaxing, bro."

"Hey, that's probably better than the crap these two will be smelling over the next few months." The group laughed.

Jazmine finished making herself a cup of coffee. Then, she took the last chair.

Eric, Jose, Laurel, and Davey all stared at her.

"Did I do something wrong?" she asked after taking a sip of the warm drink. "This coffee is garbage, by the way."

Davey laughed and appreciated her taking Cass's seat. Her essence made it feel like he was never truly gone. The air shifted, quiet but full. Grief had become something shared now, less sharp, more like a memory learning to breathe again.

"Not at all. Just glad you're here."

"Alright… so let's see the kids," she said.

"Want to hold him?" Rae asked Jazmine.

She nodded eagerly and put down the coffee cup as the chair wobbled beneath her.

"Hang on! I want to hold one too," Sara cried.

"Hah, here." Davey handed the daughter to her.

"Whoa, whoa, whoa," Ava said. "I'm the literal aunt and can't get the baby first? Alright. I see how it is." Eric laughed, and Ava gave him a smirk.

"You'll all get a chance. I promise," Davey reassured the group.

"So, names?" Miles asked.

"Right… Davey, do you want to share, or should I?"

"How about you do the boy, and I do the girl?"

"That's how you got into this mess, isn't it?" Eric laughed again, and Ava joined him.

"That's right it is," Rae responded. "And we enjoyed every bit of it. Our baby boy is Caleb Karoll."

"Baby Caleb is precious," Sara shared.

"You named him after Dad?" Ava asked.

Rae nodded. "That's right. Go ahead, babe."

"Well, our baby girl… we struggled with this one for a while, but we landed on… Cassandra."

Jazmine looked up slowly from the daughter. The room fell silent. It was nobody's moment but hers and the parents. A tear fell down her cheek.

"Thank you," she whispered. She looked back down at the baby girl. "I love you, Cassandra." The parents looked on with grins as large as their hearts.

"We love you all."

For the first time in what felt like a long time, nobody rushed to fill the silence that fell into the room. They had become each other, and they all knew it. Outside, the neighborhood cat, who had never dared to leave its stoop, decided to rise. It cautiously crossed the road and hopped onto the railing of the steps outside the home. It stared inside and offered quiet meows to the family. The parents smiled at the curious cat.

Then, Davey examined the room.

It was not the kind of victory he had dreamed about, but it was the one that mattered. The kind measured in hearts, not votes.

Friends.

Family.

Everything he had been fighting for.

Epilogue

Months later, the kids were growing, and the city had welcomed the fall air once more. Davey had won the city council seat and was eager to start making his change. Rae had taken an extended maternity leave after another hero stepped forward and into the spotlight. She was home with Caleb, while Davey took Cassandra on an adventure.

He took her to his small therapeutic office in Queens Plaza, which he needed to clean out. He strapped her into the baby carrier and moved onto the train that had once been his routine. The rumble of the tracks felt different now. It no longer carried him toward work or purpose but toward something gentler, a version of himself that finally understood what quiet could mean. She was a fan of the rattling and still heard her mom's voice over the announcement system.

When they disembarked, the screech of the brakes led her to cry, but she was quickly consoled as her father rubbed her back softly and offered gentle hums. They climbed the steps to the small office, and Davey pointed out the mural of Rae and Aunt Ava across the street.

There wasn't much that was his in the office. He wondered if it ever truly belonged to him. The place had always felt borrowed, like most spaces in the city. Even the walls seemed to listen more than they spoke. The furniture came with the place, and he was never a big decorator. What few things he had fit into the diaper bag: a book or two and an old notebook he had forgotten about, the one he used to take notes when he met with Simon Cribb. The edges were curled, and the ink had faded, but his handwriting was still there. He traced the first sentence he ever wrote about Simon and realized it was really the first thing he had written about himself.

He finished cleaning and offered the baby a bottle before they headed back home. She happily took it without a second thought. Her gulps made Davey realize that he was hungry too. Parenthood had become a quiet apprenticeship in selflessness. Every small sound from her mouth reminded him that the simplest things were sometimes the most important. So, they climbed down the stairs together and walked across the street to Central Sausage.

Boris was the constant, with his white, grease-stained shirt and lawn chair.

"David, my friend! Welcome back to Central Sausage. All councilmen eat here still, like broke student!" He stood and opened his arms to greet Davey as he crossed the street.

Davey couldn't help but laugh. "Just Davey, Boris. How's business been?"

"Good, David, good. But not as good now that you will not be here, yes?"

"Unfortunately, not. I'll miss your hot dogs, Boris."

"Then you try something new, yes?"

He thought about saying he would just have the regular, but decided to hear him out. Change, he thought, begins like this. In the pause before habit. In the willingness to try something new.

"What do you have today, Boris?"

This caught the vendor off guard.

"You like new?"

The smell of grilled onions and the sizzle of the fryer filled the air.

"I like new."

Boris grinned wide and reached for the tongs. The grill hissed, the air smelled of mustard and warmth, and for the first time in a long while, Davey felt that the city itself was exhaling with him.

Authors Note

I wrote When the City is Safe Again during a season when I was close to not writing at all. My mental health was heavy enough that finishing this book often felt impossible. There were days the story waited for me and I could not reach it. The fact that this book exists means I did. These characters carry expectation, silence, fear, and hope. They try to look steady when they are not. I know what it feels like to fall apart in private while appearing fine in public.

Part of this book pushes against a stigma. Many men are taught to endure without asking for help, to keep moving without admitting they are hurting. This story argues for something else. Reliance is not weakness. Asking for help is not failure. Vulnerability is not a flaw. Strength doesn't have to be brawn. If you see yourself in these pages, I hope you feel understood.

If you see someone you love, I hope you see them with more patience and compassion. The characters build themselves around what they fear, what they hope for, and what they feel responsible to protect. Identity is fragile and always changing. I spent a long time debating whether this book needed a true villain. Every attempt pulled the story away from what it was meant to be. I wrote a range of characters because mental health does not choose its targets. This book exists because I endured. I hope, in some small way, it helps you endure too. Thank you for reading.

Their Songs

A select few songs that accompanied me in my writing journey. Each meant something to a scene, or a character, or a couple. Some became "anthems" for the people who live on these pages.

1. First Day of My Life - Bright Eyes

2. Good Job - Alicia Keys

3. Like Real People Do - Hozier

4. Sweater Weather - Kurt Hugo Schneider & Alyson Stoner

5. FEAR - NF

6. Unsteady - X Ambassadors

7. Youth - Daughter

8. weak love - voice memo - Caleb Bachtel, Voice Memos To God

9. Rescue - Lauren Daigle

10. Banana Pancakes - Jack Johnson

11. Fine Apple - Nic D.

12. Young Folks - Peter Bjorn and John

13. New Person, Same Old Mistakes - Tame Impala

14. Davey & Rae's Anthem: Come Close - Common & Mary J. Blige

15. Jose & Sara's Anthem: Best Part - Daniel Caesar (feat. H.E.R.)

16. Cass & Jazmine's Anthem: To Build a Home

       - The Cinematic Orchestra (feat. Patrick Watson)

17. Eric's Anthem: Heavy - Booshle G.

18. Ava's Anthem: Keep On Living - Propaganda

19. Laurel & Miles' Anthem: Bloom (Bonus Track) - The Paper Kites

Acknowledgments

First and foremost, all glory and praise to God for giving me the words to write my story and being my strength through the struggle.

Special thanks to my editor, Aaron Lelito for taking on my debut. And to my support network, without whom I would not be around to write the story of Davey and everyone beside him. You know who you are.

To my kids, thank you for wanting to sit with me and "write with daddy." I hope you will always have your own support network. I love you.

I also want to shout out some of my "brothers": Casey, Andrew, Andrew (yes, there are two), and the guys at the D&D table. I appreciate you guys for talking about my book.

Lastly, thank you to my author friends who helped steer me in the right direction at times, and to my early readers for being willing to see the story I had to tell.

Reading Group Discussion Questions

When the City is Safe Again explores the quiet, often unseen battles people carry, the weight of responsibility, and the ways relationships shape and are shaped by mental health. These questions are designed to guide reflection, conversation, and deeper engagement with the themes, characters, and emotional truths in the book. There are no right answers, only your thoughts, observations, and experiences as a reader.

1) How does Davey's sense of responsibility reshape the trajec-tory of his life, and where does it cross the line from purpose into obligation?

2) When the extraordinary collides with the painfully ordi-nary in the lives of the Heroes, which characters crack, which adapt, and what does that reveal about their emotional state?

3) What does this novel suggest about the long term cost of unspoken mental health struggles, both for the person carrying them and for the people who love them?

4) The five core relationships in the book respond to the ex-traordinary in distinct and sometimes conflicting ways. What do these differences reveal about how people seek safety, love, and control when their world refuses to stay ordinary?

5) The world of this book blurs the line between who saves and who is saved. How does the story challenge traditional ideas of heroism, and what does it suggest about the people who quietly keep others standing?

6) Take a moment to think about the roles you carry that no one sees. The quiet responsibilities. The parts of your life where you hold others up without asking for recognition. How do those invisible tasks shape who you are, and where do they blur the line between love and exhaustion?

7) If being needed becomes part of someone's identity, what happens when they are no longer needed, and how does the story explore the risk of building a self around usefulness to others?

About the Author

Sean Mejias is a writer from Rochester with Puerto Rican roots. His work blends the human and the surreal to explore how ordinary lives meet extraordinary worlds. When The City Is Safe Again is his debut novel. He writes about identity, belonging, and the small miracles of everyday life. When he's not writing, at church, or with his wife and kids, he's exploring nature or being reminded of his misplaced faith in the New York Jets.

Learn more at TinyFrogPress.com.